FROM ANIMUS

CASSANDRA CIELO

Welcome to Book 2 From Animus.
As I wrote this book I found myself reflecting on what it means to be given a second chance. To have been gravely misunderstood and as a result losing relationships and connections. The characters Rina, Rei and Tae have to face ugly truths and extend mercy and forgiveness to those who may not deserve it.

I hope as you read you not only enjoy the story and romance but that you would consider the ways you have received or have given forgiveness, maybe even undeserved, maybe even to yourself.

The love, you the readers, have shown these stories make everything possible. Thank you for sharing your passion for these characters with me, it makes my day to hear from you. Don't forget to check out my other works.

Love, Cassandra

Content Warning : Their are depictions of violence and death. Heavy topics such as grief and loss. Though is a closed door romance with no explicit scenes, there are some makeout scenes but characters do not go further then kissing.

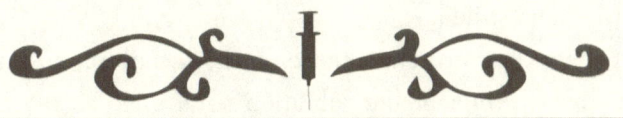

Tae's POV

Unexpected

I rolled my shoulders against the firm back of the headmaster's chair. The oblong desk in front of me was unnecessarily big and tedious. I ran my fingers through my short black hair, tilting my head from left to right, trying to alleviate the persistent tension at the base of my skull, trailing down between my shoulder blades.

Simply the sight of the paper in front of me had my shoulders tensing up and legs feeling restless. I needed to train. Burn off this burgeoning frustration and unease.

Ever since I had found Rina, the mounting tension of what I had to do was crushing me.

She was the key to everything, and at this point, my only hope. My father had abandoned me again, and Rei...

Rei was as oblivious as ever.

I absently slid the paper back and forth along the mahogany desk. *Swish* to the left, *swish* to the right. Left to right, and again, as if my subconscious was deliberating on what to do with the offensive sheet. I had gotten the answer I was looking for after doing some sleuthing into Rina's family and mine. Now the question was, did I tell her the whole truth, a half-truth, or spin a tale and send her away out of *his* reach.

My hand stilled.

I sensed her presence in the teachers' building instantly. The smooth *hmm* of her vibration so attuned to my own, something that should not be this strong yet, with us only having spent a few moments together.

Was she looking for *me*? I did not like how that thought both terrified and elated me. She needed to keep her distance, and yet...

My brother would always be my first priority, so even if I wanted to keep my distance from her, even if I knew it was the right thing to do, I wouldn't.

I stood, the headmaster's chair rolling out from under me as I skirted the table, headed to the file closet to the side of the room. The file room wasn't much, just a few rows of metal cabinets filled with the records of our current students.

The windows in the main room were massive, spanning up to the thirteen-foot ceilings; they had no latch to open, but the file room had a small square window that the lock had been broken on for many, many years.

Reaching the window, I popped it open and hopped out onto the brick molding that lined the outside of the building's second floor. I had been the one to break said lock, and had used this escape repeatedly since, to avoid teachers and my father. Perhaps not the safest way to avoid one's problems, but I never did take the safe route.

With deft ease I climbed the bricks, using my gift to propel me higher and strengthen my hold on the protruding stones patterning the outside wall. Once I landed on the roof, I straightened my suit and took a deep breath. Feeling for her again, I sensed she was waiting in the hall just outside the teachers' offices.

Opening the rooftop entrance to the building, I dropped down the stairs, sliding my hand along the railing, my stride taking three steps at a time. When I reached the bottom, I was just around the corner from where she stood.

I took a steadying breath, reminding myself that it was fear, concern and trepidation, not interest, that had my heart thrumming in my chest. It was most definitely not excitement that zinged like an alarm shooting through my pulse at seeing her hand poised to open the door.

Her profile was hidden by a mess of curls about her head. Like a crown of wild briars.

I recalled her face the day she opened the acceptance letter to T.R.E.

I had personally dropped it into the mailbox of her family's two-story townhome. I had watched her from the roof of the building next door as she came out to get the mail, her hair wrapped messily atop her head. Her skin like smooth gray agate in the bright, hot afternoon.

I studied her face, knowing full well I should not be there, watching her flip through the letters before turning to go back inside. She was in light blue pants and a matching top that made her warm caramel eyes pop. I waited for her to go, but she paused, finding the letter I had left for her.

A soft gasp left her shapely pink lips, and I took note of a bandage across the right side of her jaw. A strange sensation swirled in me at the sight, but before I could place it, she was ripping open the letter, drawing my attention to the widening of her eyes. She was surprised, but was she *happy* to receive the acceptance letter to the most prestigious school in all of Erasmus?

Then a smile broke across her face, cheeks warming pleasantly as she read the letter.

She *was* happy, she would come, and everything about my forlorn life would change.

So far everything was going according to plan.

Drawn back to the present I watched as Rina pulled her hand away from the large double doors of the teachers' room. Her pale fingers lifted to her hair. I watched her tuck and untuck her curls behind her ear, a nervous tic I was beginning to understand.

"Rina?" I called, walking down the hall to meet her. She would probably receive unwarranted punishment if she went into the teachers' room while class was obviously in session. So why had she come here and risked getting into trouble? As it was, the teachers were miffed as to why we had accepted her. I did not bother to explain, as my decisions did not need to be justified to them. But she did not need to come and poke the bears with a stick. I'd told her I would meet her in the courtyard after school.

"Shouldn't you be in class?" I pointed out, hoping she would catch on to the disapproving tone in my voice.

"We need to talk," she said, and the smile I had seen that day on the steps of her home was nowhere on her cold face. She moved closer to me, her vibration gift resonating with whatever emotion she was feeling.

I steadied my gaze, determined to keep a safe wall between us. "Control yourself. You will only aggravate your wounds." The smallest almost imperceptible twitch of her cheek told me her bruise was hurting something awful today, and despite the wall I had mentally put up, my hand reached out and touched the curve of skin over her cheek. That same jolt that had sparked in my veins moments ago was back, and I flicked my hand away just as she faltered, stepping back.

Why was I drawn to touch her? It was the same sensation that had passed over me in the arena, seeing her on the ground covered in bleeding pink scrapes puckered with sand. I'd wanted to clean her up, bandage her cuts, and put her back together in a way that screamed nurturing and care, emotions I did not want to outwardly show anyone. They were dangerous, and only meant pain would soon follow.

I cleared my throat. "Follow me to my office," I said, breezing past her to open the door of the teachers' room.

All eyes turned to us as we entered. I did not have to check to see if she followed, I could tell she had from the withering stares and whispers of the unimaginative teachers seated at their cubicles.

I blocked out their babble, as their opinions of Rina meant nothing to me. They were idiots to not see the potential in her.

"I don't care how gifted she is, trouble follows Golanites like a plague."

My eyes slid over to the offending individual. A teacher hired only a year ago, her name was Maylee, or was it Mylee —whatever it was, she would need to dust off that résumé of hers.

I stopped and turned to Jacob, my father's admin assistant, who leaned against the door to the break room, mug of tea in hand. I gave him the "look," as he called it, my chin lifting in the direction of the teacher with the forked tongue. She would be gone by end of day.

Rina had moved ahead of me, her fixed stare on the door to the headmaster's office.

My lips twitched; she would not be able to pull the door

open. Not because she was not strong enough—the door, for all its grand height, was actually quite light—but the lock to it was rather unusual. I decided to spare her the embarrassment of struggling with the door, though I could not help being curious to see how she would struggle with it. My curiosity would have to wait, as it was clear she wanted to be free of the unfiltered onlookers.

I reached around her, and pulled the door open a crack.

She huffed, whether from relief or surprise I couldn't tell, and went inside.

I followed, closing the door behind me.

Pausing a moment, I leaned back to watch her. She strode into my father's office, which was decorated to his tastes in dark cherry woods. She tilted her head, dark curls bouncing as she took in the massive windows. Windows that had an uninhibited view of the roof across the courtyard.

I could almost feel her anger then, like a flavor in the air between us. I moved to the drink bar my father kept fully stocked. Not being a fan of alcohol myself, I lifted the decanter of water and poured myself a glass.

Heat burned the back of my neck. She was looking at me now, and though my back was to her, I felt that spiking sensation over my skin.

"Water?" I breathed, hoping she would not hear the slight tremble in my voice. I took solace in the fact she could not see my face, see the way my jaw muscle twitched.

"It's all a game to you, isn't it?"

I closed my eyes, composing myself. She was fast, quick to assess my strategy. But just how much did she know?

"No water, then?" I hedged, sensing how her power flared in the space between us.

I turned to face her. "Such hostility. I thought you were

better than that? Just because you are Golan doesn't mean you have to pander to the stereotype." I carried my glass of water to the desk and took a seat. My eyes landed on the paper I had been fiddling with earlier. The one with the results from the city records office. I flicked my gaze to her, but she looked like she was still reeling from my words. Casually I slid open the middle drawer just under the desk. With drink in hand, I curved my arm around the paper, letting water slosh from the glass and on to the ink. If she noticed it now, it would not be legible. With my elbow, I slid the ruined paper into the ajar drawer. Leaning forward to take a sip of water, I let my torso discreetly close the drawer, hiding the sheet safely away in the desk.

Rina was none the wiser.

"Rina?" I mused. "You came to see me for a reason, I presume. What was so urgent it couldn't wait till we met in the courtyard tonight? So urgent you would miss class for it?"

Her eyes fell on me, her jaw set and shoulders rigid. She looked like she was trying to compose herself and was failing terribly. What was upsetting her so?

She approached the desk, placing her palms flat against the smooth wood, leaning forward. This close, I could see her warm caramel-colored eyes had flecks of gold. Like honey-swirled caramel. One could easily get stuck in such a mixture.

"You wanted me to go to the roof."

I leaned back in the chair. She was too damn close. The vein in my neck pulsed, my mouth suddenly dry. I fought the urge to lick my lips 'cause that would be incredibly inappropriate. I took a slow sip of water, nodding once.

Yes, I had wanted her to go to the roof; that was of course why I had mentioned it the night before when I drove her back to the dorm. It was clear she had found exactly what I'd intended her to find.

"You wanted me to find Rei's shed. You knew it was there?" Her gaze was like amber-tipped spears poised to strike. A strange thrill filled me at her accurate read of the situation.

Another nod and sip of water had her spilling more epiphanies.

"Did you also know he was listening in on all your calls?" My gaze shifted to her slender finger poking the dark cherry wood. If the table were not between us, would she be poking that offensive finger into my chest? Would I have let her? By the Strings, what was I thinking? I focused on her words. "That he was taking notes?" She finished with a sneer, and though I had to give her credit for her quick deduction, I had to dock her points for not catching on to my lack of words.

I suppressed a smile and nodded. I had affirmed her suspicions, all without implicating myself, because even now Rei's machine was recording this conversation, and should my little brother return to his shed and listen to this message, he would find Rina the one telling me all his secrets.

"What is wrong with you two? He has me spying on you, but you seem to know everything already!" She threw her arms out in understandable frustration.

I cleared my throat, wishing I could explain it all to her now, but I couldn't—it was too soon, and she did not trust me yet. "If I didn't before, I sure do now."

She huffed, visibly done with the conversation. "I'm not playing these games. I'm done with both of you and your twisted brother rivalry."

Without another word, she stormed to the door and pulled the handle. It didn't budge, of course, and I could feel her panic, sharp and prickling in the room. By the Strings, our vibrations should not be so attuned to one another. Was this what it was like with people of Golan? It was not this fast, this instantaneous with people from Shamar.

I plucked an excuse slip from my desk and folded it a few times. She would need it to avoid any issues when she returned to class.

She pulled fruitlessly at the door. I found no enjoyment in her fear, so I hurried to her side to open it.

My palm splayed across the dark wood.

She gasped, and the curve of her backside brushed against me. A traitorous zing cut through my insides, as if she had been the one to startle me and not the other way around.

"Didn't mean to startle you," I struggled to say as the door unlatched with a *snick*. "The lock is attuned to my vibration gift. Only my touch will open it." Why was my voice so low? Why was my mouth inching towards the top of her head? Dark curls spun with strands of gold, no doubt from time in the sun. Time in the sun that would never fix the ashen hue of her skin. Did she lie out in the oppressive summer heat in the hopes that the sun would make her more normal, more like the rest of Shamar?

She inclined her head, the curve of her lips coming into view, pink and tantalizing, like a desert rose. I found the comparison amusing, as not only were her lips a match to the flower, but her personality too. The desert rose was a symbol of strength, persistence and resilience. Traits I could see blooming in her the more time I spent around her.

I could tell she wanted to leave, intended to, but she hesitated, and for a moment I was sure it was because she felt whatever this was between us. If she turned her head a little bit more, I would lean down and kiss her. I wanted to kiss her.

If there was a way to reach through the gift to tell her as much, I would have, because they were words I would not say out loud.

A pit formed in my stomach. I was supposed to be seducing her, not the other way around.

"Earlier"—her voice was breathy, and a swell of pride filled me at the idea that she might be just as affected as I by our close proximity—"when you said things aren't what they seem, were you..."

She was so clever, quick to understand, to piece things together. Perhaps she was too good? I had anticipated it taking her much longer to see me as someone she could come to and talk with candidly. I knew she did not really feel completely open with me yet, but we had made real progress by her coming to me on her own. I had intended for her to find the shed but not to seek me out, to confront me, to be leaning her back into my chest like she was in this moment.

"You can trust me." I repeated the words from the phone call I knew she'd overheard because I had watched her crawl around on the roof and had timed it just so, once she had found Rei's shed.

"I want to leave."

I nodded, content that we had made it this far. I would not keep her here with me, not yet. I reached my hand over hers, feeling the softness, and passed the folded paper to her.

"I wouldn't force you to stay, but you are far from done with us." She was only at the beginning of, if it all went to plan, a game that would change both of our lives forever. "You will come back, and I'll be waiting," I assured her, because this was a game of cat and mouse, and I always caught my prey.

CHAPTER 1

Safe Zones

W aking up was like drinking ice water: The shooting pain in one's molars at the first splash of the frigid liquid. The way it seizes up one's back as it slides down into the stomach.

That was what it was like when I came to. Moving was impossible, my limbs were like lead on the bed.

My eyes focused on the worn stone walls that arched overhead. The room was long and narrow. Cots lined the floor, filled with silent bodies, wrapped and wired up to medical equipment. I blinked slowly, confused. This wasn't the hospital.

My eyes flitted over the King's Crest, the winged beast carved into the stone, and my body relaxed. The words "safe zone" were etched beneath the symbol of the dangerous winged beast. I was in one of the many bunkers dubbed "safe zones" littered around the city. They'd been built to be used as a last resort should the city prove no longer safe.

The narrow tunnel was lit by small lanterns along the wall, casting a warm golden light into the dark space. I tried to sit up, to remove the tubes in my nose, the mask on my face. I wanted to ask why I was there, to understand the burning in my chest every time I took a breath. But there was no one to ask, and along with my body being unresponsive, so was my voice.

I woke two more times like this. The bodies in the cots around me changed—the only indication of time passing.

———

The wailing woke me. The cry was muffled, like listening from deep underwater. My head lolled in the direction of the sound; distant as it was, it sounded familiar. The wail came again—my father ran toward me, his face stricken, hands reaching out to me. He fell to his knees at the side of my bed.

The way he ran to me reminded me of another time he had run to my bedside. The tears, his scrunched face, the way he called my name, again and again, his hands fluttering over my body as if he wasn't sure where to touch, were just like how he'd come home that day. The day my mother died. He had held me in his arms that day too, after he'd finally settled on touching me. That day his arms had been comforting, but now his touch was haunting. I couldn't place why but his touch left me trembling.

"Her fever is breaking." A voice spoke, and at the words my father's form rippled. Like an image in still water washed away at the slightest touch, he was gone, as if he had never been at my bedside to begin with.

I blinked rapidly, confused as the scene changed before my eyes. Where my father had been, a doctor hovered over

2

me. He wore a white coat with a black pen tucked into the breast pocket. My eyes focused on the pen as my mind struggled to catch up to the present moment. It took a while for the doctor to remove the tubes and wires from my face and hands, but once they were gone he helped me sit up.

"There we go," he encouraged as he pressed a needle into my upper arm. I winced, a familiar feeling bubbling up within me, but like an unpleasant memory I immediately shoved the emotion away.

The shot made my mind fuzzy, but I could see the room better now. It was much bigger than I'd originally thought, and I could tell, from the king's insignia on the walls, that we *were* in the bunker on the base outside the city. The base that had been attacked at the front line.

"Where is my father?" I asked, my voice a whisper. A nurse appeared next to the doctor and they shared a knowing look. The nurse shook her head sadly. "Where?" I croaked again, my eyes searching the room to see where he had gone.

"Rina," the doctor said, his voice surprisingly gentle, "your father is dead."

I stopped looking around and turned my face towards the doctor, my hands fisting the green blanket over my body. No. It wasn't possible. My eyes had already begun to fill with tears, taking the room out of focus and into a distorted nightmare of shapes and colors.

"He was just here," I breathed, not understanding how one second he had been here and now they were telling me he was gone? Not gone, dead. How? When? No, no, he had just been here, it couldn't have been a dream.

"I'm sorry, miss, it would seem he passed two months ago," the nurse added, her voice remorseful.

"Two months?" I echoed, the tears falling from my eyes

clearing my sight. Months. Two whole months — I hadn't even been at school for two months. It wasn't possible.

Through the tears I looked around the bunker, the base that had been attacked, destroyed in a battle. How had it been rebuilt so fast? Rei had said it had only been a week since the battle at the frontline.

Rei. The hospital.

I shook my head and closed my eyes, a sharp pain—an almost familiar pain—filled my chest. "H-How long have I been here?" I asked feebly.

"You need to take it easy, you're still very weak," the nurse said, softly placing her hands on my shoulders. I looked up, startled, and flinched away. She'd touched me? No, no one touched me, at least no one had before... Rei and his brother.

Memories of the night at the hospital, of the two weeks at T.R.E., ripped through my mind as if tearing open stitches in a barely healed wound. I cried out, clutching my stomach, bile burning my throat. I turned on my side, and, as if knowing I would need it, the doctor held up a small bin, which I used to empty the contents of my stomach. My vision grew gray and spotty as my head swam.

Heaving, I ground out. "How long?"

"You have been missing for four months. You came to this makeshift hospital about a week ago."

I rolled weakly back on the bed, all the strength leaving me.

Four months. I had been missing for *four* months?

I tried to recall something, anything that made waking up in this place possible. Anything that could make sense of what they were saying.

"I can't remember," I whispered to myself. "Four months..." How had four months of memories just vanished?

A man in a dark military suit walked over to us. He had long salt-and-pepper dreads twisted over one side of his broad shoulders. His skin was like the ocean at night, his eyes standing out like moonlight on the surface. Only a long pink scar marred the surface of his face, the length spanning from brow to lips. From what I could see, his garb was meant to have the attachments for metal armor, which could only mean he was some kind of general.

"I will take it from here," he said, his voice deep and gravelly. One hand lifted, shooing the doctor and nurse away.

"Her body has been through a lot, she needs her rest," the nurse said, and again I was befuddled by her care for me. Had my skin suddenly changed from being Golan ash to Shamarian in the months I was gone? The months I had no memory of. Instinctively I looked down at my hands still fisted in the rough green fabric. My skin remained unchanged. Somehow this was a comfort to me, and I relaxed my hands.

"I understand her condition, but as I said, I will take it from here." The look he gave the doctor and nurse was final, and without a word the doctor walked away. The nurse, however, did not.

"Rina." The general looked at me, drawing my attention. "Can you recall anything from while you were missing?" he asked sternly.

I felt defensive for a moment, ready to vindicate myself of whatever he was implying. I had spent my whole life defending myself—even now as the victim I would have to again? This was what I expected; the nurse's kindness was a fluke.

I narrowed my eyes. "No, it's all blank."

"What is the last thing you remember before waking up here?"

I frowned, but thought back to the night in the hospital. Meeting Jean, Theo and Armond. The look on Rei's face as I yelled for him to run. The cold that filled my body.

I crossed my arms over my chest, feeling the nausea crawl through me as I tried to remember anything after that moment.

"Just leaving the hospital, getting possessed. Then nothing... It's blank." The room seemed to tilt even though I was lying down, and though I couldn't make sense of it, pain like nothing I'd ever felt before ripped through my chest. What is this? Worse than bleeding out on the roof. Worse than splinters in my face, because those had all been physical. This was a pain inside, a pain invisible to anyone else but the person feeling it. The closest thing I could compare it to was the night my father had told me my mother was dead—and now he was gone too?

Was I really alone? Without a family? Without my memories?

"Rina, please calm down," the general cautioned as he moved the nurse to stand behind him.

The trembling I had felt in my father's hug had returned and intensified. Eyes wide, I gasped and sat up, my gift pulsing through me like a storm, wild and out of my control, tainted by something dark. My vibration gift, something that had always come to me like a warming in my chest, something that had felt like home and safety, was wild and angry. I tried to calm the vibrations rocking out of my body in thrumming waves, but something thick and heavy coated my senses, making a wall between me and my gift. Between me and my soul. I couldn't control the vibration. The heavy inky barrier hung unmovable, coating what should feel light and alive.

"I'm not doing this..." I panted, trying to calm down.

"Come on, you can control it! I know you can!" the general shouted, shielding himself and the nurse from the waves crashing against them. The cries and shouts of pain and protest from the other injured in the room met my ears. I was hurting everyone. I needed to stop to gain control, but it was like the moment I had become possessed—I could do nothing to stop it.

"Rina! Look at me," the general yelled, and I turned my wide eyes on him.

His hand reached out, the skin stretching and rippling against my gift as he pressed through the wall of vibrations around me.

I lifted my hand, taking his in mine. The moment our hands touched, he closed his eyes and a feeling of calm spread through me. He gritted his teeth, holding on to me till finally my power settled down, folding reluctantly back into me.

We stayed holding hands for a moment, the cries of the other patients filling the air.

What had I just done? Shakily I lifted my head.

"What happened to me? I feel so, so wrong. I feel like... I did something... more than this." I gestured to the bunker and the freshly cracked walls. "Something else, something worse, but I don't know what?" I searched his nearly white eyes, pleading.

The general closed his eyes and sighed. "That is because you did," he answered gravely.

The nurse looked at me with horror. Whatever

compassion she had felt for me was gone as she hurried from the room, the look of fear on her face never softening.

She was terrified of me, and looking down at my hands—she was not the only one.

CHAPTER 2

A City of Ruin

The general sat down on my bed, pushing his dreads back, showing a distinct widow's peak and strands of gray in his eyebrows and along his jaw. "My name is Liam." He patted my hand and smiled slightly, causing a cascade of lines to form around his eyes and mouth. "I would like to help you uncover your lost memories."

I looked at this stranger uncertainly. He was a general, and clearly from his age, one of high standing. He had just seen what I had done to the people in the bunker. So why was he offering to help me instead of carting me away as a danger, a menace, to all Shamarians? I was Golan after all.

"Sir Liam—" I hesitated. "You said I did something. Please tell me. Tell me what happened."

"Rina, now is not the time—"

"Tell me," I persisted.

He nodded, patting my hand again, whether to do the trick he had done before to calm me, or as a gesture of kindness, I wasn't sure. "Erasmus has fallen to Golan. The city is in ruins."

9

I shook my head, not sure how much more bad news I could handle. My father was already—no, I pushed all thoughts of that away. "How did the city fall? Because of the night at the hospital?"

He stood up and reached for a bag at my feet, dropping it on the edge of the bed. "That was only the beginning. It was a progressive takeover. The first wave was the Grieving. With the front line marginally defended, they forced their way into the city past the last of our defenses. They poured into the streets at night, killing and burning everything in their path. The second wave was the Wraiths, possessing the students at nearly every school. They possessed so many gifted children at once, we didn't have enough manpower to stop them. To protect them. They used children against parents, making it impossible for us to fight back. How could a father or mother stop or kill their own child? Then the children disappeared. The Wraiths would possess them and, before the sun came up, take them across the border into Golan's territory."

I covered my mouth, knowing full well what would become of those kids, how they would become slaves and be raised up to abuse their power until they became monsters: the Grieving.

"I can't believe it." But I could. It was a calculated and planned takeover, something years in the making, which was Golan's style. They were in it for the long game, and in all the previous battles it had been the same. Shamar was always on defense, reacting to whatever nefarious scheme Golan had taken years to orchestrate. After thousands of years, you would think Shamar would change their strategy, but without a king, Shamar was a lost kingdom, and Golan was ever the strategist.

"The third wave was when the city finally fell. Nearly

everyone was evacuated, but those who stayed are either dead or imprisoned in their homes to starve or become bait for the Wraiths."

"The third wave?" I asked, while everything in me screamed that I didn't want to know the final stage in Golan's terrible plan.

"A hooded figure on a dragon set fire to the city. Whoever rode the beast had such amazing power that they were able to blow a hole into the center of the city, killing thousands instantly."

"Dragon?" I asked, feeling that out of everything I had just been told, from my father to the fallen city, this had to be the most outlandish thing. Though the image of a winged beast flying over the city, flames raining down on the clay-brick homes, charring the innocent to crisps of black flesh, played in my mind, I couldn't reconcile it. Though the image was vivid, the possibility was ludicrous. Dragons were gone. Long gone, like King Roark and Queen Eline, 400 years kind of gone.

"Yes, we believed them to be extinct, lost to our world after King Roark made the deal with Skithian."

Deal? It made sense that a general would know the stories about how King Roark gave his life to save our people from Skithian, but a deal? That wasn't language just anyone would use.

"You're not just a general, are you?" I asked, wary of the older man for the first time.

"You are not just an ordinary student of T.R.E?" he countered, an almost-twinkle in his pale eyes.

My face grew hot and I became aware of how many eyes were on us, watching from the surrounding cots, heads tilted in interest at the strange pair we were.

"I can't speak to what you have heard about me, but I can say that I am loyal to Shamar."

"Yes, well, many things are yet to be uncovered. Like your memories."

"I—" I began to defend myself to explain where I had been and what had happened, but the minute I pressed my mind for answers, the room began to tilt again. The nausea was back with a vengeance as I leaned over the bed, throwing up into the bin Sir Liam lifted to meet my heaving. I nodded a weak thanks as I gripped the edge of bed, shaking.

His solid hand rubbed my back in a soothing gesture. "That's enough for now. Let's get you cleaned up."

I wiped my mouth, a little embarrassed.

He returned his attention to the black bag at my feet and opened it. "Those," he gestured to my body, "are an old model." I looked down to see I was wearing a simple Krav uniform that was covered in blood; whose I had no idea, as I wasn't even sure where I would have gotten such a garment. "These," he continued, lifting a ball of fabric from the bag, "have a built-in damping system."

"Damping?" I asked, taking the outstretched suit from him. It was strange, like black rubber, but somehow threaded with gold. The king's crest was stitched into the inside of both wrists, threads of the beast's golden wings trailing up the length of the arms. The terrible beast was sewn baring its teeth, as if it could come alive and attack the wearer. It was terribly beautiful.

"It will lessen your vibration gift."

I looked up, my brows furrowed in confusion. Why would the military design such a suit? Shamar needed to strengthen their power, not lessen it. "Why—" I began to ask, but he raised his hand to stop me.

"Full transparency, they are typically made for POWs, not that you are one, but we don't need another episode like the one you just had. It's for everyone else's protection, you see."

I blinked. "Oh." Then wrinkled my nose. Such extravagant stitchwork for POWs—why dress them so nicely? But truthfully the suit was nice. Tight and fluid, much like the Krav uniforms given to Shamar soldiers to go to battle in. The sleek design and light weight of the material seemed unnecessary to give to POWs, not to mention the gold threading. Such pointless extravagance.

I twisted the sleeve, baring the king's crest for Sir Liam to see. "A bit much, don't you think?"

To my surprise, he chuckled, a deep throaty sound. "Traditionally they would not have such an embellishment, but I didn't want you to feel like an actual POW, so I asked for a bit of a modification. It is modeled after what Shamar soldiers wear to battle, only the material is different."

I looked down at the bundle in my hands. "Why give me this, other than to stop my vibrations from going out of control again..." I shook my head. "I mean, I'm not a soldier. I haven't graduated or enlisted yet. I'm only seventeen."

"As I said, many things are yet to be uncovered. You're wearing a Krav uniform presently, are you not?"

"Yes, but I don't know where it came from, or whose blood this is." I shrugged helplessly, frustration bubbling up in me.

"The uniform you're wearing is only the beginning of the mystery surrounding you. Everything that has happened the last few months has been devastating, and you seem to be at the very heart of it."

"Me?" I asked, incredulous. "I lost some memories and

suddenly I'm a city destroyer?" Something about the idea didn't seem so far-fetched. "I just started training my gift, I'm not strong enough to take down a city." All of this doubt and inquisition was because I was Golan, because I wasn't like the rest of them. I clenched my jaw, unable to take any more, and I swung my legs over the bed, dropping the suit to the floor. "No, no!" My head was shaking, adamantly denying what he was implying. It was unjust, unfair, crueler than any slander ever said about me. I could not believe what Sir Liam was alluding to.

I staggered on my feet, the cold, hard ground sending jolts of pain up my shins. My knees buckled.

"Rina," Sir Liam warned, coming around the bed to catch my shoulder before I collapsed.

My chest rose and fell, the blood on the uniform accusing me, daring me to ask who it belonged to. Daring me to believe that I was capable of causing pain and destruction.

I swallowed, reaching out to clutch Sir Liam's forearms. With a fierce desperation I looked up into his moonlight eyes, which should have terrified me, and asked the one thing that could shatter my already fractured mind.

"Who was the figure riding on the dragon?"

His gaze was knowing but steady. "That is what I'm here to find out."

CHAPTER 3

Ward of the Kingdom

Apparently, Sir Liam had asked the doctors to prep me for leaving the bunker. Hence why they'd removed all the fluids and wires when I had awoken. The shot the doctor had given me was a painkiller meant to help me deal with the physical brokenness of my body. Not only had I lost my memories, but I had four broken ribs, a fractured collarbone, a severe concussion—no doubt leading to the nausea—not to mention the numerous lacerations and bruises across my whole body, and one very crude set of stitches that spanned the length of my forearm.

I was a mess.

Liam led me—more like carried me—to the bathroom so I could change. It was on the way that he told me all about my injuries, probably hoping to spare me the alarm at finding them all myself.

It didn't work.

Though I understood on a conceptual level the injuries he listed off, it was a whole nother thing seeing my bare skin in the cloudy mirror of the bathroom. I gingerly changed clothes, counting the tan tiles lining the wall in the hopes that the action would keep me from thinking altogether, either about my injuries or the lost memories, it didn't matter. All I knew was that thinking hurt, and I didn't want to hurt anymore.

I was exhausted.

The suit compressed my skin, making the cuts and bruises feel in an odd way supported. Strangely enough, they hurt less, like being in a full-body cast without the itching. Still, the suit allowed me to move freely, the gold threads catching and glinting in the dim light of the bathroom. I looked at my reflection, caramel eyes set in ashen skin. At least some things had not changed. I splashed water on my face and dunked my hair into the sink. It was longer than I remembered. The brown curls were kinked and dirty, my scalp horribly itchy. Dirt, blood and all manner of grime dripped from my hair into the white basin. When the water ran clear, I squeezed the extra water from my locks and exited the bathroom.

Sir Liam nodded slightly upon seeing my appearance, and took my hand, placing it on his arm to support me. Together we walked outside.

The sky was gray and the air cold. It was winter, and my thoughts shot back to the night in the hospital with Rei—the humidity in the air and the heat of summer. Any doubts I still harbored about losing four months were confirmed at that moment, as I breathed in the dusk chill. The bare trees, the crunch of brown leaves beneath my feet and the stillness that only came when the creatures of the forest were hibernating, were all unquestionable proof.

"Come on," Sir Liam said when I stopped walking.

"I think I still hoped you were lying to me," I whispered when we began the walk through the trees.

"I wish it was all a lie," he consoled, a pain in his tone that told me he too was struggling with some kind of loss.

We came to a small clearing filled with all kinds of automobiles and other vehicles, covered in nets and leaves as camouflage.

Sir Liam cleaned off and opened the door of an inconspicuous truck, very different from the fancy military vehicle I had been expecting.

"We are too close to the border here," was all he said before guiding me into the passenger's seat.

We drove in silence, neither of us having the desire or need to break it. My desire stemmed from exhaustion more than anything else. I could care about everything tomorrow; now I just wanted to be left alone. To sleep. To be numb.

The road we traveled was unfamiliar to me, the woods outside of the city spanning patches across the dry, rocky earth. He did not take me past the wreckage of the city, though I longed to see it for myself.

I didn't know if I could trust Sir Liam, at least not fully. I didn't know how much of what he'd told me was actually true, but I didn't want to fight. If he was sent to kill me, then I supposed I would be okay with that. I had never wanted to fight, but my whole life I had been expected to. For at least tonight I wanted to put down that expectation.

After a while, when the sky was dark and the stars glittered overhead, we pulled up to an old cabin. The wood was weatherworn and creaking.

"I will take you to see the city when you are better, and only during the day. Too many Wraiths roam the streets at night," Sir Liam said, stopping the truck and climbing out, answering the question I hadn't asked.

"So you know that I am skeptical of you?" I noted aloud, closing the door of the vehicle.

"I would consider you naive if you were not, and I don't consider you naive," he answered over his shoulder as he opened the door to the cabin.

I slowly ascended the wooden steps and followed him inside. The cabin was as small as it had appeared from the outside. It was all one open room, with a single door that led to what I assumed to be a bathroom. The walls and floor were less weathered than the exterior, but were creaking all the same. There was a couch in the middle of the room and a bed in the far right corner. A tiny stone hearth and rug faced the couch, a thin counter and stool behind that. I had never seen a home so bare-bones before.

Sir Liam moved to light a fire, and I stood awkwardly in the doorway.

I was in the middle of nowhere with a man I hardly knew. Who was he to me? I was an orphan, if what the doctor had said about my father was true, so then what gave Sir Liam the right to take me from the bunker, and why had I not thought to ask that before getting into his truck?

"So what is this? My new home? Did you adopt me or something?" I ventured, hoping it was not something more sinister. Sir Liam didn't give me the impression of a malicious villain, but what did I know? I had a concussion after all.

He laughed. "No, you are a ward of the kingdom, and I am a servant of the kingdom. I am to look after you till a proper place has been found for you."

I didn't like the way that sounded. A proper place would

be in Golan with the rest of my kin. At least that was what any Shamarian would say if he asked them.

What choice did I have? I couldn't control my power, and if it was true, about the city, about my father, then I had nowhere else to go anyway. At least this was a roof over my head and food to eat. I walked over to the counter and picked up a plum from the smooth clay bowl.

"May I?" I asked, holding up the fruit.

Sir Liam nodded, and I bit into it. The juice was sweet and bitter, and like in the bunker, the room began to tilt, a sharp pain splitting through my head, and I dropped the plum, falling to the floor in a heap.

Cold metal bars pressed against my cheek. Blue eyes stared deeply into mine. The weight of the plum settled in my hand. A whispered voice said, "I'm sorry."

I cried out, pain pulsing down my neck and over my ears, behind my eyes. The images came fast and jumbled, like a patterned fabric too intricate to look at in detail. The blue eyes held such love and compassion but such terrible pain. The cold of the metal felt so real. Worst of all was the fear, the wild anxiety that scoured my chest like hungry beetles whose only food source was hope. The words whispered the last piece of hope I had left in all the world.

Sir Liam was at my side. "Rina, please, you will tear the house down! Please calm down, breathe, now. Good, that's it. Easy." He held my hands in his, pleading with his eyes.

Everything Sir Liam had done and said to this point felt rehearsed in comparison to the genuine fear and concern in his body language. I closed my eyes and shut out the feelings, the voice, the vivid blue eyes, and let myself give in to the calm Sir Liam was passing into me. Slowly the pain ebbed and my screaming stopped.

"W-What is happening to me?" I whispered, looking up at him from the floor.

"Child, what you mean to ask is what *happened* to you. This is some form of post-traumatic stress. Your power, your soul is twisted and broken, like those with the sickness, like the Grieving, but you aren't suffering from the same affliction as they, this is something else. Something I don't think you wanted."

I tried to understand his words. Trauma? My whole life had been one trauma after another and I had handled it all fine. I had been fine. Sure, a little bitter, and aggressive, but I'd held on to my father and my promise to my mother and I had been okay. So what had caused me to become this broken and pained thing? Something like the Grieving?

"How do you know?"

"Well, I don't, at least not for sure." He scooped me up off the floor and carried me to the bed, placing me down gently on the green-and-red plaid. "Just rest now. The Seraphs didn't travel through time all in one night, and we won't unravel this mystery in one either."

I looked at him with a slightly raised brow. No one brought up the Seraphs in such a simple turn of phrase. It was so old-fashioned, like something from King Roark's reign. I would have questioned him about it, but my strange outburst had drained me, and though the damping suit had stopped me from destroying the cabin, it hadn't stopped the pain from destroying me.

I pressed my face into the cool pillow, determined to wake and find that all of this had just been a terrible dream.

CHAPTER 4

Little Golan Girl

I slept eighteen hours in the days that followed that first night.

When I was awake, Sir Liam had me focus on building up my physical strength again. My routine became eating, training and sleeping on repeat.

Sir Liam didn't ask me any further questions, probably to avoid whatever panic attacks seemed to get triggered when I tried to recall the last four months, and though I was grateful I hadn't had another outburst, it was getting increasingly difficult to actively avoid thinking about my father. How he might have died, if he had been buried, if I had been there. These thoughts would sneak up on me and start the beginning waves of another outburst, but I was getting good at noticing the signs.

Sir Liam helped me steady my mind when it began to tilt, but like the thoughts of my father, it was harder still to avoid thinking about the kids from the schools. I had been to nearly all the schools in Erasmus, and though subsequently kicked out of each, for every cruel jerk I crossed paths with, I encountered the same number of normal, innocent kids just trying to survive school like me. To imagine those kids now suffering in Golan, as slaves—it chilled me to the bone. Most of the kids I had been in contact with were rude and hateful. Though they had been kids who abused and ridiculed me, I would not wish the misery of Golan encampments upon them, upon anyone. Despite their faults, they did not deserve to become slaves to Golan, to the sickness, to become monsters void of free will.

One person most of all plagued my mind, no matter how violently I banished thoughts of him.

Rei.

What had happened to him? Had he been trapped, tortured? Was he one of the thousands killed instantly?

The spark I had felt with him was small, something that should have been a passing curiosity, but instead it lingered inside me, making me desperate to know his fate. Each day the desire to find him, to find out what had happened the night after the hospital attack, grew stronger till I could not fight the thoughts anymore. I had to know what had happened to him, to all of them, to my father—and hiding out in the woods was not going to help me find out.

———

The sun rose and I along with it. My body felt stronger, my wounds greatly improved, though my mind was still fractured and unfocused most of the time.

I pushed up from the bed to find Sir Liam wasn't on the couch as he had been every morning before.

Rubbing sleep from my eyes, I walked outside. The sun

hung lazy in the sky overhead as I stepped barefoot on the cold, dew-covered grass.

Sir Liam and a young man I didn't know practiced Krav at the top of the hill that rolled up from the ground to the left of the cabin. They glided, dancing through Krav movements with a grace that almost felt familiar.

The young man had dark skin like Sir Liam, his hair pulled back into a fist of short dreads. He wore a Krav uniform, but it did not have the clasps for metal adornments to show a higher station, like the one that Sir Liam had. The young man was just a soldier, and unlike the threading on my uniform, his was solidly black, blending almost seamlessly into his dark skin. Then the young man turned, showing a pattern of glittering gold stitching across the back collar of his uniform. It was hard to make out, but it looked to be a claw and wing surrounded by intricate curling threads that traversed the arches of his shoulder blades and down along his spine. I watched in awe as the rising sun caught the tessellated threads, making them glimmer like scales.

I shuffled forward on the slick ground, drawn to the way the two men seemed to float on the morning breeze with their deft movements. They bent and twisted, arms gliding on the air as if the wind were carrying them through the flow. When I was only a few paces away, the young man's eyes opened as he sensed my approach.

I could see the clear planes of his face, the gentle curve of his jaw showing he was closer to my age than I'd originally thought. He was nearly identical to the broad-shouldered man next to him, but where Sir Liam's eyes were nearly white as a snowdrop, this man's eyes were a crisp blue, like a cloudless midday sky.

They stirred an emotion in me, one I couldn't explain,

but felt familiar and akin to crippling sorrow. My thoughts flicked back to another set of blue eyes. Eyes housed in a pale-skinned, dark-haired man, who always wore a gray suit. I refused to think his name, refused to dwell on those labradorite eyes, which had compelled me too easily before. My stomach flip-flopped painfully.

"Sir Liam," I croaked, feeling the beginning tilt that warned of a coming panic attack.

Sir Liam paused his movements, though his eyes remained closed.

"Your vibrations are restless..." he said slowly, lifting his hand as if to carry the wind to the edge of his fingers, letting it gather at the tip before letting it flutter away like a caged bird released.

"Who is this?" I breathed, trying to steady myself while refusing to look at the young man with the triggering eyes.

"My nephew. Aaron," he answered without breaking his flow. I looked briefly between the two. That was why they looked so similar.

Aaron looked down at me, and I looked away, avoiding his eyes. He began to descend the small hill to meet me. I glanced at the cabin behind me, the desire to turn and run back inside surprising me. I wasn't a coward.

Boots stopped in the grass in front of me. They were standard military issue, nothing special, but I fixated on them as if they'd been fashioned by the Creator of Strings himself. Maybe in the last four months I had become a coward, because when a smooth dark hand clasped my elbow in a traditional greeting between soldiers, instead of reciprocating I trembled pathetically where I stood, my arm hanging limply at my side.

"I'm Aaron."

"Rina," I whispered.

He crouched down, head tilting, blocking my view of his boots, to peer up at me.

Though I knew it was coming, I couldn't stop my gasp at seeing his blue eyes again.

I stumbled backwards as eyes the most startling blue replaced the ones before me. His last words to me in the hospital filled my mind. "I'm so sorry, Rina." The boy I refused to remember, Tae.

"No!" I yelled, pushing away from the boy in front of me and stumbling backwards. "Sir Liam." I panted as I continued to shuffle away from the small hill and back to the safety of the cabin.

"Rina?" For the first time, Sir Liam sounded alarmed. His pounding footsteps chased down the hill after me.

His hands were on my shoulders, shaking me slightly to get me to look up at him. My whole body was shaking so hard that even Sir Liam's broad shoulders trembled from holding me.

"Breathe. Easy, now."

I complied, looking up at the older man. His face was steady and strong, and before I could stop myself, tears filled my eyes, spilling over my cheeks. I missed my father, missed his easy comfort—comfort I could never feel again.

"I'm sorry, I should have told you my nephew was coming," Sir Liam apologized, misunderstanding my distress. "Aaron, please get us some more firewood," he ordered over his shoulder, and the young man turned and disappeared through the trees.

"Why is this so hard?" I muttered weakly once he was gone.

"Your soul remembers, and in time your mind will too,"

he assured me. Maybe he hadn't misunderstood my distress after all.

I had come to realize Sir Liam was a quiet, reserved man. He was relaxed about most things and did his best to make me comfortable, but other than during training, he spoke very little, yet his eyes were ever watchful. Whether waiting for me to snap, or have another memory surface, I wasn't sure. All I knew was his calculated watchfulness was also a reminder of the labradorite-eyed boy I kept banishing from my mind. And like I had with that blue-eyed boy from months ago, Sir Liam and I fell into an easy, comfortable silence with each other. He never pressed me to remember, and I hadn't pressed him to take me to the city.

"I'm okay now." I nodded, stepping out of his hold and looking at the rising sun. I swiped at my cheeks, calling on all the stubborn determination I had left in me. I had decided today was the day I would press Sir Liam. I had planned to before the sudden appearance of his nephew, but not even that disruption would change my mind.

I closed my eyes and exhaled, focusing on what I had decided the night before. "I need your help," I began, turning to look at Sir Liam, who made a small laughing noise while raising an eyebrow. "I mean, I need more of your help," I amended, rolling my eyes. "I need to find someone. Someone who might be able to help me remember."

"Who?"

"The school I attended, T.R.E.—I need to find the headmaster's son." I shifted. "If he is still alive."

He nodded, crossing his arms over his broad chest. "Hmm. I am familiar with the headmaster and his sons. Which one are you looking for, Taegan or Rei?"

At the names of the two boys, my whole body seized up. I

stumbled back as if shoved, my heels catching on the wooden steps that led to the cabin.

Everything began to tilt again as my back slammed into the doorframe. I clutched the worn wood, not caring that splinters jabbed into my fingers.

I struggled to catch my breath —as quickly as the attack had ebbed before, it returned, but with a vengeance. I clung to consciousness even as my vision frayed and a smooth voice filled my mind.

"Tae isn't who I want to be anymore. If I could, I would be Taegan, just Taegan."

I cried out as a pain so acute it felt like being burned from the inside filled my body, making me dry heave on the grass.

"Rina—Rina, come back to me, come on. Focus."

"Rei?" I breathed, my mind confused.

"Is she okay?" Aaron's voice asked somewhere far away.

"Bring her inside, I have to get to work," Sir Liam ordered.

Arms lifted and carried me.

"I need to find Rei," I muttered to the darkness, unsure if the words were spoken aloud or in my mind.

"Very well, rest now," Sir Liam answered.

"I've been asleep too long," I protested, even as listlessness climbed through my bones and I was placed atop something soft.

"You haven't been asleep long enough."

I tried to open my eyes, but they refused. All of my energy was sapped, and though I could feel someone slowly picking the splinters from my hands, I could not tell if it was Aaron or Sir Liam. The sensation was minimal, and I found my mind fluttering to another memory—one from months ago, before my possession, before the lost time, when a blue-eyed boy had pulled splinters from my skin in much the same way.

I fought to stay awake as the memory swept me through another wave of tremors.

"Sleep, it will make more sense when you wake up."

I wanted to disagree. Sir Liam had said the same thing every single time I fell asleep and every single time I awoke, but nothing made any more sense than it had the day before. Even so, I had begun to trust Sir Liam, so I drifted, succumbing to the sleep that desperately wanted to take me.

For the first time since waking up in the bunker, I dreamed.

Four months ago...

"No, no..." I breathed, my body going numb. With all the strength I had left, I turned to Rei. "Go!" I yelled, pleading.

Rei didn't hesitate. He grabbed Jean, pulling her away from me, deep into the cover of the trees, as my vision clouded with a violet haze.

When the haze receded, I opened my eyes to a dark cell. Metal bars pressed against my cheek, I gasped as if my lungs had been empty of air for a long time. I panted, my hands roaming my body as if I wasn't sure I was alive. I hadn't died, or at least I didn't think I had.

I had been possessed, had probably done unspeakable things, but where was I now? Was I in prison? The cold stone at my feet and the bars indicated as much, but I couldn't see anything well in the dark. The faint drip of water reached my ears, and I closed my eyes to reach out with my gift.

The scrape of a metal door opening had me on my feet.

A cloaked figure came out of the shadows, approaching the bars.

"Who are you? Where am I?" I yelled, my vibration rising up in me as I prepared to attack the bars and the person on the other side of them.

"Conserve your strength. Your gift cannot help you here," a soft voice whispered, and the cloaked figure placed a tray of food on the floor beside the bars.

I backed away, though hunger gnawed in the pit of my stomach. "Who are you? Where am I?" I demanded again.

"Eat and rest. You are not in a safe place, so you will need your strength."

I faltered at her words. It was obvious I wasn't in a safe place—I was in a cell and I didn't know why—but her honesty confused me. Why admit I was not a safe place?

"Why am I here?" I asked again, my voice low and more controlled.

"That isn't for her to answer." Another voice, like embers of a fire, spoke in the dark room.

"Master." The cloaked girl bowed and scurried out. I looked to see the new person, but could not make them out at all in the dark.

"So you will tell me, then." I lifted my chin, definitely ready to reach through the bars and yank the person into the thick metal. Ready to bruise whoever was crazy enough to cage me.

"It isn't his place to answer that question either." A languorous new voice slithered in the air, making my stomach curl. All bravado left me and I shivered. This new voice was darkness itself.

"What do you want from me?"

"I want you, Relina Gilead, to help me take down a city."

The snakelike voice whispered in the air along my neck, as if somehow the man was behind me. I turned, ready to strike, but my fist connected with the stone wall as my vibrations rebounded back into me sending me flying. My back cracked into the metal bars and an arm wrapped around my throat, tight enough to hold me but not choke me.

The voice like embers caressed my ear and I bristled, finding the sound familiar. "It would be in your best interests to eat and rest now. Unless you plan to kill yourself, there is no way out of here." His breath was warm against my ear. "No one is coming to get you. To everyone you are already dead." The man held up a plum, pressing it hard into my lips till the supple flesh ripped against my clenched teeth and juice dipped down my chin.

"Sweet dreams, little Golan girl."

CHAPTER 5
Wavemaster

Present day

I sat up, my hands rubbing over my mouth and chin, feeling for any sign of the plum. I winced instead at the tips of my fingers wrapped in small bandages.

"You're awake then," Sir Liam said, handing me a cup of tea.

I smelled the sweet tea, immediately recognizing it. "No!" I yelled, smacking the plum tea from his outstretched hand—the teacup clattered to the floor, the steaming contents soaking into the worn floorboards.

"Rina?" Sir Liam asked, confused, but not even the slightest bit upset.

"I'm sorry, I... I think I remembered something." I looked up at Sir Liam and chewed my lip. "I didn't believe you before. I didn't believe I could be responsible for destroying a city, but somehow... I think I did."

"What do you remember?" he asked with a renewed seriousness, sitting down on the edge of the bed.

31

Shame washed over me. "I don't want to say it."

I had been abused, of that I was sure, but was that all? What other monstrous things had those men done to me in that cell? What monstrous things had I done while out of it? I looked helplessly at my hands, recalling the Krav uniform covered in blood I had worn in the bunker.

"Rina, I want to help you, remember," Sir Liam said, placing his hand on my knee. The gesture was meant to comfort, but it felt undeserved. Somewhere in the back of my mind I knew I was a monster. Kindness was the last thing I should be given.

"I don't even know you!" I yelled, the last week catching up to me. I had tempered myself from feeling everything, anything, afraid I would cause a panic attack, that I would lose control, but I couldn't hold back anymore. "You tell me my father is dead, that a city is destroyed and I am responsible. You nurse me to health, all while telling me nothing. I know I did something, I can feel it, I can feel the pain inside me, but I don't know what I did, who I hurt to do it. How could I possibly take down a city?" My voice wobbled, and though I knew the outburst was sudden, I couldn't stop it. I felt ridiculous for not being able to handle my emotions better.

Sir Liam breathed in and closed his eyes. As he did, something came around me like a hug—warm, soft and fluttering, akin to the feathers on a newborn chick. "Can you feel that?" he wondered patiently.

"What are you doing?" I asked, the same calm cuddling close and settling inside me, as it had before. He had done this many times, calming me, but this time it felt stronger, more intentional somehow. It was as if he had been holding back before. I was instantly soothed; thoughts of my mother playing with my hair as a child, singing me to sleep, filled my senses. I was safe, I was whole, I was loved. Every terrible emotion I had just been feeling was watered down by the peace that encompassed me. I wanted to close my eyes and bask in the calm, but my stubbornness held fast, and instead I stared at him slack-jawed.

"I am a Wavemaster," he offered simply.

I blinked, my gaze falling on his hand over my knee, and though I felt like curling into his side and sighing with complete contentedness, I chose to focus on his words instead.

A Wavemaster? No. That was impossible.

"What you are feeling now is just one of the abilities Wavemasters have." He smiled. "As you know, we all have a unique frequency, vibration, but there are vibrations distinct to certain emotions too. I can replicate those vibrations and then adjust what someone is feeling based on the emotion. That is how I can calm you."

I nodded, hearing his words, but not quite comprehending them. Wavemasters were said to be extinct, gone as the Seraphs were, thousands of years ago. "That's impossible." I breathed shakily, uncomfortable with the idea of my emotions being manipulated, but also unable to deny the 180 my emotions had suddenly taken.

"I can move through the vibration dimension, see and touch people's gifts. I have felt the tangle of your gift, the way it wrestles against itself. As the manifestation of your Nephesh," he cleared his throat, "I mean your soul, I have watched it in the vibration dimension, writhe and seethe under the weight of what you have done. It will not heal on its own, so I have been helping it unmangle itself."

"I don't understand, how is that possible? How can you

touch my soul, my gift?" Nephesh, he had called it, but that word felt old, like it was something used many lifetimes ago. How old was Sir Liam, really?

"It is because I am a Wavemaster. While you are sleeping, I go into the vibration dimension and help guide the strings of your vibration, loosening the knots that bind your memory." He opened his eyes, and the calm shell around me lifted. "It is the burden and the duty of a Wavemaster to feel and see the vibrations of the world. We were a great asset in wartime, as we could find a person based on their vibration signature, even over very great distances. We were the best trackers, and in a way weapons, as we could tangle up a person's gift, just as someone has done to yours."

My eyes narrowed. "You mean to tell me that someone, like you, intentionally erased my memories by scrambling my vibrations?"

His brow furrowed sadly. "Like me, but not—the person who hid your memories was tainted. The corruption of Skithian is all over you, shrouding you in a thick darkness that makes it hard for me to see where your vibrations are even tangled. It took me a week of you sleeping for eighteen hours a day just to get one memory back for you."

I jerked. "Wait, you have been doing this every night?" I asked, knowing I should feel uncomfortable, invaded, but I didn't. Whatever a Wavemaster was, it was not dark and sick like what was already in me. If anything, the thought of Sir Liam untwisting the darkness inside of me was a comfort, if not a bit strange.

"I know it is only right to ask your permission, and I should have from the start, but I didn't think you would believe me if I did not have proof. You are quite a strong-willed girl. Now that you remember something from the last few months and can fully understand what I can do, I will ask your permission. Do you want me to continue to help you uncover your lost memories?"

I swallowed. I had no other choice if I was going to help save the city, the city I was most likely responsible for destroying in the first place. "Yes." I nodded.

"Thank you for understanding."

I looked away from Sir Liam, and started. Aaron sat on the couch, his eyes dark in the dim light of the cabin. Without the enhancement of the sunlight giving life to his eyes, I found his presence much more bearable. He stood up and walked over to the bed, crossing his arms in a similar way to Sir Liam. He tilted his head, eyes glancing at the tea on the floor. "Now that that's settled, may I ask why my homemade tea is so offensive to you?"

My face flushed. "I'm sorry!" I hopped off the bed to pick up the cup. I glanced around for something to use to clean up the spill.

Aaron threw a rag at my face, making me flinch. "Seriously, what could my tea have possibly triggered?"

I moved the rag to the floor, about to respond but Aaron was walking away to sit on the couch, his question clearly rhetorical.

I glanced at Sir Liam, but he was smiling, which made me very confused.

"Leave it and take some fresh air with me," Sir Liam offered, standing and walking to the door. The cabin felt significantly smaller with three people instead of two.

I followed him outside. The moon was dipping down to the west—I had slept away another day and night. Winter's chilly gusts danced through the bare trees. I wrapped my arms around my middle to hold in my body's warmth.

"My nephew is here to help keep me safe," Sir Liam said, white puffs wafting into the night air. "When I am in the vibration dimension, I am left very vulnerable. Afterwards I am very weak; I can't protect you or myself." He rubbed his hands together. "The process is very draining."

"Oh, I see." I nodded. I had wondered why Sir Liam would invite someone else to the cabin. "What's with the tea?" I asked, recalling Aaron's sour mood.

"Ah, well, he makes tea when he's sorry about something. He feels like he must have upset you somehow when you met, and was trying to make up for it."

My face burned with embarrassment. "And I threw his apology on the ground."

"Yes, well," Sir Liam chuckled slightly, "it was rather ironic. Poor boy, took him all day and night to make it."

My jaw dropped, and though I was horrified that I had tossed away all of Aaron's hard work, I found it rather funny too. "I should apologize," I acknowledged between chuckles.

"Perhaps you should make some plum tea."

We both laughed, unable to hold it in.

After a few moments I controlled my laughter and turned to go inside, the night far too brisk to be standing idly about.

"Sir Liam," I began, and hesitated at the door, "you said you could find people over great distances, and you have met Rei before, so you know his vibration signature..." I trailed off, letting my question hang in the cold night air.

"To answer your question, yes, I can find him." His brow furrowed, making the scar over his eye wrinkle oddly. "But don't you want to uncover more of your memories first?"

"We can do that along the way. I just feel like Rei is part of this somehow, and I... I need to know if he is safe." The truth of that revelation had us both looking somber.

"Very well."

We shared a look of agreement that had me sighing and my shoulders relaxing. Sir Liam would find Rei, and by the Strings I hoped when we did he was alright.

I turned away and entered the cabin, ready to apologize to Aaron for my weird outbursts. It seemed like Aaron had a pretty good idea of what was going on with me, though I wasn't sure what all Sir Liam might have shared.

Sir Liam offered to stay outside, giving Aaron and me a few minutes alone to address our misunderstandings and start again.

When I walked in, Aaron was dumping the plum tea down the kitchen sink.

"What are you doing?" I asked, alarmed and ashamed. Was he dumping it because of me?

He glanced up with a confused look on his face. "It's just gonna go to waste, and will attract pests if left sitting out."

"But you spent so much time making it," I protested, coming over to the pot in his hands and taking it from him. Only, I was surprised to find I could not remove the pot from his hands. I sensed his vibration— he was using his gift to hold the pot in place, preventing me from pulling it from his grasp.

I blinked, dumbfounded as Aaron turned so the pot was between us, my hands over top of his.

"You... don't like me much," he said simply.

I let go of the pot, embarrassed, and held up my hands. "It's not you, exactly," I hedged.

"Then you just don't like plums?" He shrugged and glanced down at the red liquid.

I glanced at it too and then waved my hands. "No, um, it's your eyes." I shifted uncomfortably.

He tilted his head, a mannerism that fit his face well. The angle accentuated the cut of his jaw and the tight muscles of his neck. He was either too young to grow facial hair or he just naturally didn't have it, as his skin was smooth, unmarked by blemish or stubble.

"My eyes?" he asked, and the objects of offense widened with curiosity.

"Yeah," I said, lamely unsure if I should mention the reason for my dislike, or just let it be.

"This is a first. Normally my eyes are considered pretty attractive to the ladies." He grinned, no doubt another thing the ladies found attractive, as his smile was pearly and whimsical in a mischievous way. "So what exactly seems to be the problem with them?"

"Umm." I looked up at his eyes as if the problem would jump out at me. The dim firelight caught in the clear depths, and I was again relieved that in the poor lighting they were nothing spectacular, and did not make my insides twist painfully as they had earlier. "I don't know what all your uncle has told you about me, but I've been through some stuff." I pointed to his normally blue eyes. "They are a little triggering for me. I was surprised, is all. It really has nothing to do with you," I answered honestly, feeling sorry for making him feel bad.

He placed the pot in the sink and leaned in, eyes staring pointedly into mine. "They don't seem to be bothering you right now," he observed.

"They don't look blue right now," I answered without thinking.

"So your captor had blue eyes?" he deduced, leaning back seriously, arms crossing.

"What? No!" I held up my hands, confused as to why he would draw such a conclusion.

"Then what?"

"It's not your business." I shook my head, annoyed, and grabbed his arm, clasping it at the elbow with one hand, and with the other taking his hand to do the same to my arm. "I'm Rina Rineheart, it's nice to meet you," I mumbled gruffly, trying to change the subject.

His hand closed over my elbow, and with a wide dazing smile, he said, "Aaron Martus, pleasure's all mine." We stared at each other, a challenge sizzling beneath our unassuming gaze.

I was the first to break it. "Now, about this tea. There is nothing to apologize for on your end. I'm the one who acted out." I dropped my arm. "There is no need to dump away your hard work."

He watched my expression, carefully letting go of my arm after a few beats of awkward silence. "My uncle is allergic to plums. It's the only tea I know how to make, though, and since you seem to also have an aversion to it..." He trailed off.

"Why can't you drink it?" I asked.

"I don't like sweet things," he said dismissively as if there was more to it than that but he didn't want to say.

"Well, then..." I mused, looking at the pot.

The door opened and Sir Liam walked in, cutting through the awkward silence.

"If it's all settled, then I'm off to sleep," he said, walking heavily to the bed. "May I?" He looked at me.

"Of course," I answered quickly, confused why he would ask me. It was his cabin though he had been letting me use the bed the last few days.

"Aaron, keep an eye on her. The sun's coming up, but I need a few hours of sleep after yesterday."

I opened my mouth to ask about finding Rei, when Sir Liam held up his hand, silencing me. "Tomorrow. I will look for him tomorrow."

"Uncle?" Aaron asked, concern in his voice as he walked to the bedside.

"I'm okay, just spent," the older man assured, lying down and falling asleep instantly.

Aaron tucked in his uncle and gave a gentle squeeze to his hand before turning back to me.

"Wanna take a walk?"

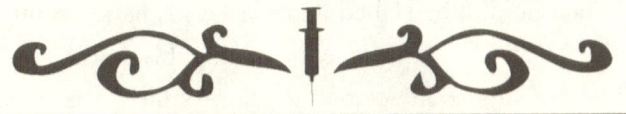

CHAPTER 6

Death by a Thousand Cuts

I hadn't realized when Aaron said "take a walk" he actually meant "go up to the small hill in the freezing temperatures to train."

We didn't speak at first. I followed his lead as he moved through different flows of Krav. I let my body, stiff and shivering, move through the dance, learning some new movements along the way.

Aaron was a unique teacher. While Sir Liam had been focused on meditation and strength training, Aaron utilized slow, steady holds and bends, which made my muscles burn in an entirely different way. Though I could barely use my gift, I somehow felt like I was still meditating in the flow.

The sun rose over us. The sky exploded with dusty blues and golds, which melted the light frost that tipped the grass.

Aaron held his eyes closed even when the sun wrapped around us, warming my skin. I relished the light as it took the chill from the ground and my bones. The sun cast golden light across his dark skin, making him look like an onyx carving inlaid with gold leaf.

The king's crest shimmered in the growing light. I was not sure how long I watched him. How many twists and turns he had done before noticing my stare?

When he did, he sighed and placed his hand on his hip, breathing heavily. "What is so interesting this time?"

I smiled, and that seemed to startle him. "The crest—it looked like a claw and a wing. I've never seen anything like it before."

He glanced over his shoulder as if he had forgotten it was there. "Oh, yes. Hm. Normally I wear a cloak."

"Why cover up such a pretty design?"

"It's rather inconvenient to broadcast my allegiance during wartime."

"I suppose that's true."

"I was in such a hurry to get to my uncle, I forgot to grab it," he said, mostly to himself.

"What does it mean?"

"I'm not sure my uncle would want me telling you."

"Oh..." I frowned slightly, then thought of something else I was wondering. "Your uncle seems rather old. Like 'talks like he's from King Roark's reign' kind of old. Which is impossible, but it's rather odd. How old is he?"

Aaron shifted uncomfortably. "I don't know if he would want me to tell you that either." He scratched the back of his head, making his mess of dreads bounce.

I crossed my arms, getting annoyed. "Fine, then let me ask something about you."

"Me?" he asked, pointing comically at himself.

"Why don't you like sweet things? And don't say it's because they rot your teeth." I lifted an eyebrow, daring him to lie to me.

The sun had moved overhead, and his eyes were starting

to shimmer blue again, but I held his gaze, determined to fight through the growing pain in my chest.

"I'll tell you, but you have to keep practicing."

"Deal."

He stood to the side and watched as I moved through a flow, grateful to be able to close my eyes.

When he didn't start talking, I peeked at him, but he wasn't looking at me; instead, he was gazing up at the sky, his expression distant.

"Aaron?"

"I fell in love with a girl. Though she was hidden away from most others her age, I was given the job to guard her. It was my first assignment as a soldier. I stayed at the capital for years watching over her, keeping her company. She was very lonely."

I blinked, surprised by his story. He was no older than me, but had been in love? "Tell me about her?" I encouraged when he grew silent as if he would say no more.

He waved his hand, signaling me to keep practicing. I did, unaware of when I had stopped the Krav flow.

"She was kindness incarnate, with hair so fair it was almost white, and eyes like the sky before a storm. She studied all things medicinal, and while I was with her, she taught me many things about natural remedies and treating wounds. Her favorite tea was plum, and she knew how to make it from scratch. One day she taught that to me as well. Her company was so gentle and calm, it was hard not to fall in love with her. I would send letters for her, as it was her only way of communicating with the world outside of the capital. One day I was sending a letter for her to a strange address; the letter was not sealed, and on the way to the post the contents fell out, and though I had not intended to read the letter, I did..."

I continued the movements, waiting for him to continue, my interest thoroughly piqued.

"It was to her lover, a man I knew well, a man I greatly respected and honored. The fervor of her passion for my superior was undeniable. I stood no chance with her. My heart broke that day, and I have been picking up the pieces since. So you see, all sweet things, especially plum tea, remind me of her. What's worse is he had been the one to teach her how to make it. I was a coward and left her after that, unable to keep bitterness from my heart, knowing everything she learned, she learned to aid him, to tend his wounds, to keep him healthy and safe."

"Oh," I breathed, sensing his anguish. Yet something about his story softened me in a way I had not felt in a long time. My life had been destruction, pain and war. Though I was sure Aaron had seen his fair share of that too, it was a strange sort of comfort to see that love could still be possible in the midst of all of that turmoil. "I'm sorry, Aaron. Do you still love her?"

"Senseless as it is, yes—yes, I do"

We said nothing more on the subject, as I was not an expert on love, nor did I know how to heal a broken heart. So instead I did the only thing I knew how to do.

"Wanna spar?" I asked.

He looked at me with the full gaze of his blue eyes. They hit me hard, and my heart pinched painfully. Was this what it felt like for him to drink plum tea? If it was, then perhaps I could sympathize on some level with his heartache.

"I'll give you a handicap." He grinned, tucking one of his arms behind his back.

Sweat poured from my brow as my body strained to stay upright. I knew Aaron was going easy on me since I wasn't able to control my vibrations properly, but one thing was clear—even after all these months, I could still pack a punch, gift or not.

After hours of sparring, we both collapsed onto the ground, exhausted and sweating. The midday sun high overhead beamed down on us, lulling me into sleep. Before I knew it, I was dozing off, the warm sun on my face reminding me of a distant day on the school rooftop from what felt like a lifetime ago, but it wasn't that day that filled my mind as sleep took me.

Four months ago...

The door opened and closed, but no light followed my captor. In the darkness, the only sounds were their footsteps and a metal tray hitting the floor.

Was this the moment they would torture me? I backed into the stone wall as far from the gate as possible. I had not seen anyone since the first night. I had been in the dark cells for what felt like days, alone and cold. My mind had been fuzzy, and my vibration gift unusable.

"Drink," a cold voice ordered, followed by the scrape of a metal container passing through the bars.

"N-No," I challenged, my voice shaking as my resolve to drink wavered.

The whine of the cell door opening had me stumbling to stand. I ran towards the sound, even though I swayed unsteadily, ready to pummel my captor and flee.

I lunged palms reaching around soft flesh. The warmth of his throat as my hands connected sent a jolt of shock through me. Had I not thought this man was alive, a person? I supposed I had not, because what kind of person caged another living thing?

So I squeezed, tightening my fingers around his neck till he gasped slightly. I didn't have my gift, but he had his, so after a fleeting moment when I thought I would win, that I could escape, I was repelled back.

My hands blew out to the sides as a sharp force slammed into my chest, tossing me against the stone wall. I coughed and wheezed, though the impact was not as bad as the last time I'd hit the metal bars.

It was clear, however, that this person meant to put me in my place.

"You wild thing... Are you a beast or are you a human? Use your head."

"Stay away from me," I rasped, pressing against the wall.

"Control yourself," he ordered, his voice worn, whether from my nearly choking him or something else, I couldn't tell.

I squinted to see in the dark, but even at close range I could not see the person; but I knew it was the same man who had put the plum against my lips.

"I won't help you! I refuse to help you!" I yelled.

"You don't have any control over that," the man informed me.

"There's nothing you can do to me that would make me help you," I said more firmly, though I continued to cower in the corner.

"You don't want the food, then?" the voice asked lightly.

My jaw clenched.

The door opened again, and another form entered.

"Why are you bothering with her?" The voice was the same slithering one as the last time. I curled against the stone.

"She needs to eat," the man in front of me answered.

"Leave me to die, I will never help you." I hissed pathetically.

"But little Golan girl, you already have." The voice of the man in front of me had become familiar again, like someone I knew but could not place.

The prick of a needle jabbed into my arm, then the door squealed closed, the other form that had entered leaving, as if satisfied just seeing me locked up.

"What is this?" I asked as my body became heavy.

Warm breath brushed along my cheek, tickling into my hair. "I'm sorry to put you through this. For making you suffer, Relina."

Then he was gone.

I tried again and again to escape my cage. But each time I fought back, I was drugged. Eventually I figured out that the serum in the needle suppressed my powers for a time, and just when my powers would begin to return, the cold would creep into my bones, telling me I was being possessed.

I was slumped on the floor, the drugs keeping me just awake enough to breathe, but unable to do much else but recall the violence I had unleashed while possessed.

I had moved through the city each night, starting in the wealthiest neighborhoods.

My gift was enhanced by the Wraiths, and with them using me I was able to topple buildings, set people on fire with the snap of a finger and split the ground with a tap of my foot.

I was chaos, I was death.

I was the face those screaming in fear saw before I reached out, my vibrations rupturing their hearts where they stood.

A clean, instant death.

The streets glowed with flames as people and buildings alike burned. The dust of the dry air carried the smell of burning flesh to my nose, and inside I gagged, vomited and screamed in pain with the people of Shamar. But my body never responded, no matter how many times it tried to fight the Wraith's control.

I drifted through the streets, the Grieving flanked around me, killing, as I continued to move forward, my arms outstretched, my vibration pulling inside me as the clay buildings thousands of years old gave under the force of my gift.

I could feel the vibrations of the hearts beating inside the building as I trapped them in the rubble to suffer and die from lack of oxygen.

Tears streamed down my cheeks as the drugs made it impossible for me to fight the images in my mind. The swirl of terror I'd wrought on my hometown. On so many innocents. How many days had it been? I couldn't recall.

"Little Golan girl, it's time to wash up," a voice said, drawing me back into my cage. The cold, damp room smelled of musk and blood. My blood? I wasn't sure.

"They are all dead, I killed them. S-So very many of them," I whispered to the voice. "I didn't want to, I didn't," I swore over and over again, till air couldn't fill my lungs.

Blood was on my hands, all over my hands. A scream was building in my throat, but my body was too heavy, too unresponsive to let it out.

"You remember?" the voice asked urgently. Something warm and wet was rubbing against my blood-coated palms. "Are you telling me you remember being possessed?"

"A little boy and girl, they were in its way. The Grieving

were killing all around me, but I didn't want to... I didn't. I didn't. I didn't, but the Wraith... so many people were in its way. So many in the way..." I trailed off, my body softly trembling with unreleased screams of agony.

I was a monster.

"Damn it," the voice snapped. "You were never supposed to remember." The man's voice quavered, as if he was fighting tears.

Somehow his emotion left me feeling less alone.

"Please, I don't want to. Please, no more," I begged, but only silence greeted me.

Sometime later voices muttered in the darkness. My head lolled to the side as I looked for the man who had cried with me, but I could see nothing. Had I imagined him?

"We can't keep using the serum on her."

"Why not? It's the only thing keeping her caged when I'm not around," the snakelike man answered.

"I think the serum is affecting her in an unexpected way. She is remembering what she is doing while possessed." It was the man who had apologized and tried to wipe the blood from my hands. His tone was informative, but it held an edge of something else.

"What an interesting side effect," the languorous snake mused, making my body shiver. "A fascinating discovery."

Anger bubbled in me. How could my pain be fascinating, how could my killing and remembering it seem like a good thing to these men?

"This isn't good for us. When she goes back to normal life, after this, she will recall all the things she has done, the people she killed, and us." There was fear in the man's voice, no doubt fear for his own neck, because once I was free I would turn them both in or kill them myself if I had to.

"Whoever said we were letting her go?"

"After the city falls, you set her free—that was the deal."

"Then get me the other half of the journal so we can end this," the sinister voice snarled.

"Of course, Master Logan," the other man said in a clipped tone.

"Don't get too attached," the snake, Logan, warned. "She most likely won't survive."

The creak of the door closing met my ears as my eyes fell closed again.

I was going to die.

I deserved to, after the things I had done.

I would welcome any end to this pain, but not before they suffered just as much.

The drugs left me in such a stupor so I hadn't noticed the man kneeling before me in my cage.

"I'm sorry, I'm so sorry." The man who had argued with Logan lifted his hand to my cheek, brushing away the rolling tears.

He was close enough that I should have been able to see his face, but in the dark all I could be sure of was his black hair and light skin.

"I hate you," I rasped as my eyes closed, too heavy with unbearable pain to keep open.

"I know." He sighed and wrapped his arms around me, pulling me against his chest.

It was a comfort that only made me cry harder.

CHAPTER 7

Honesty

I sat up, startled to find the sun kissing the treetops, and smoke billowing out of the cabin chimney down the hill from where I had fallen asleep.

Aaron lay in the patchy yellow grass next to me, eyes watching me.

I shivered, the wind drying tears on my cheeks. "Were you watching me sleep?" I asked, too startled by the memory to reason out a rational question.

"Yes, actually." He grinned, a single brow raised. "You were crying in your sleep."

My eyes narrowed. "And you didn't think to wake me from my nightmare?" I scoffed, annoyed that he had seen my pain, and a bit ashamed too, because though the things I was remembering were untwisting my soul, they only seemed to tangle up my heart in return.

"You have to remember, even if it's painful, even if you cry. It's not for me to take those memories from you." He sighed, propping himself up on his elbows. "I would have woken you under different circumstances."

"What circumstances are those?"

"If it had actually been a nightmare and not a memory."

I frowned, looking down at the grass. "Do you think it's possible for someone like me to have destroyed the city?"

A beat passed and I peeked up at him through my mess of curls.

His boyish face had turned serious. "Yes, but only with the support of a tremendously evil power." It was his turn to frown. "My uncle is helping you because he knows within your memories are the answers to who and how that evil power came to be."

"Oh." I looked down at my hands. Which one of my captors had such power. If I had to guess, I would say it was Logan. He was a monster—not that the other man wasn't, and not that I had the right to rank evil after all that I had done. Most of which I still couldn't recall, but the flashes of thought in that memory told me that the sorrow and shame I felt now was only the beginning.

"Uncle has been working on finding your friend the last few hours."

"Really?" I stood up, my body sore and aching from sparring and sleeping on the ground. "Has he found him yet?" I couldn't hide the urgency in my voice. Rei would help me; I just knew he would have answers for me.

Aaron stood up too, surprise lifting both his brows. "I don't know, it can take a while for him to find someone, days even." He continued to look at me, his head slightly cocked like he was trying to figure me out.

"What is it?" I asked, confused by his surprise.

"You just look excited, is all. It's startling after seeing you so upset."

My cheeks grew red and I shrugged. "Come on."

We jogged down the hill to the cabin.

It took only a few hours more for Sir Liam to locate Rei.

I shifted anxiously next to Aaron on the couch, watching Sir Liam stir on the bed after what felt like forever.

Sir Liam sat up and opened his eyes tiredly, his broad shoulders slightly slumped. My heart hammered against my chest as I waited for him to tell us what he had discovered.

"Rei is still in the city," Sir Liam finally said.

Though the city was not a safe place, I was relieved to know he was close by, and not in Golan, beyond my reach.

Sir Liam coughed slightly, and Aaron hurried to fill a cup with water for him.

"Where in the city?" I asked impatiently.

"It seems he is at the estate."

"The estate?" Aaron asked, handing his uncle the cup. Sir Liam took a big gulp.

"Yes, the headmaster's home is located on the school property; it's all one very large estate."

I hadn't recalled seeing another building on campus, but if the estate was as large as Sir Liam seemed to think, then it was entirely possible that I hadn't seen it. "Okay." I clapped my hands together and stood up from the couch. "When do we leave?"

Sir Liam just shook his head. "Finding Rei has used up too much of my energy, plus the sun has set." He gestured to the darkened window. "The city is the most dangerous at night. I need sleep, and despite your eighteen hour nights, you need sleep as well. It is just as draining for you as it is for me to untangle the mess of your vibrations." He stood up and walked over to the couch I had just vacated. Gently, he eased himself down on the couch and rolled his shoulders till he was settled deep in the cushions. "We will have to wait till the morning."

Even though I knew he was right, I found myself protesting. "But—" I sighed. "I don't feel tired. I feel..." Tangled, twisted, dark. All of those feelings did make me tired, but it was more of a hopelessness than fatigue. "I took a nap today," I said childishly.

"Did you have a memory return?" Sir Liam asked, his eyes shut.

I glanced at Aaron—I wouldn't be able to lie about it. I walked over to the bed and sat down next to Aaron. Despite just meeting these two men, I felt oddly safe with them, in a way that spoke of family bonds and a joint purpose.

"I did."

Aaron reached over and placed a hand on mine, encouraging me to share.

"I-I was held in a cage, in the dark," I began as tears pricked my eyes against my will. So many things had been done against my will. "I was possessed often." I continued as Aaron's hand tightened over mine. "When I wasn't, I was drugged, but the drugs did something that made me remember everything I did while possessed."

"What?" Aaron balked, looking between me and his uncle.

Sir Liam remained unfazed. "Continue, Rina."

I swallowed. "Two men held me captive. I only know one of their names, though..." I took a deep breath, building the strength to say the name of the snakelike man. "Logan."

Sir Liam's eyes opened at this, and a deep rumble of displeasure rolled out from his chest.

Aaron and I both looked at the older man, surprised.

"Uncle, do you know who that is?"

"Rina. Anything you can remember about that man is of critical importance to the Kingdom of Shamar," Sir Liam said hastily, his eyes cutting over to meet mine.

My palm began to sweat against Aaron's hand.

I thought back to the memories and to the argument the two men had seemed to have about me remembering the possessions. "They mentioned something about the other half of a journal, and using me to destroy the city."

"What of the journal? Did they say anything else?"

"No, I don't believe they did, at least nothing I can recall right now."

"Let me know the moment you learn anything else about Logan or this journal."

"What about the other man? What of him?" Aaron asked.

I considered the other man—how he could be cruel, and yet apologized, cried with me and held me. Was it all out of pity? "I'm not sure," I whispered uneasily, because I truly wasn't certain of the man's motives.

"That's enough for now. Rina, you know what to do— even if it's scary or shameful, you tell us anything you remember about Logan and the journal."

"Yes, okay." I nodded, feeling nervous about what other things I might recall.

Aaron patted my hand and moved to the spot against the door, settling in to sleep just as his uncle had.

I curled up on the cot and sighed. "Sir Liam?"

"What?"

"If you aren't... um... working on me tonight, will I..." Still dream of the memories? I had wanted to finish, but the words plugged in my throat. I didn't want to face more of the memories, but I knew somewhere in them was the answer to what had happened to my father. An answer I was too afraid to ask Sir Liam for.

"A knot has been loosened, and the effects will ripple through your vibration for some time, till it hits another knot. The more I loosen at once, the more memories will hit you at a time. It is better for now for us to go slowly." His voice was heavy and sluggish with sleep. "As slow as the moon passes the sun."

I thought of the moon's orbit. "The moon doesn't pass the sun." I yawned, rolling onto my side. Aaron leaned against the cabin door, knees bent and eyes closed. Was that how he had slept the night before? It hardly seemed comfortable.

"Yes, but it does follow us around the sun..." Sir Liam began, but when his voice trailed off, Aaron finished the phrase.

"... and like any good lover, it comes between that which it protects and that which could burn up its love."

"I don't know what either of you are talking about." I groaned, rolling to my other side, too tired to make sense of the strange poetic imagery they both seemed to know by heart.

"You will." Aaron's whisper met my ears just as sleep darkened my conscious mind.

Three months ago...

I was back in my cage, slumped on the floor, the idle drop of water on the cold stone ground the only thing passing the time. I counted the drops. Where was the water leaking from? I mused about killing my captors by breaking the source of the water and drowning us all.

It was all I could do besides cry.

The drugs were still in my system, but I was less sluggish than before. I could stand with support from the bars, but fighting was out of the question.

I had no strength. Where had my fiery spirit gone? Was I finally broken?

The door opened, and the man who had shown me tenderness entered. I knew it couldn't be Logan, because whenever he entered the room I shivered, and the bars around me took on a new vibration. It was he who controlled the rebound power. And despite the argument the two men had had, Logan continued to give me the serum.

"Get out," I growled, as if I had the authority to send the empathetic man away.

"It's getting colder out, I'm sure you felt the change in temperature," the man answered, a softness to his voice I hated. Whether because it made him more human or because it sounded familiar, I wasn't sure.

"Get out," I said again, using the bars to pull myself to my feet, sensing he was about to come into the cell.

The bars opened and he walked in, closing the metal door behind him. "Here," he answered, holding out a bedroll and blankets. "You don't have to freeze to death."

"It would be better to die sooner than later," I snipped, weakly shoving the outstretched blankets away.

"No." His tone was as cold as the hard ground. "No, don't you dare give up." The man sounded angry. "You have to be stronger than that."

His anger gave fuel to my own. How dare he tell me to be stronger, to not give up. He was my captor, he was a monster! Everything I had done was because of these men.

"Do you even know what it's like to be caged?" I demanded. "Because I'll make sure you do, I'll have you behind bars," I sneered, gathering a little strength—not my gift, because the serum subdued that, but my own physical strength—to land a punch to the man's face. In the darkness, I had to guess where he was, and despite my fairly certain estimation of his height, I was off, and my fist connected with his shoulder.

The blankets dropped to the ground, and the man, with a speed I had forgotten I used to have too, pinned me against the bars.

I gave out a yelp of pain as a bar pressed along the bones of my spine. My wrists were held to my sides, the man's body flush against mine as he leaned into my ear.

"Keep that fire and fight in you, no matter what." His breath was warm and I turned my head away, surprised. "I want you to survive this." I felt him shake his head, but even with him so close I couldn't see his face. "I need you to survive this," he whispered.

"You need me to live to assuage your own guilt," I hissed back. "My survival will not redeem you."

"I don't believe there is anything that can redeem the things I have done." He sighed, and the sorrow in his voice made me certain that his guilt was wholly felt.

He released me in a gust, and was out of the cage and through the door without another word.

CHAPTER 8
Homeward

I stretched my arms high over my head, woken by a new day, and eager to push the memories from last night from my mind. Since it had not been about Logan or the journal or even about the city, I felt it wasn't necessary to share. Besides, today was the day we were going to find Rei.

My stomach flip-flopped with anticipation and dread.

As we prepared to head out into hostile territory, an air of determined cautiousness descended over us. We all understood what it meant to enter the fallen city. Though thankfully we didn't actually need to enter the city, as T.R.E. was in the hills outside the city limits.

Sir Liam seemed to know his way to the estate. We drove in silence, the anticipation of an attack present in all of our minds.

We pulled up to the gate of T.R.E., and much as it had been on my first day, it was in pristine condition, as if the horrors that had decimated the city had forgotten to touch this one structure. It almost had me believing that T.R.E. would also be standing in all of its glory, but as we drove up the winding path, I saw it was not so lucky. The once impressive building was in shambles. The gabled structure looked a sad and lost sort of thing. The once pristine grass and landscaping were overgrown and dead from lack of attendants and the turn of the season. The windows were all shattered, roof caved in and the doors to the grand white staircase hung open on their hinges like a mouth left agape. As if the building itself was in shock at its current state.

I took it all in, feeling blindsided. It had only been a few days for me, but months had passed and the proof of that passage of time jarred me once again. I pressed my forehead against the truck window and looked up, recalling the way I had felt that first day. Honored, excited, determined and weary, but most of all, awed. Now I was awed for a different reason.

"You okay?" Aaron asked, tapping my shoulder from the backseat.

"It's odd, I mean, I was just here. I can't reconcile the differences..." I reached up and touched my dark curls and the extra length again. It was strange to think I had been living a whole life the last four months that I couldn't remember.

"It is rather unprecedented, what you have been through," Sir Liam said, stopping the vehicle. We climbed out and followed him through the small gate and into the school courtyard.

Labradorite-blue eyes flicked in my mind as we walked over the dead grass.

The courtyard appeared mostly unchanged from that first day... the day I met Tae.

"It would have taken a very old, very skilled person to do

what they did to your memories," Sir Liam continued, pulling me from my thoughts.

"Very old?" I asked as we reached a set of stairs that traversed a steep hill at the back of the teachers' building.

"Yes, perhaps someone in the king's court even," he answered as we ascended the narrow stony steps. The path was overgrown; branches protruded sharply on either side.

"The king's court?" I mused.

"Yes, do you know of them?"

"Just that King Roark established a group during his reign to help him rule. The Steward has maintained the tradition," I answered, trying to recall anything else while avoiding being stabbed in the eye by the relentless brambles.

"Uncle?" Aaron asked from behind me, his tone a warning.

"The door is just ahead," Sir Liam responded as a large wooden door came into view.

Panting from the steep climb, I waited as he pressed against the door. "Ugh, locked." He glanced to either side of the door, but the overgrowth of vines and branches made it hard to see anything, even around the door.

"Aaron, find another way in," Sir Liam ordered, stepping to the side.

"Couldn't we just break it down?" I wondered aloud, shifting forward to test the door myself. It didn't budge, the surface jagged and thick, like a door made for a castle, not a house in the hills. Then again, it was supposedly a mansion.

Aaron slipped into a Krav stance, and in a blur of enhanced speed, he cut through the thick brush to the left of the door.

Sir Liam followed the path Aaron had made, and I hurried after them both.

Aaron waited for us a few paces down. He stood next to another door, this one covered slightly by overgrown ivy that still held its rich green color despite the cooler temperature.

"It was likely there was a trap on the other door. This one, however..." Aaron answered, using his vibration to break the door off its hinges. He grabbed it before it fell and awkwardly shuffled it to the side.

"Let's find the headmaster's son." Sir Liam grunted approvingly and dipped inside the dark corridor.

Inside, all the windows were boarded up, but I recognized the small passage to be a servants' corridor.

Just how wealthy was Rei's family?

"Where is he?" I asked, hoping Sir Liam could sense Rei in the mansion.

"My power isn't active all the time. I have to be in meditation to search someone, and sensing for another vibration only works when in close proximity. We will have to look around for him."

"But he was here yesterday, right?" I asked, needing reassurance. I didn't fully know why finding Rei felt so important, but I was anxious to see him.

"If he's not here now, he most likely is coming back," Aaron said behind me.

We came to the end of the corridor and opened another door that led into the main hallway.

Light filtered in from half-moon windows far too high to be boarded up. Once my eyes adjusted, I took in rich tapestries and dark woods, sconces of elaborate brass and a yawning emptiness that made the tall hall feel as dark and eerie as the servants' passage.

I grabbed Sir Liam's arm. "Is he here?" I asked again, a bit desperately, reaching out with my vibration, but finding it rebelling against being used.

"Stop that," Aaron snapped. "Are you trying to have another episode?"

I frowned.

Sir Liam moved down the hall. "We should be close enough to sense him if he is here. Plus, he would have definitely felt us use vibration to open the outside door."

I slapped my hands over my face. "Or he felt it and thought it was an intruder and will one, attack us, or two, flee and never come back." I groaned, aggravated that I hadn't considered any of that before.

Sir Liam snorted. "You are such a pessimist." He patted my head. "Have a little faith."

I rolled my eyes and sighed. "Where do we start looking? Or would you like to do your Wavemaster magic and find out if he's actually here right now?" I put my hands on my hips and raised my eyebrows.

He pinched his brow with his hands, but smiled. "Okay, let's find a room where we will be less exposed, and I'll search for him."

"Great," I chirped, and hurried down the hall till we found a room with no windows and only one entrance. After barricading the door with an old desk, Sir Liam sat down and closed his eyes.

I waited patiently—or as patiently as I could—for him to find Rei's location.

Aaron glared at me as I paced the large empty room, which looked to once have been some kind of storage or record-keeping room. After a few moments, Sir Liam grunted.

"Hmm, he isn't here right now."

I stopped pacing, fighting a wave of disappointment. "Then where?"

"A moment," he answered, holding up a finger.

I resumed my pacing, my hand unconsciously reaching up to my ear to untuck and tuck my hair.

"Could you not?" Aaron whispered from where he sat cross-legged atop the desk blocking the door.

I narrowed my eyes at him, my body bouncing with nervous energy. I kept pacing.

He sighed and closed his eyes to meditate.

I crossed my arms and stared at my shoes.

"Hmm," Sir Liam grunted.

I lifted my head. "What?"

"He's in the low-town district. Near Corpel and Vine Street."

"Uncle, how did you find him so fast?"

"The city is mostly empty—fewer vibrations to shift through to find him," Sir Liam answered, standing up and brushing off his pants.

"Why there?" I whispered, my face scrunching with unease.

Aaron raised an eyebrow as he hopped off the desk. "Are you familiar with that area?"

"Yeah." I nodded, shifting my weight. "It's where I live." Or at least where I *had* lived.

CHAPTER 9
Low-town

With daylight burning, we hurried back to the truck and into the city limits. New nervous energy buzzing about us.

We couldn't get far, as the roads leading into the once lively metropolis were blocked by fallen buildings and pileups where automobiles had crashed, no doubt in attempts to flee the city.

So we set out on foot.

I kept my eyes forward, forcing my mind to focus on the path back home and not on the decimated streets around me, on the flickers and flashes of memories that danced in my mind, begging me to fall apart. To go on tilt and be the uncontrollable monster I had been.

When we got to low-town, all my attempts to stay calm and controlled crumbled around me like the rubble at my feet. I shuddered. The whole city was in ruins, but low-town, my part of town, the familiar streets and shops, was unrecognizable in a way the rest of the city hadn't been. But the rest of the city didn't matter much to me.

I ran ahead, my heart hammering in my chest, pulsing in my ears.

Large metal supports were speared through entire blocks, like big black needles in red claylike flesh. Was this how my father had died? Our townhome thrust through by black knives, impaling him along with our home? Killed by whatever had rolled through this part of town tossing metal lances through storefronts and homes.

I ran to the corner shop where I used to pick up eggs and salted mushrooms for the traditional Golan breakfast we made every weekend.

It was where I had first learned about how different I was.

A Saturday morning when I was five, I went with my mom to pick up the food, desperate to go to the park and get out of the house. Mom said Dad would take me to the park after breakfast, but we needed to get the supplies. In my eagerness to go to the park, I hurried my mom out the door and demanded I go with her. She always took forever if she went on her own. I had never gone to the store before without my dad, and I understood later that day why.

When we walked into the shop, the patrons that looked up at the dinging bell grimaced at the sight of my mother and I, before quickly looking back at the shelves before them. The shop owner sat up straighter in his chair behind the counter and slid closer to the register.

I normally would run through the aisles with Dad on my heels, grabbing everything we needed with a smile, but that day I gripped my mom's hand, feeling the sweat in her palm.

My shoulders were tense, and I moved closer to my mom's legs.

I understood later that as a small infant, even as a young child, when I was next to my father I could pass for being very pale, nothing more. But next to my mother, next to what I really was, it was obvious I was Golan, and the tension in the shop that day taught me that some people, most people, had a prejudice against my skin.

I watched how an older lady shoved past my mom, elbowing her hard between the shoulder blades and yelling at her to move when there was more than enough space in the aisle for her to walk by. I watched as my mom shrunk close to the shelves, making herself as small as possible to let the angry lady pass. I didn't fully understand then, but I understood enough. My mother was hated, and I would be too. My only option was to become small. So I had learned that day to shrink and try to be invisible.

After that day, I did everything I could to be inconsequential and hide my skin. Like my mother, I wore long sleeves, never tied my hair up, and grew it long so it could be a shield. From behind, I could almost be mistaken for being Shamarian. I had hoped all these things would protect me from the stares and cruelty, but when my mother died two years later, I slowly adopted a new approach. My father was strong and willful, and it was only a matter of time before I too showed the evidence of his upbringing. Though I still attempted to hide my skin, when I was confronted I didn't back down.

It was that determination and spirit that had me running ahead of Sir Liam and Aaron, only to pause at the sight of the crumbled park where I had gotten into my first fight.

Sir Liam caught up to me. "Rina, what is it?" he asked, breathing hard.

I stared unseeing at the wreckage. The swings were half under the sand and half mangled in the rubble. The very swings the bratty boy from across the street had pushed me off of while jeering, "Haven't seen your dirty mother walking into my uncle's shop—did she finally go back to Golan? Why didn't she take your dusty face with her?"

It had only been two days since her burial and the pain was raw, so I did the only thing I could think of at the time—I slugged him, hard. His hate was uglier than the ashen skin of my heritage. He lost two teeth in the sand, and I was labeled the neighborhood menace, but that was only the beginning. A few days later, he gathered his friends and beat me within an inch of my life.

I shook my head, clearing the memory of the fight from my mind. "It's nothing." I sighed, picking up the broken chain of the swing and squeezing it tightly in my fist. Perhaps some people did deserve the destruction wrought on them by my hand. Anger and fear warred inside me. The chain pinched my palm and I threw it down, but not before it left angry red blood blisters on my skin.

"Rina?" Sir Liam pressed as Aaron came up beside him.

I looked at them, the light of the sun casting golden shadows over their dark complexions. The light only meant one thing—the sun had gotten far too low. It had taken us too much of the day to get here, and soon the Wraiths would fill the streets once more.

"We should have stayed at the mansion and waited for Rei to come back," I warned, turning to look at the lowering sun. Did we have time to take cover somewhere?

"You said you're familiar with this area?" Aaron said behind me.

"Yes, we aren't far from the townhome I grew up in..." I blinked hard and sighed, gathering my courage. "Let's go." I took off in a sprint to the old clay-brick building that had been my whole world for the last seventeen years.

The front of the building seemed relatively unscathed as we ran up the steps. My heart jumped to my throat as I pushed open the door, which had been left ajar. I shouldn't have been alarmed by the open door—the city was deserted and I knew my father was dead, but it didn't feel real. Like everything I had seen was some kind of alternate world. My father should have been on the other side of the door waiting for me. Happy to see me. What greeted me instead was the dimming sky, as the whole back of the house had been blown out. Charred tatters of my life taunted me, asking me where I'd been, how I could have let this happen. Daring me to reconcile the last four months.

My legs became flimsy, and I reached for what was left of my father's armchair. The scraps of papers he had left scattered around our home were nothing more than little piles of black soot, mostly blown away, but I could still see them. Still see the things they had been only weeks before in my memory.

My vibration power flickered under my skin like a warm, wild friend I had desperately wanted to see but feared all the same.

"Rina, take a breath, control your power. You will draw them to us!" Sir Liam whispered aggressively, reaching for my arm.

"Who did this?" I screamed, futilely, because I knew deep down who'd done this.

What had done this.

The dragon.

A beast I would slay.

The entryway of my childhood home began to tilt as a memory, fast and fierce, assaulted my mind.

Three months ago...

I sat in the corner of the cell crying. It had to have been weeks since the hospital now, and every time I went out and destroyed another part of the city, hopelessness set in a little deeper. The only thing left for me to do was cry.

I barely noticed the groan of the door opening.

"Don't cry, little Golan girl."

My back stiffened, and though I had tears across my face, I still had a backbone. "I have a name," I growled through my tears.

"Yes, a beautiful name, Relina Gilead Rinehart..."

I flinched at the use of my full name. No one called me Relina; no one except my mother. "How do you know that?" I lifted my head angrily.

"Did you think I wouldn't do my research on you? It was the name your mother gave you. Though your father refused to use it."

I sniffed, my jaw tight. "Who are you?"

"A friend, if you let me be." The clip of his steps in the dark came closer.

"You are a kidnapper and a monster!" I snapped.

"Shall I prove my allegiance, then?"

I shifted in my corner, unsure how to respond. I felt my distrust of him had been clearly conveyed. Nothing he could say would sway me from the truth. I was his prisoner, his thing, only alive to kill and destroy.

"Your mother, do you know where she worked as a maid?"

My head jerked in the direction of his voice. "What does that have to do with anything..."

"Do you know?" he pressed.

I thought back. "It was some wealthy guy's mansion... no one special..." Then, like a horrible puzzle I had never wanted to see, things my mother and father had done and said snapped into place. My mother had wanted me to attend T.R.E., talked endlessly about the quality of education, and had brought home pamphlets and flyers to decorate my bedroom wall. A wall my father cleared of all its paraphernalia after her death. The memory of the way he begged me not to go in the days after my offer letter flowed through my mind, as did the knowledge that the mansion she'd worked at was on the north side of the city. In the mountains. Only one man's estate was so connected to T.R.E.

"She worked for the headmaster?" I breathed.

"Yes, at the headmaster's home. That is where she worked during my childhood," he began. "I was no older than eight when she came to us."

Bile was rising in my throat. "Are you saying you lived in the headmaster's mansion?"

A quiet, almost hesitant "Yes" filled the darkness.

"Who are you?" I said angrily, this time only asking for confirmation because deep down I knew. I think I had always known. His voice was different when it was just us, softer, kinder, unlike when Logan was around his voice and he became cold and calculating as it had been in those days. In the days I had spied on him for Rei.

"I think you know," he hedged, slippery as always.

"The headmaster's son."

"Yes but which one?" he urged, daring me to call him by name.

"Tae."

He scoffed low and angry, as if the name offended him. "Taegan," he whispered after a moment, sounding a little deflated, "my name is Taegan."

I narrowed my eyes—Tae or Taegan, what did it matter? He still had kidnapped and caged me, so why was he revealing his identity now?

"I offered you my blood to help you, and you kidnapped me! Why?" I unfurled from my corner, attempting to stand. "Why are you doing this to me!"

His steps drew closer. "She was the closest person to me in those years," he said, ignoring my outburst. "When I lost her too, it was like losing my mother all over again," he continued, reaching the bars of my cell.

I didn't have time to dwell on his wording as anger and possessiveness filled me. "She was my mother," I snapped predatorily, not liking how he was taking ownership of her. As if he'd known her better than I had. How dare he act as if he could sympathize, as if he knew her well enough, to be sad about her passing. What did he know of my mother's death anyway, had he been there? Thoughts of the article I found in Rei's shed filled my mind. His mother and mine had died on the same day so why did Tae make it sound like they happened at different times?

"Yes, she was, but did she tell you stories of her home in Golan, the meaning of her family name?"

I leaned against the bars opposite to where he stood. "I was too young," I answered, still trying to understand what he was saying. Either he was lying about knowing my mother or our moms did not actually die on the same day as the article stated. Or, more likely, Tae was messing with me. "I only knew her family name was Gilead, but neither she nor my father had told me about it meaning anything."

"Well, she told me," he said with an air of smugness. "Story after story of the people on the other side of that senseless border. Of their way of life..." He trailed off, an edge of sorrow to his last words. I hadn't expected him to feel such passion about the border. To call it senseless was traitorous. That border was our first line of defense; it was hardly senseless, and yet... his words made some sense. The border was simply a line on a map; it didn't do anything to keep Wraiths out or the Grieving from crossing, not really anyway.

"I don't believe you." I lifted my chin, defiantly brushing the last of my drying tears from my cheeks. At least I had stopped crying—anger was easier to manage than tears, and Tae was doing a right job of keeping me in my angry box.

"I didn't come here to argue with you, in fact the opposite: I thought you might want a piece of home." He shifted, entering the cell. "This was one of her recipes. She and I made it together every winter around this time of year." His voice shook slightly as he held out what looked like a bowl. "I thought you might enjoy it."

I wanted to toss the contents in his face, but in the dark I didn't even know where that was, and the contents smelled like the red bean soup my mom would make at the turn of the seasons when I was a child. The smell was as inviting as it had been then, and despite myself I felt for the bowl in the dark.

Tae took my hand in his and lifted it to the curved edge.

His hands were warm from holding the soup, and I shivered at the contrast from the cold cell. When the bowl was secured in my palm, he lifted my other hand to the spoon.

I drew the bowl close. The steam of the contents moistened my face, and I shivered again in delight at the idea of a warm meal.

I lifted the spoon, then hesitated. "Is it poisoned?" I asked. My stomach growled angrily, seeming to not care if it was.

The spoon moved in my hand, and Tae shifted closer. In the darkness I still could not see his face, but I found myself imagining his features. Pale skin, haunting blue eyes, and pink lips... His breath tickled my hand as I imagined his lips closing over the curve of the spoon. He swallowed, drinking the contents, and for a moment time seemed to stop.

"No, it's not," he answered smoothly.

My heart rattled in my chest painfully. He dipped the spoon in the bowl, lifting the serving to my lips before letting go of my hand.

The warmth of the spoon at my lips was distracting enough to pull my attention away from Tae and back to the thoughts of a warm meal. I ate, and it tasted exactly like my mother's cooking, making my eyes fill with fresh tears. I sank to the floor to eat greedily.

Tae spoke over my slurping which was echoing embarrassingly in the dark.

"She told me that her grandmother taught her this recipe only after weeks of nagging when she was thirteen. Her grandmother had made her grow and harvest all of the ingredients for the soup before she would teach her. She said it was to help your mother understand the importance of ingredients, and that it's not just the making of the soup that shows love, it's the cultivation of all the elements that gives the meal its medicinal powers. Something about that story always sounded... nice to me. That some things are more than what you see, that there was intention and reason, even love, behind the final product."

I had listened to him silently, taking the curve of the bowl in my mouth to down the rest of the contents hungrily. Finished, I sighed, content and a bit sleepy. "Why are you telling me this?" I asked, still not sure if I believed him.

"Because your whole life you have been trying to fit into half of who you are. While you never got to learn the other side."

"You expect to teach me?" I laughed bitterly. "I don't trust you, nor like you—why would I believe a word out of your mouth?"

"Because they are not my words, but your mother's."

I narrowed my eyes. "One bowl of soup doesn't prove anything." I shoved the empty bowl in the direction of his voice.

"I suppose you're right," he agreed, taking the bowl and leaving the cell. "Though I do wish you would humor me anyway." The door closed behind him and for only a moment, though my stomach felt full, the silence and lack of his presence made me feel a little empty inside.

CHAPTER 10

Rei

The grunt and groans of creatures in more pain than they could bear met my ears, shaking me from my memory.

I sat up startled from where I had fallen to my hands and knees, and looked around the area.

Sir Liam and Aaron took defensive positions, against the growing threat. The Grieving were slowly drawing closer as the orange sky warned of a worse danger on the horizon.

I had gotten us trapped.

"We have to move," Sir Liam said, quickly reaching for my arm and hauling me to my feet with a swiftness that left me a little dizzy.

"Where?" I asked, trying to calculate which buildings we'd passed that had seemed intact enough to hide in. It was only a matter of time before one of us got possessed, though, and killed the others. The city wasn't safe, and I had forced us to come here.

"They know where we are. Don't hesitate to use your gifts now," Sir Liam warned us both.

Aaron nodded.

"I don't even know if I can," I said, desperately looking at my hands, but the power warmed in my chest, lacing down my arms at my call. It was still weighed down, and odd feeling, but it would be enough to pump into my legs and outrun the slowness of the Grieving. But that still left the Wraiths that would slip in after sunset.

"You had another memory." It wasn't a question. "I could feel your power loosen. Whatever memory it was, it was a significant piece of your struggle," Sir Liam said.

Aaron had been right—my captor had blue eyes. Labradorite I knew well. To think, the last four months I had been with Tae. I shivered but it wasn't the time to dwell on that.

With renewed energy I nodded to Sir Liam, and we took off, pumping power into our legs and speeding through the streets in a way we hadn't been able to before.

We didn't get far, though, as a familiar and strong vibration met us on the road outside.

He was the same as he'd been that day in the hospital, dressed in all black, his long hair tied loosely away from his face. His olive skin was so much warmer and more inviting than my own.

"Rei!" I cried out with more enthusiasm than I thought my voice should have. He and I weren't that close. The hospital had bonded us some, but my joy at seeing him alive and well was greater than what either of us had expected. His two differently colored eyes widened as they looked at me, a strained weariness and surprise in their depths.

"R-Rina," he breathed, his tone incredulous but as melodious as it had been the first day of school.

"Brace yourselves!" Aaron warned as a mass of the

Grieving, at least twenty, poured into the street. We were surrounded. Our only shot at avoiding the Grieving vanished.

Sir Liam, Aaron, Rei and I all crouched into Krav stances, ready to take on as many as we could before the Wraiths showed up. Rei said nothing as he dove and rolled closer to Sir Liam, tightening up our small party.

Six of the Grieving broke off and descended upon Sir Liam.

I couldn't watch what happened next, as I had my own party of Grieving to contend with. I focused on pulling my gift out and flowed through the movements of Krav. With more effort than it should have taken, I dodged, kicked and thrashed against the enemy. But even as one crumpled to the ground, another would appear in its place. Sweat beaded across my brow, my hair sticking to my neck. I reached out to grab the withered and blood-soaked skin of my attacker; the face that could have once been kind was twisted and sunken in. The smell of decay hung off of the creature in a dizzying aroma. The Grieving were tremendously strong with the gift, but their physical bodies were flimsy and sponge-like. Gripping his arm, I easily snapped it, twisting it to an unnatural angle. I whipped around as another Grieving shot a wave of power towards me. Using the Grieving I held as a shield, I blocked the brunt of the blow, but was thrown back by its force. The attacker I had been holding turned to dust, molecules finally loosening into nothingness.

I rolled backwards into broken glass. The sharp edges of the blown-out storefront ripped into my uniform. I winced as the cuts dripped red along my left arm. The dampening power of the suit was troublesome, as I could feel my gift staying just under the force I needed to win this fight.

I glanced up to see three Grieving blur in front of me.

Together they drew their power into one blast that threw me backwards in the air, through the broken window into the dark rubble of the storefront. I barely had time to use my vibration to shield the attack, but my power was pathetic compared to three Grieving at once. I had nothing left in me to break my fall as their power shook every fiber in me. The sound of my scream rang out far away as I flew through the air. My limbs pulled away from my body and snapped back together from the force. Any second I would crash into something, and surely my spine would shatter.

A solid warmth formed around my back.

"Got you," Aaron assured as he carefully used his power to slow our momentum till gravity pulled us to the ground. His arm around my waist was firm as his hulking form moved to take on the three that had attacked me. With a flick of his wrist, a blade materialized from pieces of his suit, the edges locking into place. Aaron sent vibrations into the blade, making it glow red as if it was on fire, being forged into one solid sword. The long blade seemed to almost dance as Aaron pulsed vibrations into the hilt. It was a dance I could barely follow with the naked eye. The Grieving charged him, and without hesitation he let me go and met them blow for blow, impaling one in the head before turning and flipping the blade to slash another through the gut.

The Grieving were dwindling as I looked out to the street, Rei and Sir Liam were holding their own.

Rei wielded an ivory staff shot through with streaks of black metal. He moved like water, the staff pushing and pulling the vibration waves as if they were the current and he was bending to its flow. It was enchanting.

I shook my head, I needed to get back in the fight. But the fight found me first as a Grieving slipped past Aaron and into the store. I braced myself as the fight to wield my power raged within me.

"Come on," I growled, forcing more vibrations into my legs as the Grieving threw wave after wave at me. My only option was to sprint and jump out of the way over and over again. It was wearing me down. I panted as I rolled, losing my balance and smacking my shoulder into a shelf. It toppled over at the force of my impact, the bolts that held it to the ground giving way, and the items on the rack flew across the floor with a loud crash. The Grieving was distracted for only a moment, but it was long enough for me to sprint into close proximity. Finally on the offensive, I powered my fist and battered the sad creature till it had no choice but to hold up its flimsy arms, crossing them to shield its face. The raw flesh that hung from its arms had my stomach churning. My fists connected again and again with its grotesqueness, protected by a thin layer of vibrations.

I pushed it to the window edge. Crouching low, I uppercut my fist at the junction of the creature's wrists, breaking them apart, giving access to its head. The upward momentum intensified by the added vibration in my legs lifted me off the ground as my body tilted back, twisting, my left leg wheeling around as my right fingertips grazed the floor. I heard more than felt the heel of my left foot connect with the Grieving's head. The crack of bone and squelch of liquid met my ears as my heel swiped the creature, going clean through its fragile skull.

My body, as if floating on the air, twisted right back into a basic Krav stance, and for a moment I was stunned and confused as to how I had just done what I had. Then a wave of exhaustion gripped me and I fell to my knees, the corpse of the creature turning to dust before me.

On shaky legs, I looked up to see the hungry night take the sky.

Rei too was looking up at the foreboding night, as Sir Liam continued to fight outside the storefront, taking one Grieving after another down with his fists.

Though we had almost won the fight, we would not win the one about to start.

I moved to jump through the storefront window and help Sir Liam, but froze in place as something cold and dark grew from the shadowed street.

"Sir Liam!" I called, trying to warn him even as the last of the silhouetted buildings gave in to the darkness. It was too late.

The Wraiths had arrived.

Despite wanting to help Sir Liam, my body moved on its own, shutting off the flow of my gift and disappearing into the store once more. I pushed through the rubble, finding a pocket deep in the back of the store to crouch and hide. My eyes quickly adjusted to the complete darkness. I didn't understand why I was hiding. I just knew I had to. Had to disappear, to make myself as small and unnoticeable as possible. Sinking unease settled in my stomach as the sounds of the battle died down and an eerie chill filled the air.

The incorporeal darkness that I had only vaguely seen that night at the hospital fluttered in and out of my peripheral vision. Hiding had been pointless, the Wraiths had found me all the same, and a fear that felt too strong to be my own squeezed my heart.

Again, I would be possessed. Again... and again and again, my mind cried over and over, as if I had said those words a million times, never to be heard or heeded. No one would stop them, nothing could save me from the violet haze soon to smother my senses, forcing me to yield all control.

I wanted to scream, but a voice I was beginning to know as well as my own spoke in the darkness of the hollowed-out cavity I had shrunk into.

"We had a deal... not them," the voice ordered harshly.

As if born of shadow, he walked out in front of my hiding place, and my breath caught as his face came into view. "T-Tae." I quivered, a war of emotions turning my already uneasy stomach into tight knots. The feathered black vapors of the Wraiths vanished into the corners of the dark store as if they had always been there, but also never at all.

"You should have never come back," Tae said gently, his voice full of a tenderness I couldn't comprehend. He knelt down and took my hand in his. Slowly he lifted me out of the crumpled hole.

The feel of his hand in mine did strange things to my insides. Even in the darkness, I could see how his slender pale fingers seemed to blend so well into my own. A fluttering sensation mixed awkwardly with the genuine disdain I felt towards him. Once I was free of the cavity, I lifted my chin, ready to confront him. To confront the memories I had pieced together of him holding me captive, sedating me, showing twisted kindness to me.

My eyes narrowed as his blue eyes, full of compassion, looked over the blood on my left arm from rolling over the broken storefront window. All my growing rage seemed to freeze inside me as his hand slid from mine to the cuts, his fingers gentle and slow as they peeled back the uniform to reveal the crude stitches along my forearm. Stitches I didn't remember getting.

"What—" I began at the same time he leaned in, his hand

moving to my neck, and with a sharp flick of his wrist I passed out.

Two months ago...

I stood in a dark hallway, the purple haze of possession over my eyes. A door to my right was ajar, letting through arguing voices.

"What is taking so long! Time is of the essence, Tae."

"I am aware, Master Logan, but the city was never going to give up easily. You knew that."

"She isn't doing enough, then. He wants the city now."

"She is doing everything the Wraith is making her do. If he is dissatisfied with the results, then perhaps he should make the Wraith work harder," Tae answered icily.

"Where are we at with finding the journal?" Logan demanded.

"Still looking."

"Tae, my patience is wearing thin—get me the city or the damn journal within the next week, or else."

"I will give them a chance to at least bury their dead before taking the rest of them from the city alive."

"Your sentimentality will cost you." Logan warned. "One or the other by the end of the week. I don't care which," He said with a tone of finality.

CHAPTER 11

The Lab

Two months ago...

"Good morning, Relina."

"Tae," I clipped.

He sighed. "You really ought to be nicer to me. I was thinking you might want to wander out of your cell for a bit today, but if you're not interested..." He turned, his hand jangling the door handle.

"My dear captor! Good morning, I would love to take a stroll around my prison," I sneered sweetly.

He sighed again. "Little Golan girl, you are indeed a true delight." The latch of my cell opened.

"Will I be drugged for our trip?" I asked, unsure exactly what he was planning. He hadn't drugged me with that awful serum the last few days. Though I would still get possessed—Logan made sure of that—Tae seemed to be actively avoiding giving the serum to me. I wasn't sure what to make of that. I also wasn't sure what to make of Logan's ultimatum. From what I could tell, it had almost been a week since Logan gave his demand, and as far as I knew, the city was still fighting back and Tae had not found the yellow journal. What would Logan do if Tae failed him again?

Then there were the questions I had about my mother. It didn't make sense that Tae would know her, not if what I read in that article was true. Though I hadn't brought it up, it seemed inevitable as Tae had come to see me each day, bringing a fresh plate or bowl of Golan food. It was unnerving, and yet was doing more than I cared to admit in disarming me around him.

"No, no more drugs," he answered, his voice coming close to where I sat on the bedroll and blanket he had given me. I had rejected them at first, but the cold of the cell had felt like it would never leave my bones, so despite myself I had begun to make good use of them, staying curled up in them even when I wasn't sleeping. They smelled like Tae, like the ground after heavy rain. I clung to them because the smell reminded me of being free, outside in the light—not because I was interested in the way he smelled.

He knelt in front of me, the blanket and bedroll paling in comparison to the warmth and scent radiating off of him.

"What are you doing?" I asked, startled. He only got this close if he was going to give me the serum, or sometimes food.

I jumped as his warm fingers brushed my temples.

"You haven't seen the sun in over two months. These will help your eyes adjust," he said simply, his fingertips, like feathers, dusting past my cheek settling a pair of glasses over my eyes.

I only realized I had been holding my breath when he stood up and I exhaled in a gust. The sound resounded in the quiet cell.

A chuckle came from Tae, and I was grateful for the darkness as heat crept up my neck.

"Now, I know your temptation will be to run, but I'm asking you, please don't. I have no desire to fight you, and you would not get very far even if you did."

I stood up, all traces of embarrassment gone. "We will see," I answered noncommittally. I *would* make a break for it if I saw an opening, regardless of his request. His few kind acts did not mean I owed him. Nor did they make up for kidnapping and imprisonment.

We left the room containing my cell and moved through a dimly lit windowless corridor. The door at the end of the hall opened to a wide room filled with tables of strange equipment, vials, and papers strewn about. I took in the room, feeling my palms sweat. The floor was gray stone, along with the walls, as if this could be just another, albeit much bigger and well-lit, cell. I flinched behind the lenses—the space was much brighter than the hall and cell we had come from, but it wasn't from sunlight, as this room was windowless as well. Instead, large overhead lamps hung from the low ceiling, making my eyes water slightly. I bumped blindly into Tae's arm.

He wore a long blue lab coat that only seemed to make his blue eyes more intense, even through the tinted lenses I wore. His black hair looked a little unkempt, and as my eyes passed over him, I saw behind him what looked to be a bedroom.

"You live in this lab?" I asked, pointing to the bed.

"I have to sleep somewhere," he answered simply.

"I didn't think monsters slept at all..."

His brow furrowed and he looked away, as if I had actually hurt his feelings. "I suppose *you* would think of me as some inhuman creature, incapable of having human needs," he replied, voice cold and calculating like it was whenever Logan was around. It felt odd, like, somehow, it was more of an act than when he was kind to me.

I turned as a flicker of something sickly and dark caught my eye. On the wall hung a small clouded mirror, and I peered at the girl reflected there. She was gaunt, hair dirty, and where there was once a school uniform was now a skintight black Krav suit. Thick-framed black glasses covered over what would be caramel-colored eyes. I didn't know this girl yet she wore my skin, had my face. Tears pricked my eyes for a wholly different reason.

"Relina?" Tae asked gently.

Was this who Relina was, then? A gaunt creature, made to destroy? Was I Rina or Relina? Somehow I wasn't really sure anymore. Rina felt like a different person, someone else, and yet both Rina and Relina were caged—one by society, the other by tangible bars. Which was worse?

I backed away from the mirror, unable to look at myself any longer.

Tae's expression was soft, almost as if he understood what I had been thinking.

I changed the subject quickly. "Where's Logan? Has he permitted this little outing?" I asked, scanning the room for exits, returning my thoughts to escape.

"He doesn't know about this," Tae said, his voice guarded. "Follow me."

I lifted a brow and followed him through the lab. I had thought that "the lab" Rei had wanted me to find was the place Tae took me to after Shila attacked me, but it was clear now that had been a decoy. This lab was the one Rei had wanted me to spy on. If I hadn't been brought here against my will, finding it would have been difficult, as judging from the lack of windows and doors, I was certain we were in some kind of bunker.

"How many feet underground are we?" I asked as we moved towards a door.

Tae turned as he pushed the door, saying slyly over shoulder, "Take a look for yourself."

The amount of sunlight that poured through the door had me stepping back. My hand lifting to cover my eyes even though the glasses had dimmed everything considerably.

Tae's warm hand wrapped around my raised forearm, pulling me through the open door.

The air was cool but humid, and filled with the sweet smell of earth after heavy rain, the smell of Tae.

My eyes were still shut tight against the abrasive light as I let him lead me further away from the door.

For the last months, behind my lids had always been darkness, but now with my eyes closed they held a red tint from the light of the sun.

"Watch your step," Tae said, his hand sliding along my arm to my elbow and guiding me away from whatever I had been walking towards.

"I can't exactly "watch" anything." I snapped.

"Give it a moment." Tae chuckled again. What had made his mood so mirthful?

"What is this place?" I asked. Wishing it didn't hurt so much to open my eyes.

"One more second," he encouraged.

Then the warm sun coating my skin turned cooler, as if I'd stepped into a shadow. My eyes cracked open then, and though I had to squint, I could see we were outside, but instead of a forest or rolling hills, I gazed at a lush garden in a large circular shape. My eyes drifted up to a huge fig tree, and in place of the cool blue sky above, stood walls of red and brown earth.

I stepped forward, keeping in the shade of the tree, but trying to see just how high the wall of earth went up.

Tae dropped my arm as I edged closer to the shadow line.

"What is this?" I asked in terrified awe, as the wall of earth spanned the whole way round the circular garden.

"The lab," Tae said, and came to stand next to me. "Part of it, anyway. We walked through the other part before."

I noticed then the different plants, all kinds of vegetables and herbs, most of which were not native to Erasmus. "The meals you have been bringing me?" I asked, pointing at a squash and recalling the stuffed squash Tae had given me the day before.

"Yes, I grow everything here myself. Making good meals begins with good ingredients," he quoted from the other day.

I frowned. Tae was supposed to be a monster, heartless, but somehow he was able to care for these plants, tend them and have them flourish. Just like the memory he had shared about my great-grandmother, Tae had grown and prepared all the food I had eaten. It didn't make sense. He wasn't a caring person.

"How far are we underground?" I asked again. My eyes had adjusted enough to not have to squint, but it still hurt if I tried to look up at the opening overhead where the light was brightest.

"Far enough that it wouldn't be easy to climb out of," Tae answered, catching on to my musings.

I ignored his easy read on me and deflected. "Some of these foods are not native to Erasmus?"

"Indeed, I am able to grow them because this is a

greenhouse designed to mirror a variety of climates. The sun moves like a sundial overhead, and the insulated glass dome on top holds the heat in, allowing it to even be possible to grow plants this low underground. Plants that need a particular intensity of sun are segmented off into quadrants..." He trailed off, seeing my amused expression. I had never seen him so animated about anything before. "I don't wish to bore you." He cleared his throat. "I thought you would enjoy being outside for a while today." He gestured to a wooden bench under the tree.

I walked over and sat down. The wood looked new, the seat sanded down and the nails untarnished and shiny. Had he just gotten this bench?

"The craftsmanship is very nice," I mused aloud, my hand running along the wood. I glanced up to see Tae's cheeks flush. His pale skin showed the blush almost as much as my own ashen complexion. It was off-putting. "Don't tell me you made this..." I tapped my finger on the smooth wood.

"One has to do something to pass the days." He looked away, and the red on his cheeks crawled down his neck. "I thought you might want a place to sit..." He muttered uncomfortable.

"Thank you," I said quietly, unsure if it was necessary. I didn't owe Tae anything... except he had saved my life that day on the roof.

"I'll be inside when you're ready to go back in." He turned to leave, running his fingers under his ear and down the back of his neck, clearly awkward.

"You're not worried about me escaping?" I teased a little, pointing at the earthen walls.

He smirked. "Like I said, it's nearly impossible to climb

out, but you're welcome to try if that's how you would like to spend your time today," he offered, and began to leave again.

"When I go back inside..." I called, and he stopped and waited, "will I have to go back to the cell?" I was beginning to think he liked putting me in that cell just about as much as I liked being there.

He tilted his head towards me over his shoulder, and though I couldn't see all of his expression, it appeared he was smiling. "Not until Logan comes back," he answered, and something fluttered in my stomach. I tried to ignore it, unsure if it was fear at the mention of Logan, or something else at the curve of Tae's smile.

"Oh, and Relina," he called, drawing my attention again. "Even with your vibration power, you won't be able to climb out, but when you get tired of trying, come inside for some tea." He waved his hand overhead, his dark hair shining in the sun.

CHAPTER 12

Heir

Two months ago...

Once he had gone inside, I moved around the garden, looking at all the different plants and herbs, not really knowing what most of them were. The truly exotic ones pulled my attention, leading me deeper into the vines and tallest growth. The garden seemed easy to navigate while standing next to the large fig tree at the center of the ring, but once I'd left the center, I learned the ground was unlevel. Trenches of various depths made traversing the circle rather difficult. It wasn't long before I lost sight, through the thick of the foliage, of the cavernous dirt walls.

After a while, however, I found myself before the earthen border. The greenery covering the wall made it appear as part of the ground itself, instead of perpendicular as one would expect.

Pushing the leaves aside, I tested the dirt wall, feeling to see its firmness or if it was as moist as it smelled. It was both wet and firm. My hand slid down the wall, getting no traction.

I closed my eyes and tried to pull on my vibration gift. Though I could feel it moving in me, I couldn't tap into it.

I had thought it was only the serum or Logan's presence that dimmed my power, but it would seem there was something else blocking my access. I attempted to run at the wall, reaching as high as I could for a hold. After repeated failed attempts, I decided to return to the fig tree. I climbed its branches till I broke through the canopy. The sun was harsh, making me squint. From the high vantage point, I scanned the cavity and concluded it really was impossible to climb out. Though it looked like there were spots that might be dry enough to get a hold on, they were far too high to get to without my gift.

I wouldn't give up, though. I *would* find a way out.

Slightly disillusioned, I dusted off my hands and walked to the door of the lab.

If I went back inside, I would have to go back into my cage. Back into darkness.

I had used up my time in the sun trying to escape, and now the light that had been so blinding was a soft golden alerting me of night's return anyway.

Steeling myself, I turned my back on the garden and pushed open the door to face Tae and my growing list of questions.

"Tae," I began, letting the tone of my voice warn him that I was going to disrupt whatever little truce or peace we had made for ourselves. "Why am I here? Why does Logan want the city destroyed and why is he looking for a yellow journal?"

Tae was sitting at a table mixing something. Slowly he set

down the beaker he was holding and turned on the stool to face me. He had removed his lab coat, showing a simple gray sweater pushed up on his forearms and beige slacks.

His shoulders tensed, though he was smiling as he spoke. "I'm surprised it took you so long to ask. Come, let's have some tea. I'm sure you wore yourself out today and a hot drink will revive you." He gestured to my mud-stained palms and fingernails.

A little flush of embarrassment warmed my cheeks at his noticing. I rubbed my palms against my pants and changed the subject. "Does it have to do with my blood?"

"You can wash up over there." He tilted his head in the direction of his bedroom and pushed away from the table. I watched him glide over to a kettle that had begun whistling softly the moment I walked in. Back to me he silently poured the hot water into two mugs, clearly not planning to say anything else.

Frustrated, I squared my shoulders, determined not to be unnerved by his sleeping arrangement. I was not thrilled by the idea of going into his bedroom—if one could call it that—but I wasn't fond of the dirt under my nails either. So I walked briskly past him, through the maze of equipment and into his personal space.

A part of me wanted to scour his living quarters for anything I could use against him, something to bargain or blackmail him with, but I wasn't so bold as to do that with him standing there watching me. Nor was I interested in getting anywhere near his bed. Instead I kept my eyes forward and beelined to the sink and mirror.

Silently I washed my hands, my back to him. I vigorously scrubbed my palms as the sudden urge to be clean gripped me. Flashes of the blood-shed, of the violence, I unleashed while possessed burned behind my closed eyes. It's not that I wasn't clean—the Wraith usually showered while in my body —it was that I never got the chance to feel the water, to cleanse myself of the awful things I had done. Angry tears filled my eyes, and though my hands were clean I couldn't stop scrubbing them.

I looked up into the cloudy mirror only to see Tae's face reflected next to mine. His long pale fingers reached around me and switched off the tap. Turning me he wrapped my hands, which had become red and raw, in a white towel.

"I-I..."

His blue eyes softened as he gave my hands a soft squeeze as if telling me not to explain. As if he already understood.

"Your blood is part of why you are here." He answered my earlier question with his hands still wrapped around mine in the towel. Suddenly the moment felt too intimate, too serious, and I wondered if he would be forthcoming enough to tell me the other reason I was here. "As I told you once before, you have a rare genetic trait." He let go of my hands and reached behind himself for something. I quickly wiped the tears from my cheeks with the towel, unsure if he had seen them, and grateful for the dimming glasses that still covered my eyes.

"I can't be certain but you are probably the only living person with this trait." He sighed, holding out a clipboard between us and pointing to a chart of lines and numbers I didn't understand.

"I-I can't read this—you could be showing me a chart on beetle migrations, and I wouldn't know." I frowned, pushing the chart back at him.

He looked affronted for a moment glancing at the chart as if he had been mistaken and had shown me the wrong one.

Then he smirked, "Would I keep a chart of beetle migrations under my bed? The one place I knew you wouldn't go near, even if I asked you to?"

"*Especially* if you ask me to," I corrected, eyeing the offensive area, my stomach flipping uneasily.

He shook his head, smiling, and walked over to the tray of tea he set up at a small table on the other side of his bed.

I followed skirting around his bed to get to the table. "And of course," I sneered, " you were so honest with me before, that the reason you want this trait is so that you can use it to stop Wraith possessions?"

"I didn't lie. Not really. I misappropriated information." he sat down lacing his fingers on the table. "It is true that a certain individual's blood can stop possessions, and that blood is carried by the descendants of the king's bloodline."

"Too bad King Roark didn't have any children, regardless of the speculations in the latest history books." I grumbled taking the seat opposite to him.

"*That* is not the king I am referring to." He said slowly watching me take the seat in front of him and slid a warm mug towards me.

"Who do you mean?" I asked uneasily, fingers tapping the sides of the ceramic cup.

"I'm referring to the descendant of Gilead, the once king of Golan corrupted by Skithian."

"Gilead? You mean the old king?" I breathed, my head throbbing.

The old king was practically a myth, said to have been given the Kingdom of Golan by King Roark himself long before the wars began and Skithian's darkness took control. Still no one ever really spoke of the king who had brought darkness on us all. But if, on the rare occasion, he was mentioned, like he had been that first day at school, it was always with the title of the old king; never had I heard his actual surname before.

It was a surname I knew well, as my full given name was Relina Gilead Rinehart.

I shivered as Logan's words repeated in my mind. "*I want you, Relina Gilead, to help me take down a city,*"

"T-That is my mother's maiden name," I stuttered, looking up at Tae's labradorite eyes, daring them to tell me everything. To tell me the whole ugly truth, because if somehow it was true that he knew my mother, then perhaps he knew all the answers she never had the chance to tell to me.

"It is as you think," he nodded, lifting his cup and taking a long quaff of the hot liquid.

I didn't know what to think. Was he implying that I was somehow related to the old king?

"My mother was—"

"A direct descendant of the old king," he looked up from his mug blue eyes blazing, "and you, Relina, are the heir to the Kingdom of Golan."

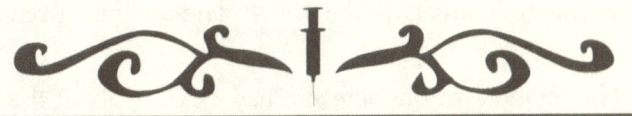

CHAPTER 13

Monster

Two months ago...

I shot out of my seat, my cup of untouched tea rattling against the tabletop. "No." I shook my head, letting the world spin. "No!" I nearly shouted. "They would have told me, my parents would have told me." Shame swelled in my chest. I couldn't be the descendant of such a man, such a foolish king, someone so hated and despised in Shamar. Hopelessness slammed into my heart. Would there always be strikes against me? I would always be an outcast, a pariah? My skin had already seemed an insurmountable odd placed against me, but this...this was beyond overcoming. No matter how I proved my worth to the people of Shamar I would never be accepted as one of them. Not when my forefather was the reason for the darkness that has plagued this land for thousands of years. The reason for so many deaths.

I looked at my own hands, still raw and red. Was I cursed? Cursed to be just as destructive, to have just as much blood on my hands as are on my kins?

"I'm sure they intended to, someday," Tae suggested gingerly, sensing my distress.

"How long have you known?" I turned on him, the chart—showing proof of the trait—glared at me from the table.

The memory of the note Rei had written, about the call Tae had with their father, flooded my mind. Tae knew about my lineage before I even set foot on campus. Anger flushed over my skin and I slammed my palms against the table getting in Tae's face.

"You monster!" I grabbed the collar of his gray sweater, forcing him to look at me. "You *knew*, you brought me to T.R.E on purpose! You used me like a pawn! I offered you my blood—if I'm what you say, then how come you didn't take it then? Huh? Or how about when I was bleeding out of the roof, there was plenty of it! Or better yet, why not just snatch me off the streets? Why make me attend T.R.E.?" My eyes blazed behind the lenses and I was sure he could see the unadulterated hate in their depths. "Was watching me get messed with and picked on just part of the twisted sick game of yours?" I fumed in frustrated fear because I was breaking my promise now but I didn't care. I was letting my anger loose in a way I hadn't for a long time. The fear of being related to the old king, the lies and secrets my parents had left me with were all making my head spin. I was more than afraid, I was terrified, because not only did I not recognize the gaunt girl in the mirror—suddenly I had no idea *who* I was inside.

Tae's eyes narrowed as he stared up at me, eyes twin pools of inert water with rip currents underneath. He placed his tea down and stood to his full height.

My arms stretched to keep hold of his collar.

"Take a breath Relina." He warned but I was beyond calming.

"Make me." I sneered, unphased by his cold gaze.

Grabbing my wrists he ripped my hands free of his sweater and took a step forward crowding me.

"Despite what you may think, I am *not* a monster. *I* wanted to give you a chance at a better life." He stepped forward again, and this time I stepped back. "A better one than you were on the road to having." Another step. "I got you into T.R.E. so you could become strong, to fight back against those who oppressed and belittled you. Yes, I knew who you were," another step, "but I grew protective of you, and when Logan showed up to get the results I had..." He hesitated, his voice that had been hard turned to a whisper. "I had burned them. I burned them to keep you safe, but it was too late. Logan knew, knew because of your last name. *He* asked me to bring you here." Another step.

"And you *love* Logan so much you had to help him with this favor?" I snapped, provoked by the mention of Logan.

"Logan did something for me in the past." Tae answered, sounding defensive. "I'm repaying a debt," he stepped forward again, and with each step he took, I had taken one back until there was finally nowhere else for me to go. The backs of my knees connected with the metal frame of his bed.

My heartbeat quickened as I absorbed my situation. I was trapped in an underground lab, without my gift and fighting with someone I didn't have the hopes to overpower. The panic must have shown in my eyes because Tae loosened his grip on my wrists, his face softening. I blinked behind the lenses feeling my body slacken with understanding.

"You owe him," I accused. "Or he's blackmailing you," I surmised. They are almost the same thing, especially if the participant is unwilling. I sighed. "And judging by how you let me out of my cell and stopped giving me the serum to suppress my powers, you aren't a big fan of how he has been going about things?" I concluded as Tae finally released my wrists, but he did not back away. "What does he have over you?"

His smirk was back, but the anger in his eyes smoldered under the surface. "I thought you wanted to know *your* role in this, not mine."

"They are one and the same now, aren't they?" I said sadly realizing it was true, whatever bed Tae had made for himself it was not only him who would have to lay in it. Because even though I believed him to be a monster, I understood well enough now that he cared for me. Whether pity or curiosity was his motivation I wasn't sure, but I was certain he cared. And his caring about me got me mixed up into whatever trouble he was in.

His smirk faded as he closed his eyes. "You are the heir to the kingdom, but that is not why Logan wanted me to bring you here."

Overwhelmed by my outburst, I closed my eyes too and folded my knees so I was sitting in the one place I had been determined not to go near—Tae's bed. It was surprisingly uncomfortable, nearly as awful as sleeping on the floor in my cell. I ignored the parallels in our situations, knowing it would only make me soften my feelings towards Tae even more. Something I could not afford to do. He had kidnapped me after all.

"Why does Logan want my blood? If not for the trait?" I opened my eyes and glanced up at him, his brows furrowed in what seemed to be pain.

"He is looking for a yellow journal, as you already know.

We have one half of it but we need the other." He tilted his head back, exposing the pale skin of his neck, and sighed. "I know you are going to ask why, but the truth is I don't even know. He hasn't told me why we need it. All I know is the half we have states we need your blood trait," he dropped his head to look down at me, "but, no, I don't believe it is to stop the Wraith possessions."

"If my blood can stop possessions then why do I keep getting possessed?" I asked, feeling like I should have some kind of immunity.

"It must be activated, right now your blood is no different than mine."

I rolled my eyes, "except yours is Shamarina." I pointed out.

Tae cleared his throat as if annoyed I had interrupted him. "I've been trying to find a way to activate your trait, so that Logan can't keep using you. It's just proving to be rather difficult." Tae bent, sitting down next to me with a sigh of frustration. "Your blood and the journal are to repay my debt, but your freedom comes at the cost of the city." He admitted leaning forward, his forearms pressed against his knees.

"Then once I destroy the city, I'll be set free?" I asked, feeling like the floor was moving under my feet even though I was sitting down. My freedom at the cost of a whole city. It was wrong but I didn't really have a choice. It's not like I was choosing to destroy the city.

"That is the deal." Tae nodded, shifting to rest his hand over mine, which had a white-knuckled grip on the bed covers.

"Then... I guess my job is almost done," I whispered, recalling the night I overheard them talking while possessed. It was that night when I had taken out the last of the east side defenses. The memories of destruction, courtesy of Logan, because even though Tae had stopped giving me the serum, Logan, whenever he was around, still did.

Most of the people had fled the city after the first month of attacks. Those too foolish or stubborn had stayed, but night after night I ate away at the city's defenses, giving the Grieving and Wraiths greater leeway into the city. It was only a matter of time before the final stand would take place and the city would be lost.

Tae shook his head. "Neither of our jobs are done, not really, until Logan finds the yellow journal and does whatever it is setting up for. I don't understand most of it, but I can tell it's some kind of ritual." He stiffened suddenly, his whole body becoming like a steel cable next to me. Tightening his hold on my hand he stood, pulling me up with him.

We were barely two steps away from the bed when a presence entered the room.

Logan. I was certain it was him from the shivers radiating across my skin.

When I looked I was surprised to see the man Tae had argued with the day I nearly died on the roof. He looked the same; tall, svelte, with hair as white as cotton, skin smooth like ivory stone and vacant eyes the color of sea glass.

So this was Logan. He looked no older than Tae and wore a Krav suit of red and black; a worn, almost picked-apart patch of stitching that could have once been the King's crest was tattered on the side of his collar. He could have been handsome if he didn't look like he'd sold his soul to Skithian himself—which, if I had to guess, he probably had.

Logan slinked past the table Tae had been working at,

tapping a long finger against the beaker he had left there. The rhythmic tapping only added to the disquiet.

"What is happening here?" Logan asked, his voice slicing, eyes cutting to the wrinkled bed covers behind us. Tae was nothing if not meticulous, and it was clear Logan knew that.

"I needed more of her blood and it was too hard to see in the cell..." Tae answered coolly, his tone calculated and withdrawn. It jarred me for a moment how different he actually sounded when it was just us. He was either crazy or had gotten very good at hiding behind this persona. It left me wondering which one was really Tae.

"You never seemed to have a problem before..." Logan mused, narrowing his eyes at us. "I thought you had already isolated the gene?"

"Yes, however, to meet the standard laid out in the journal, I need to completely separate the isolated gene into a drinkable fluid... which is proving to be more difficult."

"Not so difficult that I need to find someone else, I should hope," Logan said, his tone dripping with condescension.

"Of course not," Tae answered smoothly.

"Will it take long?" Logan asked, looking bored.

"Not at all," Tae said, leading me to the stool he had been sitting at earlier.

"Why is she not sedated?"

"It was affecting my previous samples. Worry not, her powers are still subdued," Tae assured him, gesturing to my suit.

"Subdued does not mean no threat." Logan narrowed his eyes. "Are you sure it's for no other reason?" Logan hedged, looking like he knew Tae had stopped giving it to me because he did not want me to remember the horrors I committed each night. "When you're done taking the blood, please be sure to give her some of the serum," he ordered, eyeing me suspiciously.

Tae looked at me, then at Logan, unsure, before nodding and leaving to the garden. I wondered for a moment why he had left, before realizing he'd hidden the serum somewhere else, not in the lab, so that I wouldn't find it and perhaps use it on him. He was too clever and seemed to know me too well.

Logan and I were left alone for only a moment, and though I wanted to, I would not fight him. Not yet. Because if I tried now, I would not be able to win. I had to bide my time for the right moment.

Tae came back and quickly took my blood, not meeting my eyes. He said nothing as he gave me the serum and my body slowed, my power disappearing entirely from my control.

"It is finished," Tae said, taking the now full vial and the empty one to a glass cabinet across the lab.

Logan walked up to the chair I sat in, placing his hands on either side of me and leaning down. "Good, because I have an extra special mission for our favorite Golan princess." Logan sighed, his white-blond hair looking translucent under the overhead lights. "You are going to see your daddy tonight."

CHAPTER 14

Fatal Flaws

Two months ago...

Our small two-bedroom townhome was as cramped and cluttered as the day I had moved out to attend T.R.E. I looked over the piles of papers, research and articles my father would pore over night after night for his job in journalism. He read anything and everything he could get his hands on, and they would be left in the spot he had finished devouring their contents. Coffee tables, chaise, kitchen counters, toilet seats. He wasn't a slob, he just recalled the content best by the location he read it in, so our apartment was his filing system—every location or surface was a drawer of sorts, to hold whatever he had read there. The clutter hadn't always been so bad, though; when Mom was alive, she worked as a maid, and perhaps she did that because she couldn't clean our house the way she wanted to. So she and I had made a game of it. Finding his new papers and articles and guessing where they might get abandoned. The closet hall, the cutting board, or on the radio we never used. When I guessed correctly, Mom would take me out for ice cream. The owner of the ice cream shop was always kind to us, treating us, despite our skin, with a dignity I received from no one else outside my family.

"Rina!" my father called, running down the stairs to me from my old room.

I stood in the living room, my body not my own. The purple haze marred the once familiar home. I'd been sent to do Logan's bidding; seeing my father but being unable to be with him was my punishment for being let out of my cage. Or perhaps punishing me was Logan's way of punishing Tae for not completing the demands for the city or the journal by the week's end.

My body moved despite the effort I tried to expend to make it stop. My father didn't have the yellow journal. My family couldn't be part of the Gilead line. Tae was wrong. A liar. A monster.

"My gir—" He froze on the last step, finally seeing me in the dim light of the lamp in the living room. I had told him many times to change the dull bulb to a brighter one. If he had, then maybe he would have seen my eyes sooner. Seen their purple glow. He would have been able to run away. "No. No," he repeated fiercely, turning to grab a vase from the table next to him.

It was pointless—he didn't have the gift, he would not be able to fight me off, to defeat the monster controlling me.

The Wraith moved inside of me, hungry to complete its mission, hungry to find the yellow journal and kill anything in its way.

If only my father hadn't been home. If he had been anywhere else, he would have been safe. I wanted to scream at him, to tell him I was sorry, but I was a host, no more in control of the situation than the scraps of paper left idly on the floor.

"Daughter..." His voice broke as he held the vase up, hesitating to throw it.

"Father..." I thought painfully as the Wraith moved my body ever closer.

Finally he threw the vase, but it was too late—the Wraith had sent a blast of my power out. I screamed as my father flew through the air, bouncing from wall to wall as the Wraith whipped his long slender body around like a stuffed doll.

His legs bent, and his twisted arms spread out as if he could keep from hitting the ground when the thrashing stopped.

The Wraith left him there, crumpled on the floor of the hall, as it scanned the contents of the room, study, kitchen, bedrooms and even the bathroom.

The scattered papers that had made our home ours were in disarray. The contents of every cabinet, drawer and closet were strewn across the floors in the Wraith's search for the yellow journal.

Inside, I was crying. The horrible creature had just left my father broken on the floor. I didn't even know if he was dead, but I doubted anyone could survive being thrown into a wall repeatedly.

It was only after the search proved unsuccessful that the Wraith brought my body back down the hall, stepping over my father's mangled form. I wanted to turn around to see if he was breathing.

"Rina..." my father rasped, his fingertips reaching out to catch my ankle. I sobbed for joy that he was still alive, but the Wraith, swift as the shadow it was, pulled the blade I had around my hip and turned, plunging it through my father's still-beating heart.

"NOOO!" I screamed, wishing with everything in me to be free of the Wraith.

I watched in horror as my father's green eyes bulged with pain and shock. I wanted to stay with him, to kneel down next to him and be with him in his last moments, but the Wraith turned my body away and carried me down the hall towards the entryway.

At that moment the door burst open, the morning sun peeking in behind Tae's heaving silhouette releasing me from the Wraith that held me captive.

"Relina!" Tae yelled. But as soon as the Wraith left my body, I was on my knees crawling on the floor towards my father's corpse.

I couldn't breathe. I could barely see through my tears as I sat cradling my father's limp head in my lap, the sounds that left my lips like a wild animal.

Anger at finally being free of the Wraith that slaughtered my father was the last thing I wanted to feel, but felt all the same as Tae dropped down next to me, his hand reaching out to touch my shoulder.

"I'm so sorry," was all he said as rage filled my senses and I closed my father's green eyes, knowing full well that the last things he saw was his daughter, possessed, lifting her hand to send vibration after vibration at him, until finally plunging a blade through his heart.

"I hate you," I growled low, my fingers inching to the blade, already imagining plunging the sword, covered in my father's blood, through Tae's chest.

I had never wanted to be a killer; I had been terrified that I had killed Rei. Now, sullying my hands felt like the only thing I could do. I'd killed the only family I had left. There was no blood worse to have on my hands after that.

"That is probably very true, but you hate *yourself* more in this moment, than you do me," he answered calmly, his other hand coming to rest on my other shoulder, forcing me to turn to look at his horrible blue eyes. Eyes I wanted to see lifeless, cold. Like my father's. How dare this captor, this beast of a man, presume to know me, to know my heart.

I *hated* him.

"What do you know of my pain? You're a monster. Rei was right to not trust you!"

With a scream, I yanked the sword from the floor and lashed out, only to be rebuffed by Tae's vibration gift, which tossed the sword out of my hand.

He grabbed my wrist and shoulder, gripping them with such force it was impossible to move.

"Killing me might give you peace, but wouldn't you rather say goodbye?" He nudged his chin towards my father's body. "Send him off well. You can attempt to kill me after."

The tears came then, angry, vengeful, but most of all hopelessly broken. My father had begged me not to go to T.R.E., and now because of me he was dead. None of this would have happened if I had listened to him, if I had never set foot in that school.

I turned to my father's body and knew exactly where I would take him—to the plot where my mother lay.

Tae reached out to take hold of my father, but I slapped his hand away.

"Don't you dare touch him."

"You can't carry him alone."

Even with my gift to help me carry his weight, I wouldn't be able to get him all the way to the cemetery on my own. So

I silently tipped my head, indicating for Tae to help me, hating that I needed to.

We wrapped my father in a sheet, and together carried him out of my childhood home through the empty streets. The red clay buildings cracked and crumbled from the damage I had wrought the weeks before. The corner shop where I would get ice cream as a child with my mother was unrecognizable. It took nearly the whole day walking to get my father to the gates of the cemetery.

The sun burned hot, even as I knew snow fell at the capital this time of year. Erasmus was a dry, hot city, save for a few weeks each year. And that day it felt more blistering than any other before.

I cried the whole time, tears falling numbly over my face, though I didn't make a sound. I couldn't, I could barely breathe. This was my chance to run, to escape Tae and Logan and this horrible city. But I could never leave my father, not dead in our home, or abandoned with Tae on the street. If we finished burying him before sundown, then I would fight back. I would escape, but... why even bother anymore? I had no one to escape to. No one was looking for me.

Tae stopped at the gate, the sun casted his face in orange light, making his skin look almost as bronzed as Rei's.

"Relina, I need you to know I didn't mean for this to happen. Your father was never supposed to be harmed."

I clenched my jaw. "Shut up."

"Relina..."

"Don't," I said angrily, carrying my father with new determination.

I would escape.

He stopped talking and helped me carry my father to our family plot.

When we got to my mother's headstone, a simple curved top and epitaph of "Beloved wife and mother, Nivera Rinehart, 4156-4190 AR," I collapsed. Tae laid my father down, and I sobbed, looking at the plots.

An old red maple hung overhead, it's leaves danced in the evening breeze, casting pointy shadows over the stone face.

After every fight, I would come see this empty place of stone and dirt to apologize. Apologize for not keeping my promise, because after every fight, my hatred for the people of Shamar grew a little stronger. A hatred my mother had never wanted me to have.

I had not been to my mother's grave since the day I'd gotten my admission letter. After fighting with my father about my acceptance, I had come here to tell my mother the great news. That the school she'd always wished for me to study at had invited me, and I would be going despite what my father said. I had thought she would be proud. Now I knew differently, carrying my father to the plot saved next to her for him.

"Nivera," Tae whispered, saying my mother's name with nostalgia.

I glanced around for a shovel, but when I saw nothing, I began to use my hands. Blindly I dug up the dirt, when Tae's hand fell onto my shoulder, giving me pause.

"Let me," he said, gently lifting me by my shoulders and guiding me to stand by the tree. I looked at my dirty hands and then at him.

He was smiling sadly, and something about it made me feel understood, like he did, somehow, know the aching anger and pain clawing inside of me.

I watched in awe as he closed his eyes and carefully began to use his vibration gift to cut into the earth. Beads of sweat rolled down his cheeks as he concentrated on separating the ground, shifting it so that the opening was just deep enough and wide enough to fit my father.

Tae's dark hair fell over his eyes as his hands slid over the dirt, his long pale fingers straining and flexing with tense control. No one I had ever met showed this kind of prowess over their gift. Tae moved the earth without disturbing my mother's plot or the red maple.

When he finished, he dropped to my mother's stone and leaned his head on the etching. I wanted to scold him but I didn't; instead I guided my father into the hole.

"I'm so sorry. I love you," I whispered, and began to use my hands to push soil over him. Tae seemed to have caught his breath enough and began to help me, shoveling the dirt at a much faster pace than I.

"Why didn't you stop it?" I asked, my voice raw. "If he wasn't supposed to be hurt, why didn't you stop me?"

Tae paused and looked up at me, his hand falling next to mine in the upturned earth. "Logan sent the Wraiths after me... I couldn't get to you without being possessed myself." His blue eyes were steady but bleak, as if he thought I wouldn't believe him. "I knew your father didn't have the journal. I told Logan as much."

I shook my head. "You expect me to believe you had nothing to do with this?" I bit out.

"Yes, because," he clenched his fists, his blue eyes glistening with tears, "I have been seen as a monster by everyone, and I accepted that, but I couldn't accept it with you. I wished for you to *see* me. I still do. Because when I'm with you, Tae isn't who I want to be anymore. If I could, I would be Taegan. The whole of me, not just the part I let everyone see, not the person I've created to protect those I love." He lifted his head and gave me the full force of his blue eyes. "You have to believe me because I would never have wanted you to suffer the pain of losing someone precious, when protecting someone precious to me has been my sole purpose all along." His brow furrowed.

"Who? Who are you protecting?"

"My brother," he answered defensively, then softened at my wide-eyed expression. "The other half of the journal... Rei has it. I saw it the day I visited you in the hospital." Tae sighed.

I recalled the book Rei had been reading, the yellow cover with no title, or author. My eyes narrowed accusingly. "Why didn't you take it then and prevent all of this!" I gestured widely to the graves of my parents.

Tae flinched slightly, jaw clenched. "I tried that day, but Rei came back. He found me taking it and fought with me."

"If you fought in the hospital room, I would have woken up." I countered.

"I had already sedated you by then. The hospital could have burned to the ground and you wouldn't have woken up." He had the good sense to look at least a little shame-faced.

"You expect me to believe you couldn't beat your brother and take it?"

"I could have beaten him, but it is precious to him. I figured I could get it from him discreetly later on, but then Logan attacked the hospital, and here we are."

"You were really there that day?" I settled recalling his forehead on mine, his words of apology.

He looked ashamed. "I knew Logan would go after you. I sedated you long enough for the other serum I made to soothe your mind from the trauma and pain leftover from healed wounds. I told the nurse to discharge you before sunset. A moving target is harder to hit and you were a sitting duck in the hospital."

So that had been the pinch I'd felt. The serum he had given me then was so different from the serum that subdued my powers. The serum from the hospital had left me feeling so refreshed and good when I had woken up.

"You tried to get me out." I breathed realizing not for the first time that everything Tae did was for a reason.

He looked at me, blue eyes a tempest of emotions I couldn't begin to understand. He held my gaze, and the temptation to reach out and take his hand in mine was like a burning compulsion in my chest.

A cool breeze passed through the leaves of the red maple and Tae broke eye contact.

"I don't know if Rei even still has it, but I would assume so, and now Logan knows and will send you after him next."

My brows knit together. "You told him?"

"Yes," Tae turned his desperate gaze back to me, "I tried everything I could to stop Logan from sending you to your father."

"So I'll be possessed again as soon as the sun goes down." It wasn't a question.

Tae grabbed my forearm, holding me in place with his gift. I flinched.

"I will not let that happen," Tae nearly snarled. "I will stop you myself."

I narrowed my eyes for a moment, confused by his ferocity. "You won't let me get possessed? Why?" I glanced at the setting sun, the sky pale blue and pink, the golden light nearly gone. "How?"

He stood and lifted my arm, pulling me to my feet. "You can't be possessed if you're already unconscious." Then he yanked me into his chest, and before I even had the thought to register the embrace, to fight back, his hand chopped hard against the pressure points in my neck.

The last thing I heard was his voice in my ear.

"Sleep now, little Golan girl."

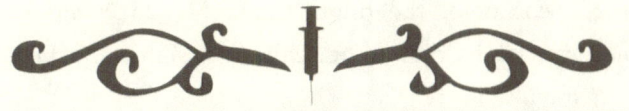

CHAPTER 15

Comparison

Present day

When I woke, I was disoriented, taking in the sunny room. My head throbbed from the onslaught of memories.

Tae had tried to help me. Rei had the yellow journal, or at least he'd had it at one point. My father was well and truly dead, and I knew the culprit; me. I'd destroyed everything, all for Logan's desire for a stupid journal and my blood. Blood of the old king. It wasn't possible, was it? Logan had called me a princess. Clearly, they believed it to be true, but did I?

My face grew hot with tears of anger and sorrow.

I lay on a small cot, a thin blanket and fresh clothes over me. The clothes were all black, just like the ones Rei always wore, except these were loose and clumsy on me like they had been in the hospital. Light streamed in from two skylights, making the dark wood room seem lively instead of old and dusty like it actually was.

"Oh, you're awake?" a voice, willowy and small, chirped from the corner of the bright room. Her face was round, framed by dark hair cut to her chin. Her skin was ashen, just like my own.

She was Golan.

I sat up, alarmed, wiping my face.

Had I been taken to Golan somehow? Was I at one of the slave camps? I looked around, and that thought quickly seemed impossible, as the room was dripping with an elegance that couldn't exist in Golan. My brow furrowed. The walls were panelled with dark wood, the furniture— dressers, end tables and chests—colored like warm chocolate, set upon a rich red carpet. It all made the room seem dated and somehow more elegant than any room I had been in before, even with the cobwebs. Shelves of ivory towered to the ceiling along the dark walls. The grandeur reminded me of the grand staircase of T.R.E.

I looked back at the girl.

"Seojin," she whispered. "My name is Seojin. I'm a healer." She came over to me, her head tilting to get a look at my arm as she pushed up the oversized sleeve.

The cuts from the broken glass were gone, as if never there. The crude stitches were also gone, but in their place was a long white scar spanning the length of my forearm.

She had said she was a healer, so had she healed me, then?

"You're Golan?" I blinked, confused.

She gave me a meek nod and fluttered her lashes. "Isn't it obvious?" she answered in a tone slightly more annoyed than a moment ago.

I frowned. "Where am I?"

"The mansion, of course. You arrived last night. Sir Liam carried you back here."

"Where is he? Where is Rei?" I asked, looking around the room once more, this time for a door.

She knelt beside the cot, her hand closed over mine tentatively. My whole body tightened, not used to being touched by anyone, but especially not by someone who was Golan... at least not since my mother.

"Has he kissed you?" she asked softly, looking up at me with dark eyes. My head whipped to look back at her, a knot in my throat. Who was she talking about? Tae? Rei?

I shoved her hand away and stood up, tripping on the too long pants and falling into a nearby dresser.

She stood up as well, her hands folding together over her chest in a fragile gesture.

I righted myself, fists at my sides. I had always thought if I met someone else who was Golan, they would be just like me, but I realized then, being confronted with this girl, that we were nothing alike. She was soft in the ways that I was hard. Her mannerisms were like a porcelain doll prone to cracking. I could see from her slender form that she was too thin and weak, whereas my body was toned from excessive fitness and training, even if a bit malnourished. My hair was long and wild, while hers was like thinning black feathers smoothed around her slight face. What had happened to her to make her so drawn and feeble? It made me angry, so very angry.

The door opened and Rei stepped into the room.

"I see you're up," he said, his jaw tight.

A ball of black fabric flew at my face, and instinctively I caught it, while Seojin behind me flinched, lifting her arms in reflexive fear. I raised an eyebrow at her, again noting the intense difference between us.

"Sorry, Seojin," Rei said gently, crossing the room to put his hand on her shoulder. My eyes narrowed as she leaned into his touch. Surprised by the strong jealousy I suddenly felt, I stepped away from them, unsure what to make of the foreign emotion. I hadn't thought I was that interested in Rei. The almost-kiss we'd shared in the hospital was the farthest thing from my mind, but I could see now that even if I did grow to like Rei, I would definitely have competition in Seojin.

She looked up at him, her gaze soft and caring, whereas my gaze was fierce and speculative. I found myself becoming more jealous, more from the *way* she cared for him, with a reverence I didn't have, that my personality couldn't afford, rather than from primal female competition.

Rei smiled at Seojin before turning towards me, his gaze becoming hard and jaw tight once more. There was ire in his eyes, but also apprehension.

"You should have told me as soon as she woke up. What if she hurt you?" Rei said, stepping slightly in front of the meek girl.

I shook my head at his odd behavior. "Why are you acting like this?" I asked Rei, more confused than ever. In my memories, Tae was being legitimately nice to me, and in a not creepy way, while Rei looked at me now with genuine trepidation.

He walked carefully around the cot till he was face-to-face with me, his towering height very annoying. I stared at him like he was more than a little crazy, but his gaze remained hesitant, searching.

"Why do you look so confused?" I pressed.

"Me?" He scoffed, his face relaxing as he pointed to himself. "Confused?" His other hand that was still clenched, flexed slightly. "The last time I saw you, you nearly killed me and took my mother's journal. So forgive me if I think you're the one who is confused."

I flinched. So then it hadn't worked. Tae had tried to prevent me from becoming possessed and going after Rei, but he'd failed. Somehow I'd gotten the yellow journal—a memory soon to come back to me, no doubt—and Logan got what he wanted. All of it. The city, my blood and the journal. How many more things did I still need to recollect?

"You wouldn't remember, you were possessed," he said, the look in his eyes telling me he was not lying, not embellishing. I sank back onto the cot, holding the ball of black fabric to my chest.

He had no idea how many things I remembered despite being possessed. How many pieces were slowly finding their way back into my memory.

"Change—we have a lot to talk about. Seojin," Rei said, signaling the small girl to follow him.

I stood up quickly. "Where are Sir Liam and Aaron?" If they had brought me here last night, where were they now? Were they hurt?

Rei continued to walk away as if he had not heard me. I was about to ask again when he stopped his long dark hair shadowing his face as he informed, "Sir Liam left at first light for the capital. He said he would be back soon."

"And Aaron?" I hesitated, unsure if he had made it out of the fray alive.

"I don't know." Rei's fists clenched at his sides. "Sir Liam said not to worry about him, though. He is apparently quite resilient," he answered, a clipped edge to his words as the door closed behind him, leaving me alone.

I looked down at myself, then at the bundle of fabric in my arms. The clothes I was wearing were probably Rei's, and the ones I was holding, as they were much smaller, were either Seojin's or his twin sister Emi's.

Neither girl seemed to like me much.

Who had Seojin been asking me about, anyway? Her question was probably in reference to Rei, judging by her obvious interest in him. She probably didn't even know Tae.

Shaking my head, I changed slowly, taking the few moments I had alone to breathe and rationalize everything up to this point. As Rei's clothes fell from my skin and I slipped into the tight black Krav uniform—not military grade, but still sturdy—I wondered if seeing Tae in low-town had actually happened, or if it was some kind of weird hallucination?

My hand traced the long scar across my forearm, and his words to me—"You shouldn't have come back"—twisted in my mind. My memories had slowly begun to return, and with them the realization that at least for a good part of the last four months, I had been with Tae, or rather Taegan, as he wished to be called. What did he mean by that? His desire to be Taegan with me. Was Taegan who he saw himself as when we were alone, and Tae with everyone else? We hadn't become friends in my memories, so why did I feel like we were... somehow more? Somewhere in my memories, something must have changed between us, because I could not deny that seeing him earlier in low-town had done bizarre things to my heart.

I sat down again on the cot.

Why had Sir Liam left me? I was his ward, his responsibility, after all.

I wrapped my arms around my shoulders and squeezed, trying to control my breathing. Without Sir Liam's calming effect, what if I had another meltdown? What if I hurt someone else? The warmth of my gift filled my chest, and I gasped with hope. I could feel my power again; it was less turmoiled, less out of control than before. More than half of my memories had returned—did that mean half of my power was freed from the inky sludge coating my soul?

Sir Liam had said the knots inside me had been loosened, and from there the memories would just flow. So far, the memories only came on suddenly, and usually against my will, but if I tried... would I be able to recall pieces of my past, now that most of the blocks were gone? Could I start to control when and what memories returned?

I closed my eyes and focused on the last images—painful as they were—with Tae. I concentrated on what might have happened next, after leaving the cemetery. I sifted through pictures, flashes, looking for something new, something I had not fully seen yet. What came to me changed everything I thought I knew about Rei and his brother.

CHAPTER 16

A Deep Scar

One month ago...

T he hollowness that consumed me with the loss of my father left me numb and cold.

I had no one.

Curled into my dark cell, I wished for nothing more than to waste away.

Though I refused every time, Tae came to see me regularly to invite me out of my cell, when Logan wasn't around. And as promised, when he was, Tae did everything he could to keep me from getting possessed. All to protect his brother.

A brother who hated him.

It didn't make sense, nothing did, because despite his efforts to keep me from getting possessed and destroying everything, I wanted to get possessed because I wanted oblivion. I would have even welcomed the serum that could keep me just on the cusp of consciousness, but Tae refused to give it to me. Refused to let me give into the animus I had for myself.

I didn't know how long it took for me to finally leave my cell; time didn't seem to matter anymore. But when I finally did, I was surprised to find the garden had lost some of its initial splendor, the trees and plants worn down from the change in season. Some even looked as worn down as I felt.

I followed Tae to the center of the greenery and sat down next to him on his bench.

The sun was warm, far too pleasant on my skin after days in the dark. It was an enjoyment I didn't deserve, so I curled into myself, away from the light and into the shadows of the fig tree.

Tae handed me a cup of tea.

We sat in silence most of that first day.

In the ones that followed, much the same would occur. Occasionally, Tae would talk about the plants. Sometimes I would cry into my tea, and Tae would wrap his arm around my shoulder and hold me. Days passed like this, but he never pressed, never apologized. Tae was just there every day, bringing me meals I hardly touched and giving me comfort in the form of nature, hugs and hot tea.

Slowly, during those days, I began to see him as Taegan.

As I watched him tend his plants, explain his interest in the earth and its many wonders, he seemed far removed from the calculated man I had met in the school courtyard. He shared stories from my mother, about Golan foods and traditions that I would have probably never learned otherwise. He shared with me a part of myself I had never been given the chance to know.

The day I called him Taegan for the first time, I knew something major had shifted between us.

We were sitting on the bench under the fig tree. The morning was gray and overcast, so I didn't need the glasses he had given me.

"So when the leaves change in the southern kingdom, they nearly blend into the sand because of how golden they become. It's apparently like nothing we have here in Shamar. When golden hour hits the sand, it looks like the whole land is covered in gold, and then add the leaves on to that!" he explained with boyish excitement. "Nivera used to say this was the time of year she missed most in Golan. I hope to one day see it for my—"

"Taegan..." I whispered tentatively, looking down at the cooling cup of plum tea in my lap.

He shifted next to me, and I peered up. His ears had turned bright pink. I fought a smile by biting my lip. How long had it been since someone called him by that name? Was he embarrassed?

Tae cleared his throat, placing his cup on the bench next to him. "Relina?" he asked with an apprehensive smile pulling his lips.

I offered a timid smile of my own in encouragement as I let my gaze fully meet his. He wore the blue lab coat that gave an extra special glow to his eyes, and without the lenses, I found the color in the depths to be far more enchanting than they ever had been before.

"Taegan," I began, this time with a serious edge to my voice, letting the use of his name convey far more than any other words of thanks would have. He hadn't rushed me to feel better, to act normal. He hadn't belittled or lectured me to behave differently. He had protected me, comforted me and in his own way guided me to a place where I could begin to hope moving on might be possible. But to truly move on, I needed answers. "Taegan, you said your mother died before my mother came to work at the manor."

He nodded, face solemn, as if he knew what was coming next.

"In truth, I haven't fully believed you all this time, because of an article I read the day you saved my life on the roof. It said that your mother died the same day as mine. How is that possible?"

"I was wondering when you would ask this." His eyes crinkled at the corners, as if he was recalling something painful. His pink lips thinned as he spoke. "My mother was the first servant my father had. They were no older than you or I when they fell in love. She... She was from Golan, and as such, unequal to my father's family status."

I gasped nearly spilling my tea, but quickly covered my mouth as he continued talking, giving me no time to process his words.

"Still, he had come to love her, and much to the disdain of my father's family, he married her. They were happy despite the ridicule my father received for his choice. His family disowned him, however, so we didn't live on the estate, at the manor, nor did my father run T.R.E., which was his birthright. We struggled to make ends meet, but we were happy."

I grit my teeth, brows furrowed, uncomfortable with how similar his story was to my own family's. The hatred for Golanites ran deep in Shamar. Would there ever be a time when lines would not be drawn against love?

"Y-You're telling me your mother was Golan?" The still air in the garden hung heavy as if holding its breath.

His blue eyes closed as he took a dragging inhale, head

lifted slightly. "Yes." He exhaled as if the moment of this admission had been bearing down on him for far too long.

"Then that would make you—"

"Half Golan, just like you," he confessed, stealing my thunder.

"Then, your siblings?" I paused, looking at his pale skin, his blue eyes. He must have his father's eyes, as those of Golan descent typically had my color or a darker pigment. "So that is why you look different, paler than the twins."

"Naturally." He smirked, holding out his arms as if it was a joke.

"Do they—"

"Shh." He pressed a finger to my lips, making my cheeks flush. "Let me explain. It's a long story and a hard one for me to tell."

I nodded, his finger leaving my lips after a beat.

"When I was six, my uncle came to see us. He was the only person from my family who seemed okay with my father's choice. He stayed with us for a week, then left. When I was seven, he came again. This time my father was away on business. My mother asked him to leave and come back when my father returned. I didn't understand why until the next year when he came again. I was... in the next room... when he attacked her." Taegan stopped, fisting the blue fabric of his coat on his lap. "He murdered her when she refused to accept his advances."

My hands clasped over my mouth again, this time in horror.

"More than anyone, Relina, I know the suffering you have experienced. Because I have had painful losses and I am half Golan too. Half of the thing our country hates; half a person, half a secret."

"Taegan, I'm sorry," I breathed, reaching to lay my hands over his white-knuckled grip.

"My father was reinstated as headmaster after her murder, and has remained a coward since her death. Less than a month later, he married a nice Shamarian woman from a good family to make up for his "failure" of marrying a Golanite. It was his second chance to have a better family, and as I was so young and never introduced into society, his family doctored the paperwork to say that they—he and his new wife—had been married for the last eight years, and I was their child. He erased my mother entirely and gave me a new one legally, but even still, I..." He lifted his pale arm, nothing like the deep olive of Rei and Emi's skin. "I was forever a reminder of the woman he lost, and a blight to the people enslaved by the secrets unearthed in his lab."

I was about to ask what he meant, but again he stopped me with a finger to my lips.

He took a dragging breath, as if preparing himself to speak the next words. "A few months after my mothers death, my father hired a Golan servant, whether for his benefit or mine I couldn't say, but she quickly became my whole world."

It was my turn to look somber. "My mother," I answered.

"Yes, Nivera."

Then it was true—he had known my mother after all. I had wanted the stories he had shared with me to be true. I had wanted those pieces of her to keep and cherish as if they were my own memories, and now I could.

Tears filled my eyes. "Do you know how she died?"

He nodded grimly.

"It wasn't an accident, was it?"

He closed his eyes exhaling sharply. "No, my little Golan girl," he said, the nickname a sad endearment I was only just beginning to comprehend, "it wasn't."

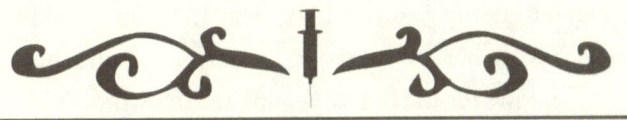

CHAPTER 17

A Mother's Love

"Tell me, Taegan, what happened that night. Why did she die?!" I put down my cup of tea next to his cup on the bench and fell to my knees in front of him, my hands laced over his in a plea. "Taegan," I breathed, squeezing his hands tightly. Rei had said a random possessed Golan soldier had killed his mother. What more was there to the story?

He looked down at me, tears wavering in his blue eyes. The sight of them caused a pit to form in my stomach.

"Your mom was the closest thing I had to knowing my own—our—people, our heritage. Somehow she knew I was Golan, like her, when no one else had been able to tell; she saw me for who I really was."

"She was like that," I acknowledged sadly.

He nodded, his face hardening for what he had to say next. "Logan has been looking for the yellow journals for a long time. He discovered that Nivera had one. I can only suppose she refused to give it to him, so that night, when she stayed late to help me build the planter boxes for the garden we planned to grow together, he came to take it by force."

Taegan looked off into the distance, remembering.

"He found my brother first, bringing him outside as a hostage. Nivera begged Logan to let him go. He did, but as he shoved Rei towards us, Rei's eyes opened, glowing violet."

"Rei was possessed." My eyes widened as Taegan continued his voice conveying horrors I would not wish even on my worst enemy.

"Rei drew a knife on Nivera, and at the moment he was about to strike her down, his mother got in the way. Rei twisted the knife through her heart, killing her instantly."

"By the Strings." Pain and anguish swelled in my chest. Rei couldn't know; he must not know that he'd been the one to attack his own mother.

"It was a blur after that. Rei lunged for Nivera again, but she fled, drawing Logan away after her. Leaving my brother and I to deal with the aftermath. The moment Rei was released from the Wraith, he began to piece together what he had done—his mother dead on the ground, and a knife covered in blood in his small hands. It wasn't hard to come to a conclusion. He understood enough, and it was his cries of utter despair that drove me to chase after Logan."

Taegan exhaled, folding himself to the ground next to me, our hands still tightly clasped together.

"I caught up to them. Nivera was fighting Logan off, and it was like I was there again. Eight years old, watching my mother fight off my uncle. I did the only thing I could—I ran at Logan. I don't remember much, or if I even landed a punch. I loved your mother; I believed I could save her. This was my punishment for believing I even stood a chance." He leaned back and lifted his shirt to reveal a deep groove, a long faded pink scar across his otherwise perfect torso.

"Oh..." My brows furrowed in a new level of confusion and uncertainty. I had been so convinced Taegan was the villain—he was my captor, he was the evil I needed to destroy —but this was a side of him I didn't want to see. He had a history, beliefs of his own. Convictions and battles he was fighting, just to keep those he claimed to love safe. Could it be possible that we weren't all that different? I had judged him and condemned him for his choices, his wrongs, and though they were still wrong, I could see now that *he* was not evil, even if the things he did were.

"I wasn't able to stop him. Even as she offered the journal to him, to spare my life, he struck her down."

Logan had killed my mother. *Logan.* My blood boiled and I stood up, needing to hit something, to rage, to fight for her, because again my heart was being ripped from my chest and there was nothing I could do about it. Logan had ruined everything, and for what—a damn journal. He'd even taken my father from me.

"Ahhhhh!" I screamed, slamming my fist into the fig tree. The leaves rustled in protest at the impact, but Taegan wasn't finished.

"I was bleeding on the ground when Logan walked past me. I grabbed his pant leg and begged him to spare my brother. I was only fourteen, I didn't have the gift, I couldn't manipulate memories. I didn't know if Logan could either, but I begged him to, in exchange for my servitude."

"By the Strings, Taegan, I-I—" I didn't know what to say. He'd given up his freedom to save his brother from the trauma of knowing he had murdered his own mother. At fourteen, to decide something so life altering... No, to have *lived* through something so life altering, and not for the first time, either. It was inconceivable.

Taegan stared blankly, tears rolling down his cheeks as in his mind's eye he watched it all happen again. "H-He took me up on my offer."

I fell to the ground in front of him, and even in my anger, in my rage, I reached for him, holding the fourteen-year-old boy in my arms, and whispered, "It's okay. You're going to be okay. You did what you thought was best."

Taegan seemed to come back to himself as his arms wrapped around me, pulling me into him, sliding me so I was partially in his lap. His arms trembled as he held me tightly to his chest, his head leaning against mine. "Relina..." He breathed my name into the space between my ear and shoulder.

I shivered, and though I knew this hug was made for comfort, to assure him I was there, that he had not lost me too, I could not help the way my heartbeat quickened at his touch.

I pulled back to wipe the tears from his cheeks, and to my surprise, he let me. His skin was flushed, nose cold and red, and for a moment I could see the child in him, the boy who had lost so much and then had to survive all alone.

I leaned in until my forehead pressed against his. The words of remorse, apology, of empathy seemed less valuable than this. Than letting my nearness tell him everything I couldn't, because he needed to know he was not alone. That he was understood and I would not leave him to suffer in his shame and guilt, but most of all that I would not abandon him for it.

Slowly, as if all the air was being sucked from the garden, Taegan moved, lifting his head away while his hand slipped up my back, over my shoulder blade, along my neck to cup my cheek. The tips of his fingers threaded into my hair. "Thank you," he breathed, and for a dizzying moment I was sure he was about to kiss me, but what was more unsettling was that I knew I would let him.

Instead, his lips curved into a knowing smile as they came to rest against my forehead. The brush of his lips across my skin was so faint, so fast, I almost questioned if it happened at all.

In a blurred movement, he lifted me up and set me back down on the bench; the tension of the moment passed as he settled next to me once more.

After a few beats, I found my voice again and asked, "What is the memory Rei has, then? The one he told me in the hospital, from the night his mom died and he saw a possession for the first time?" Was that the altered memory Logan had given him?

"That was my memory of the night my mother died, except Logan could only alter so much. So he had my uncle become a random possessed soldier and changed my mother to Rei's mom. It was the cleanest way to twist the memory. This is why he hates me. Because it is my memory, not his. And in my memory I hated myself for not saving my mother from my uncle. It was the only way to keep him from unraveling the events, the cleanest way to cover it all up."

"So he doesn't know you are half siblings?"

"No, he doesn't, but memories are tricky things. He has associated that night with all Golan people, making them all the villains. He does not know that I am Golan, but he has an innate distrust of me because of that memory, that night, because he knows it's off. You can trick the mind..." He placed his hand over his heart, the slight pulse of his vibration gift reaching me through the bench. "But you can't trick the Nephesh. The soul knows."

"But now Rei hates you?"

Taegan snorted. "He thinks he hates me. He has no idea what real hate is."

"And I do?" I asked, eyebrows raised, making him look at me.

"We both know you do." He stared at me, his perceptive blue eyes pulling at something buried deep inside of me. An emotion I worked hard to keep locked up. "Rei has lived a hard life, but a charmed one because of what I did for him. I wanted to protect him. I was a child myself then and did what I thought was right. I love my half brother and half sister. I did what I believed could save them the pain I lived with after my mother died."

"Where is your father in all this? What did he do?" I demanded, recalling how Taegan had called his father a coward.

He sighed and kicked his foot against the ground. "He knows about my little arrangement with Logan. He knows all of it."

"He didn't try to help you, protect you, anything?"

"He's a coward."

"That's not an excuse!" I said in outrage. "He should have dealt with Logan long ago. He lost his wife because of him! He should have done something..." I cooled.

"Your passion in my defense is rather ironic, don't you think?" he mused, his blue eyes glittering with mischief. "Seeing as how you were calling me a monster not too long ago." His tone was sardonic.

I huffed, crossing my arms. "Logan is the real monster."

Taegan's eyes darkened. "Logan is as much the villain as I

am," he whispered. "I am not the things I have done, just as he is not the misdeeds he has committed."

"How can you defend him?" I glared, appalled. "After everything he has done?"

"He had his reasons, just as I had mine." He lifted my hand, which was clutching the rim of the bench. Slowly he turned over my palm, and flashes of my father's blood across my skin, the ash from the destruction of the city under my nails filled my mind.

I had done monstrous things, but I wasn't a monster, was I?

"A sullied character is not so black and white, is it, Relina?" His blue eyes held no judgment, only the question. Only the hope I had blooming in my chest that maybe just because someone has done monstrous things... those things do not define them, those wrongs do not make *them* a monster.

CHAPTER 18

Trust

Present day

A hand rested on my arm as I started from the onslaught of memories.

"You good?" Rei asked, his face unreadable. I stared unseeing at him for a few moments, everything I had just recalled causing a whiplash of emotions inside of me and no doubt across my face. Rei had no idea about his mother, about Taegan.

I was curled in a fetal position on the floor, surprised Rei wasn't more alarmed by my sudden withered position. "Ugh, yeah." I grunted sitting up, his hand not leaving my arm. I gazed at my arm again, realizing something.

"That day in the hospital, your injuries—you were healed by Seojin?"

"You remember that?" He raised an eyebrow at me, his one blue eye making my heart flutter. "What is it?" Rei asked as I quickly stood up and moved around his crouching form on the floor. My back was to him as I opened my mouth and shut it. Should I tell Rei about Taegan? About what I had learned, about the last few months? No, that didn't feel right. I opened my mouth again and shut it. Something in me didn't want to tell Rei that I'd been with his brother all that time, but I couldn't understand why.

"I don't really remember the last four months," I said instead.

"I know." Rei's clothing rustled behind me, and I turned to see him looking out the window.

"You do?" I asked, unsure of what Sir Liam might have told him about me.

"It's obvious. You recalling that conversation in the hospital, that was ages ago." He scoffed. "I barely remember anything that happened before the night the hospital was attacked."

Something in the way he said that made me doubt he was telling the truth.

"Also, your vibration is all wrong. Heavy and warped, like the way the Grieving feel."

I flinched at his comparison. It was too cruel of a thing to say, even if it was true.

"Yet you felt it all the same, right? That's how you found me last night? Why were you in my neighborhood, anyway?"

He turned around and brushed past me, walking quickly from the bright room into the hall. I didn't hesitate as I stormed after him, doing nothing to hide my annoyance at his evasiveness.

"I was looking for you," he answered as we moved down the dark corridor, the big windows boarded up. The room we had been in had a view of a forest while these windows faced south towards the city. They were boarded for protection, and the darkness they provided did nothing to help me discern Rei's expression.

He continued down the corridor till we reached stairs that led down to the first floor.

"Rei?" I asked, unsure why he would have been looking for me. It didn't make sense. He hated me. Sure, we'd bonded a little those few days in the hospital, but I was Golan and he was from a powerful Shamarian family.

I reached for his arm, stopping him midstep, and though this stairwell was nothing like the marbled grandeur of the one in T.R.E., I couldn't help but think of that moment as he turned to face me.

Light from the boarded windows filtered down across his face as I moved to block his descent down the stairs.

"Even when the city burned, I didn't stop looking for you." He sighed, his face pained, and for a moment I recalled Taegan, the distant look in his eyes. How similar these brothers were, but were both too stubborn to see it.

On instinct, whether from the memories I had just relived with Taegan or from the look of misery in Rei's eyes, I reached up, wrapping my arms around him. His head fit easily in the curve of my shoulder as I stood on my toes, arms circling his neck.

I felt the overwhelming urge to tell him that I was sorry, but other than attacking him, which I didn't recall yet, he would not understand why I was apologizing. Because I was sorry for the pain he wasn't even aware that he was in. Because I knew he'd killed his own mother while possessed, just as I had killed my father, and that anguish was something I could understand fully, even if he had no idea that it had happened.

His arms circled around my torso as he squeezed me

tighter to him. We stayed that way for a few breaths before I pulled back to look at him.

Was this need for comfort because we both had lost everything we knew in the span of four months and even though we didn't like each other, we were one of the most familiar things to each other now? A piece of the past that reminded us of life before. Was that all this was? Was that why he had looked for me? Somehow I needed to know the answer to that question. Needed to be assured that was all it was. A weird form of camaraderie.

"Why did you look for me?"

The shuffle of footsteps had us jumping apart. Rei glanced at the top of the stairs before turning around, the moment broken between us, and disappeared down the steps.

I blinked, confused to see Seojin at the top of the stairs.

"He has always been strong, even when his mother died. That's when his father bought me," Seojin began, coming down the stairs to me.

I shifted uncomfortably at her words.

"I have been here with his family ever since then, like a daughter but not." Her words did not match her expression. She seemed to say everything as if it was rehearsed. "A creature, really. My family was from Golan too." She half smiled. "Someone bought me from a slave trader in Golan and brought me here, but I don't know who or how I ended up here, with the headmaster's family." She reached me on the stairs and lifted her willowy hand to tuck her dark hair behind her ear. "Rei was the only one who treated me like a person."

"Then you know Taeg—" I stopped myself as her face twisted.

"Tae." She spat his name. "He just ran experiments on

me. Rei used to bring me sweets after Tae would run his tests on me. Rei knew how much it scared me, being poked and prodded. Treated as a thing or animal. Less than human."

Her words made me angry. She was wrong, she had to be. That person wasn't the Taegan I had come to know.

"And Emi..." Seojin continued. "She never much cared for having a sister. At first she liked to dress me up, making me her living toy. Nothing more than a doll, till eventually she got bored of sharing her things with me." Her voice was void of anger or disdain; she spoke as if it all was just fact. Cold, cruel fact. "I never asked for any of this. I never asked to be sold. Yet I'm glad I was taken in by the headmaster—at least I have a friend in Rei."

I wasn't sure why she was telling me all this. I wasn't sure why she felt the need to open up her life story to me when I hadn't been particularly interested. Moreover, I was confused as to why Rei had ended up being so kind to her, while treating me like an outcast when we first met. Was that her angle? To draw a line, to show again how different she and I were?

I tried to speak, but even with her meek demeanor, she was able to talk over me. "Come. Rei went to go eat, we should join him."

The food was incredible. How did they have such delicious food in a city completely ruined? The room was small but as ornate as the rest of the manor. Circular windows framed the warm-toned room. A round table that could seat up to six encompassed most of the space.

We sat eating in silence, a plate of wild-caught fish and

pine-roasted potatoes making the room smell heavenly, though the atmosphere was anything but.

The silence dragged on till I finally asked, "So where do you get the food?"

Rei responded without breaking stride on the bite he was finishing. "My father keeps a storehouse. Living on the front lines keeps one prepared at all times."

I nodded and frowned slightly.

"Rei, what do you intend to do now that we have found her?" Seojin asked, her voice almost inaudible compared to how clear Rei's voice had been a moment ago.

"I have to go across the border," Rei answered coolly, clearing his plate of the last few bites.

A gray cloak hang off the back of his chair. It looked vaguely familiar.

He stood silently and tied the fabric over his Krav uniform. He wasn't looking at me, and Seojin too kept her eyes downcast.

It wasn't a long trip across the border, no more than a few hours; the trip could be made there and back in a day, but why Rei wanted to cross had me reaching for his arm to stop him.

"Why?" I asked. Rei froze at my touch. Even through the layers of clothes, I could feel his bicep flex, as if he was holding himself back from reflexively attacking me. My frown deepened.

"My sister was taken." Rei looked down at me over his shoulder; his brown eye, the mirror of his sister's, gazed down at me. "Would you stop me from freeing her?"

I dropped my hand, startled by his question. I had no family left, no siblings to try and save. I could not understand his desire to save his sister, but Rei was not heedless; he would know what he was walking into, and more than likely he would need backup.

"Well then, I'm going with you. It will be a few days till Sir Liam returns anyway," I said simply. Another cloak was folded on the kitchen counter in the other room. I walked over and took it, wrapping it around my shoulders.

Rei whirled on me, eyes narrowed in suspicion. Striding over, he grabbed my hands, stopping me from clasping the cloak. The dark fabric pooled at my feet as I looked at him, alarmed and defensive.

"I don't trust you. Why would you want to save the very people who have scorned you, who would have condemned you and left you for dead the first chance they got?" His two differently colored eyes searched my face with an indignation I still was not sure I deserved, even though I knew now the large role I'd played in destroying this city. I was the reason my peers were enslaved across the border. The reason men and women were dead and families like my own destroyed forever. I knew all this deep down, but I gazed back at him with the same fierceness I had the day he told me to leave T.R.E. Because if I had learned anything about myself, it was that I don't back down from a fight or a challenge. I won't ever cower in fear again, and I will never be made to live with my suffering if I have the power to change it.

"Because *I* won't scorn, condemn and leave anyone for dead if I have the strength in me to save them." His hands fell away, and for only a moment I saw the boy who had leaned into me at the hospital, the boy who had begun to trust me. "I may have done some things while I was possessed that hurt you, but I am not the things I have done, just as you are not." I spoke with an inflection that had us both thinking back to the night in the hospital when he was possessed and killed that nurse.

Rei leaned his head in, and I found myself lifting my chin, the same magnetic pull I had felt in the hospital with him causing my stomach to twist in delightfully painful knots.

Seojin cleared her throat, and we stepped apart.

"If you're both going, then I am too," her soft voice whispered. The sun cast long beams of light in through the windows across the table.

Rei laughed low and humorless. "No, you're not."

"I'm your healer. You need me to go," she protested with little backbone.

Rei walked over and tucked a strand of hair over her ear in a familiar way that felt like a punch to my gut. I shook my head, turning away. Whatever was going on between them, I did not want to see it.

"It's a short trip. I'll be back before sundown."

"You don't even trust her, yet she can go with you?"

"Rina can hold her own."

"You taught me to fight."

"Not well enough for you to cross the border," he grimaced. "Wait here, that's an order."

I turned around when silence was all that followed, to see Seojin nearly nose to nose with me. I hadn't even heard her footsteps. She was as silent as a Wraith.

"No harm comes to him," she said, but her tone was a gentle wind over water. It struck me again that she was a broken shell of a girl, a fragile thing—even when she was trying to be strong, she could only exude fragility. The most aggression she seemed to have had been at the mention of Taegan earlier.

"You won't be mending any bodies tonight," I promised, and I found it strange how sure of that I was. I knew I would not let anything happen to Rei. The strength of that certainly felt like a force all its own, as if I could make it a tangible thing.

Rei sighed and brushed past us to the door. "Let's hope you're right."

CHAPTER 19

Don't Look Back

W e stuck to the rooftops as we bounded across the city towards the border. The rubble of some buildings made for a very precarious trek that left little space for anything but complete concentration on the jump ahead.

Rei did not acknowledge me as his vibrations shot out of his legs, making him fly over the ruined city. He knew I would be able to keep pace with him. At least he must have assumed so, because he never looked back once to check on me. I was thankfully able to keep pace, though it took a concerted effort. My gift was still resistant to me, the heavy darkness making it feel like I had to swim through mud to access even the smallest amount of power. But Sir Liam would not have left me with Rei if he did not think I would be able to manage well enough. The knots he had loosened in me seemed to set off a chain reaction, no doubt triggered by seeing Taegan in low-town. But was that everything? Would

Sir Liam have to treat me again in order for the last of my memories to return?

"Stop here." Rei's voice pulled me from my thoughts and caused me to skid to a halt at the edge of town. The dry desert land of the border rolled out in front of us in dips and peaks, daring us to come closer, daring us to do the very thing as children we were warned to fear, warned never to do: cross over into Golan.

Across the sweeping land were flags of Shamar indicating the edge of our kingdom and the beginning of the land of the blue volcano. The land of my people. My heritage. My kingdom.

The enemy.

I swallowed the dry, acrid air, a strange sadness overcoming me at seeing the land before me. A sadness that was confusing. I should feel as all other soldiers feel—eager to fight, to defend, to rally for my homeland, for Shamar.

"We can't use our powers here if we hope to get in undetected," Rei breathed, unstrapping the supplies and tucking them under debris on the roof. "If we make it, we eat when we come back. Nothing can slow us down."

"Why were we not detected in the city?" I asked, looking over my shoulders at the sloping roofs behind us. The sun was still high, but could we make it back and through the city before nightfall? What if Emi was injured, or worse, dead? Hauling an injured or dead body would make the trip not just harder but longer too. I was about to say as much when a familiar vibration power came barreling straight towards us.

Rei was instantly in a fighting stance while I breathed a sigh of relief, relaxing at the sight of the person before us.

"Now where are you running off to on the eve of battle?"

Black dreads flopped on the top of Aaron's head as he landed between us and the border of Golan.

Rei was less than impressed, holding his fighting stance, eyes fierce. "We are going to the camps to get my sister back."

Aaron looked equally unimpressed, his light blue eyes incredulous, as he gestured between us. "Just the two of you, against an entire encampment of Golan soldiers?"

Rei stepped forward, fists raised. "I have a plan." He said through gritted teeth.

Aaron looked me over, checking for injuries though he knew well any real damage was to my Nephesh more so than my body. His eyes narrowed sensing the way my gift moved like oil through me.

"Without her at full strength?" Aaron crossed his arms like a disapproving father. "So your plan is to get her killed, then?"

Rei flinched, jaw working. "This is none of your business."

"Actually, it very much is," Aaron said, lifting his chin. "As she is a ward of the kingdom and under my protection."

Rei's shoulders tensed, looking like he was about to clobber Aaron. It was time I stepped in.

"Okay, let's all just take a breather." I placed a hand on Rei's shoulder to soothe him, but it only proved to do the opposite. He was a charged wire ready to maim the first person to touch him, and unfortunately that person was me. His movement was swift and volatile. The arm I had touched shot back, slamming into my nose while he twisted, turning to face me, his other hand swooping low and striking my gut. The force of his vibration gift sent me flying. The last thing I saw was Aaron and Rei's horrified faces as I tumbled over the side of the roof.

. . .

One month ago...

Taegan had done everything he could to keep me from going to Rei, giving me sleep aids, telling Logan I was sick and unconscious. But our excuses eventually ran out, and Logan had had enough.

The night I became possessed, Logan had stayed the whole day at the lab, watching over me and Taegan. I stayed in my cell in complete darkness for the first time in what felt like weeks, even though it had only been a few days since Taegan had told me everything.

Staring through purple-hued eyes, I approached the manor. It was dark, unlit, making my purple eyes the only thing glowing in the dark halls. The Wraith seemed to know exactly where Rei was in the great building.

A small part of me was excited to see Rei, even through the eyes of a monster, because he was the last thing I remembered before this strange nightmare had begun. Maybe he would be able to help me. Save me from being trapped. But my hopes stopped there because if Rei had really wanted to find me, how difficult could it have really been to do so? I was out nearly every night, gallivanting all over the city, wrecking, killing. If he had been looking for me, he would have been blind not to have found me by now.

The Wraith pushed open the door, taking me inside the dark room. Tall ivory cases filled with volumes and volumes of books surrounded me. A second level with more shelves, beyond that, rose high up, meeting a coffered ceiling with small murals painted in each panel.

It was more than the simple study my father had—it was a full-on library. I would have liked more time to be impressed, but the Wraith was not interested in the least in these tomes.

The Wraith moved deeper into the room, scanning the shelves for the yellow journal, and I realized the Wraith wasn't here for Rei; it was just looking for the journal. It would only fight Rei if he got in the way. Problem was that Rei was sleeping on a chaise in the middle of the large room.

The Wraith seemed to know this and didn't care if it woke him, almost as if it was interested in a fight.

The Wraith scoured the rows, moving books violently from left to right, tossing them haphazardly onto the floor. I was positive Rei was awake but pretended to be asleep, when the patter of footsteps running down the hall caught the Wraith's attention. Someone else was in the mansion with Rei?

The door opened, and a small cloaked figure came through.

"Rei?" The voice was light and confused, like a small child, but judging from the height, it was not a child. The girl entered the library, and everything in me wanted to scream for her to run.

The Wraith did not allow the girl another word before I was in front of her, eyes ablaze and power rolling from me. The Wraith reached for the girl to silence her when a hand clamped over my shoulder, twisting me around.

"Rina!" Rei said, his voice too happy, too surprised, until he saw my eyes. His face became disgusted, even enraged.

The foul violet glow cut into us, drawing a line between the happy reunion we might have looked forward to and the dismal one we were having. Rei stepped back, fists raised.

The girl behind me stood forgotten as the Wraith used me to share blows with Rei.

It would be impossible for Rei to win against the Wraith. Its inhuman ability far exceeded someone in the early years of their gift.

The Wraith would use me to kill another person I cared for.

Rei fell into a shelf, his back cracking the wood and stone as mine had once done to a window in the hospital when Rei had been possessed.

But there was no one to save Rei like there had been for me that night.

Out of the corner of my eye, the girl was running up a spiral staircase, and the Wraith seemed to take an interest in her, more so now that Rei was proving to be less of a challenge.

My feet flew over the wood floors and launched me up the stairs after the girl.

The room the girl stopped in was small, and unlit like the rest of the manor. The Wraith's attention shifted from the girl to what the girl was holding.

"If I give this to you, will you leave, promise not to hurt Rei anymore?" the girl pleaded, tossing the book on the floor towards my feet.

The Wraith understood its mission, and taking the book, it hurried across the room and out onto the adjoining balcony. The moon was bright, bathing the stone terrace sliver. The stars sparkling behind thin clouds moving swiftly against the black sky.

"No!" Rei yelled, eyes wide as he ran at me, eyes fixed on the book in my hand.

The Wraith sent a blast at Rei, but he dodged it, jumping onto the pitched roof to avoid the attack. He dashed across the shingles, leaping down to where I stood. The Wraith twisted, blocking the punch Rei had thrown. Rei lunged for the book again and again. It was almost as if the Wraith was playing with Rei, but that was impossible. Wraiths felt nothing, neither joy nor sadness.

My body took hit after hit—Rei was not going easy on me at all, not even the slightest bit distracted that it was me he was fighting. His eyes were focused on getting the journal back. I understood why Taegan had decided to find a more discreet way of getting the book back. It clearly meant a lot to Rei, as he was fighting with everything he had to get it back.

The Wraith took the fight to the next level, and after conceding a few hits, the Wraith shot out my vibration in a hammer of attacks; Rei had no hope of blocking them all. He crumpled to the floor like a broken child, eyes wide with fear and anger.

"Rina!" he yelled, but even as he called for me, I knew that he didn't expect me to respond. He knew I wasn't really there, even though I was watching the whole thing.

The Wraith lifted Rei by the throat, choking him as I had done to so many others before him. My hand flexed against his bronzed skin, the Wraith preparing to snap his neck. Inside, I watched Rei's eyes plead with me, plead for his life. I curled up inside myself, horrified and hating what the Wraith was about to do. I wanted to shut my eyes; I couldn't watch Rei die right before me. I couldn't watch the blue and brown of his unique eyes fade to vacancy.

My body convulsed. A power slammed into my side, and

I only had a second to see that the person who attacked me wore a blue lab coat before I was falling over the edge of the balcony, down to the ground below. Rei's life safe from my murderous hands.

CHAPTER 20

A Knife to the Heart

I screamed as I woke up, arms flying out to my sides, trying to break my fall.

Rei, Aaron and Seojin stood there, looking down at me where I lay on a blue couch.

I swallowed, embarrassed by all the eyes watching me.

Aaron, seeing my distress, cracked a smile of his big pearly whites and sat down next to me on the couch. "Had yourself a little fright there, huh?" he teased.

I slapped his arm. "Why are all of you just staring at me —" I broke off, a sudden realization snapping into my mind as I looked at Seojin. Really looked at her.

The figure that first night in the cell, the one that had warned me to keep my strength up, that I wasn't in a safe place, the cloaked girl in the library and the girl before me lined up like ants in my mind. Seojin. It had been Seojin, the meek, weak girl who'd never come back to the cell after that first day.

I was on my feet, even as the room swayed a little.

"You knew! You were there, Seojin! You let me stay

behind bars!" I yelled, feeling my blood boil in a way I knew better to control. I should not hold her responsible. I should not place blame on her; after all, I had done to this city, and yet...

Rei, seeing my overwhelming anger, shifted to stand between me and the object of my rage.

"Rina, what is wrong with you? Calm down."

"Move!" I growled and shoved Rei hard, hard enough to make him stumble but not enough for him to lose ground. He was using his vibrations to secure his footing.

"Please." Seojin's soft voice came from behind Rei's shoulder. "I was desperate. Master would have done something far worse to me should I have disobeyed. You were safe in the cell."

Aaron's vibrations sparked as he came up behind me, ready to intervene if needed, but I was calming down— enough that I wouldn't shove Rei again, at least.

"Cell?" Rei's face darkened, and he turned to look at Seojin in distrust.

"Taegan wouldn't have hurt you. Did you even bother to ask him? He would have kept you safe from Logan," I defended. A surge of protectiveness gripped me over Taegan. The way she had called him Master made my stomach churn. He wasn't the slave driver everyone thought him to be; he was so much more.

Rei slammed his fist into the wall, forcing us to look at him. Though he glared at me, he turned around to yell at Seojin.

"I asked you, I *begged* you to help me find Rina. You knew how much I wanted to find her. How much it meant to me, but you lied to me. You knew where she was these last four months and you said nothing?" Rei concluded, pulling the fragments of our exchange together to build his own narrative. "Tae had her prisoner this whole time in the *cells*, under the manor, beneath the lab?!"

"Y-Yes," Seojin stammered, shame filling her voice. "B-But the only time I saw her in the cell was the day after you came back from the hospital, the night she vanished. I-I didn't know she was still there."

"Why didn't you tell me?" Rei demanded, his voice leveling, but only just.

"Tae threatened me." She clutched his hands with shaking fingers, her brown eyes wide and desperate. "You know how scared of him I am, and even though I wanted to tell you the truth, I didn't actually know for sure if she was still in the cells after that first night."

I interrupted them, malice in my tone. "You left me there! You didn't even try to help me escape. You just left me," I accused.

Rei whirled on me then. "You don't get to speak. You..." He dropped Seojin's hands and took one long stride till he was chest to chest with me. "You defended him. Taegan." He spat the name and I paled, realizing that I *had* called him Taegan before, not Tae. I had shown a crack, a flaw in the perfect portrayal of Rina I was trying so hard to be. With every new memory, every new revelation, my world apocalypsed again and again till I was left with no other conclusion to accept than that I was more Relina than the girl Rei had come to trust.

"I-I..."

"What did he do to you?" Rei was shaking me now, searching my eyes for some shred of the girl from the hospital. The one who had nearly kissed him before, the one who'd felt confused and fluttering emotions towards him. The girl who he had promised friendship and loyalty towards. I wanted to yell that I was still her, I was still Rina, but in so many ways I wasn't anymore. I was the heir to the Golan kingdom, and I had more secrets inside of me than I knew how to manage.

Rei's hands moved to my face, his fingers lacing into my hair as he pulled me into him, as if holding me again, once more, would somehow bring me back.

"I saw her the day she was released, and what Tae did to her," Seojin interrupted, glaring at me with suspicion.

Rei pulled away from me.

"What did he do?" Rei and I asked in unison, though our inflections were completely different. Mine oddly hopeful and Rei's full of dread.

"He asked some creepy white-haired boy to wipe her memories."

I reeled back, a pain bursting in my chest that had me gasping. It was unbearable. "No." I shook my head. "No, no, he promised he wouldn't. He promised." Tears, maddeningly confusing tears, pooled in my eyes as I struggled to recall that moment, the moment I knew I was feeling but couldn't remember.

"Why did he do that?" Aaron asked, joining the conversation.

"I don't know," she answered, finally angry. "I wish he had done the same for me, because after that moment, you," she threw an accusing finger in my direction, "*you* somehow turned the white-haired boy into the beast that destroyed our home." She turned to face Rei. "The beast that took your sister away and ruined everything."

Like a flash of light behind my eyes, a piece of the memory bit into my mind, making me scream as the image of a blade cutting my forearm crossed though my mind.

I fell into Aaron, my back crashing into his chest. His hands gripped my shoulders as he guided back, to sit on the couch.

"Rina?" Aaron said gently, keeping his arm wrapped around me, holding me to his chest as I drew ragged breaths.

I looked at my forearm. The white scar burned along my skin.

My blood. The ritual.

I looked up just as Seojin slunk out of the room.

Rei stared down at me with his two differently colored eyes, eyes that were accusing as they passed between me and Aaron. His jaw was clenched so tight it looked like it would snap.

"What did you see?" Aaron asked softly, his focus completely on me and oblivious to the boy in front of him who was fuming.

"Aaron, I..." I couldn't say it in front of Rei. He hated his brother so much, I didn't want to add to it. Taegan wasn't completely at fault, but Rei would not see it that way. I glanced at Aaron and then Rei, signaling that I wanted to talk with Aaron alone.

"Can you leave us for a moment?" Aaron said politely to Rei, still not looking his way.

Rei's eyes widened like they were about to pop out of his head.

"Absolutely not. You might be her temporary guardian, but I was looking for her endlessly these last four months. She isn't leaving my side." And with his declaration he grabbed my wrist, hauling me to my feet and out of the room.

Taking a note from Seojin's book, I followed dutifully behind Rei as he dragged me from Aaron, through the hall, into the library and up the stairs to the room where Seojin had bargained for Rei's life with the yellow journal.

Sunlight shone in from the French doors that led out to the balcony. I hadn't been able to see the room that night when the Wraith attacked, but what I saw now was not what I would have expected. It was a round room, a tower, designed to be a lady's dressing room. Sheer pink curtains and embellished gold wallpaper painted the room in a gentle, almost too feminine light.

Rei stopped us in the middle of the room.

"What is this place?" I asked.

"My mother's private chamber. She kept secrets here," he answered, popping one of the floorboards up with his foot and showing a small cavity under the panel. "This is where I found her yellow journal. After she died, I came up here often, and one day I just found it. I had been trying for years to read it but couldn't. It was written in some other language."

I looked at the hiding place, chewing my lip.

"Do you remember that night?" He sighed, closing the cavity, and walking over to sit on the chaise, his forearms rested on his knees as he leaned forward to look up at me.

I closed my eyes, recalling the night I attacked him, the night I took his mother's journal from him.

"I'm sorry. Seojin's right—my blood, the yellow journal, I don't know how, but it was some kind of ritual, and I think I turned Logan into..." I moved to sit next to him on the chaise. "If there was a way for me to get it back, I—"

"It's passed now. It was clearly used for its purpose and is probably long gone." He shook his head. "I just wish I knew why she had it?"

I ground my teeth together as I fought the urge to tell him

the truth about that night. The night our mothers died. No—
the night they were murdered.

"Rei, I—"

"No, I'm sorry. I attacked you earlier at the border. I was
so angry, but I never meant to hurt you. I just—" He ran his
fingers through his dark hair. "I'm not a big fan of your
boyfriend."

I snorted. "Who, Aaron?" I asked incredulously.

Rei glanced at me from the corner of his eye. "Yeah?"

"Aaron is..." I considered the right word, then smiled
because the truth was I didn't understand Rei or Taegan's
attention towards me most of the time; I hadn't understood
what it meant to have friends, but not with Aaron. With
Aaron, I wasn't confused. He *was* a friend. Perhaps even my
first real one, one without other mixed-up feelings getting in
the way. "Aaron is a friend." I grinned goofily at the
realization. I had a friend.

"Oh?" Rei sat up and looked at me, tilting his head as if
considering my words carefully.

I waited a beat, wondering if I should bring us back to the
topic of our moms, and if it was right to tell him everything.
At the last moment, I chickened out.

"I'm sorry we couldn't get across the border to save Emi."

"I intend to try again." He nodded seriously.

"Rei, I promise you we will get Emi back. We *will* get her
out," I assured him, because I intended to make up for all of
the awful things I had done, and starting with Emi seemed
like a good place to begin. I place my hand over his long tan
fingers.

We will get them all out, I thought, solidifying that intent
deep in my bones.

CHAPTER 21

Possession

"I 'll go alone. Aaron was right—I shouldn't have brought you, not with you as sick as you are." Rei whispered looking down at my hand over his.

"Excuse me?" I asked, affronted.

"Sir Liam explained it to me the night he brought you in. He was working on restoring your memories when I walked in and demanded to know what he was doing to you. I wasn't sure I believed him, but Seojin just confirmed it by admitting she saw Tae have... that guy, do it to you." He closed his hand over mine. "I will do whatever I can to help you take back the memories Tae stole from you."

I wanted to correct him. To tell him it wasn't Taegan's fault, though in a way it was, because I knew somewhere in my memories I had begged him not to ask Logan to take them, but Taegan hadn't listened. Why? Why hadn't he listened?

Rei sighed loudly, his free hand running through his long hair that at some point had come loose from its usual ponytail.

"I need to tell you..." He swallowed as his eyes shifted

from me to the floor. "I'm ashamed of the way I treated you that day at school. I think I hated you more because when I saw you I was instantly attracted to you, curious about you. But you looked like them. Like the possessed Golan soldier that killed my mom." His hand grew hot against mine. "I saw her lying there, dead, and when I saw you, I saw that day again. A smile frozen on her face, a smile directed at me though it was empty, lifeless."

"R-Rei," I breathed, unsure what to say.

"I hated all Golanites after that. All of them, until Seojin. She has always been different, a broken thing. It's hard to hate a broken thing." He scoffed.

I was really confused—why was he telling me all this?

"So then, you pity her, Seojin?" I asked. If it were me, I would find that worse than being hated.

"Why do you care what I feel towards her?" He raised an eyebrow mischievously.

"I don't." I shrugged, backpedaling.

He moved closer till our shoulders touched. "Did you miss the part where I said I was instantly attracted to you, or are you strategically avoiding addressing it?" he asked, his voice low and thoughtful.

I swallowed, my cheeks warming. I hadn't been avoiding it, necessarily, I just couldn't quite comprehend it. "Do you mean that in the way it sounds, or more of a 'you were an anomaly' kind of thing?"

He smirked. "It was my own prejudice and the anger I had for myself that first made me hate you. So, no, my interest was and *is* not because 'you were an anomaly.'" He tucked my hair behind my ear, making me shudder.

"Then, do I still remind you of that day?" I needed to know if when he saw me, it pained him, because I didn't want that. To add to his pain, his hatred of his brother, of the Golan people. I wanted to be sure that I was not still causing him to recall that night.

His eyes were intense; needing. Asking for something I wasn't sure how to give.

"No," he breathed, our lips a breath away, and though I knew what he was going to do, on some level I hoped he wouldn't.

Panicking, I quickly tried to derail him into changing topics. "You still never answered why you were looking for me?" His aggression towards Aaron and assumption of our closeness should have made it more than obvious, but I wasn't used to being wanted, pursued, liked. Taegan had won me over slowly over months of time together, even months where I hated him. Rei might have been the first boy to trust me, to make my heart race, but he and I really only had a few conversations together, only a few moments that added up to be less than two weeks.

Rei pulled back and smiled, a patience in his eyes I was grateful for. "I looked for you because I had made a promise to trust you, to be your friend, but I never gave up looking because I felt more for you than friendship." His bronzed cheeks flushed. "You have this pull about you, and I find myself unable to stop." He leaned in again, his hands cupping my face, freezing me in place. "I told myself I would, at least, do this much if I found you." His lips were a breath away again, and slowly, gently, he molded our lips together.

I was surprised to find I didn't hate being kissed, being held, as I often imagined I would. For so long I had believed no one could be this tender towards me. That tenderness could feel this good. Like a summer breeze, tantalizing against one's skin. His lips were warm, his fingers in my hair feather light. I had never been kissed before—wait, no, that didn't feel right. Had Taegan and I kissed? If we had, then I should know what to do. I should know how to kiss back, or how to stop.

My stomach flipped, and a wave of shame hit me. It didn't make sense for me to kiss Rei while I was thinking about Taegan. I at the very least knew *that* was wrong. So I pulled back, slightly nervous that I might offend or hurt Rei's feelings.

He looked at me with hazy eyes. "So, isn't it obvious?" he whispered and kissed me again. This time his lips parted, the softness of them taking me by surprise as he grew more passionate. His body pressed into mine, his arm wrapping around my back, pulling me to him. Carefully, he leaned into me, guiding me back against the chaise. My hands hovered over his shoulders, unsure what to do, how to push him away, or if I even wanted to.

"Geez, you two, I know there is a lot of sexual tension between you, but did you have to *actually* go get a room?" Aaron laughed, making Rei jump off of me and halfway across the round room. Rei looked like a startled cat, the death glare he gave Aaron nearly comical.

"Aaron..." I blinked, brows furrowed. I looked at his blue eyes and something in me seemed to shatter. No. No. Something was not right. I was falling into those blue eyes.

The room began to tilt, and as I gazed into Aaron's knowing gaze, I was seeing someone else's. My vibrations came to the surface, and a memory pushed its way into the forefront of my mind, sharp and stabbing. I gasped, turning my head away from them and collapsing to the floor as the memory I feared most became clear.

Three weeks ago...

The splash of running water met my ears. I sat up slowly to find I was in a simple white shirt that hung to my knees. I shifted on what I quickly realized was Taegan's bed. How had I gotten here? I looked around. Taegan rinsed his hands at the sink, his back to me. I shifted, the mattress protested beneath me, drawing his attention. He whipped around alarmed.

"Relina, by the Strings..." He exhaled. "You are giving me daily heart attacks." He placed his hand over his heart, walking over to me. "Please, I don't know how much more I can take," he teased, sitting next to me, his hand resting on the bare skin of my shin in a familiar way.

"What happened?" I asked, looking down at my clothes, confused.

He tilted his head, his expression quickly turning calculated but in a way that was less Tae and more blue-lab-coat science geek. "We agreed to test the serum I made, the one that would activate the gene trait. So you wouldn't get possessed anymore."

It came back to me then, the days following getting the yellow journal. Taegan had worked tirelessly to figure out how to activate the gene, and ironically the answer happened to be in the journal itself.

He'd set to work finishing it before Logan returned from wherever he had gone.

Taegan had said Logan would be returning tomorrow night, so that day we'd tested the serum to see if it would work. If the blood trait would take effect. It seemed a little too late, but if it did work, Taegan hoped with my gene activated he might be able to reverse engineer it into a cure for everyone, Golan and Shamarian alike.

It felt good to help with something that could save lives after having my hands bloodied with so many. Of course I had agreed. So, unsure if the Krav suit that subdued my power might affect the process, Taegan had given me one of his shirts.

"Did it work?"

He slid his hand from my shin to my shoulder, a glimmer of excitement in his eyes. "Let's find out."

I stood, following him out into the nightscape of the garden. We walked a few steps along the path.

Nerves filled me as I looked around the shadowed greenery. The Wraiths had taken up residence in the garden, no doubt on Logan's command. "You will stop me if I do get possessed, right?" I checked, not wanting this experiment to go south.

Taegan leaned his head close to my ear as he came up behind me. "I don't need to," he whispered, a smile in his voice as he lifted my arm up to see the black smoke I dreaded wrapping around me every night. This time the smoke ebbed and flowed over and through my skin, but the cold never took root; my vision remained clear of any purple haze.

"It worked..." I breathed. "It really worked." I turned around to face Taegan, my smile wide and hopeful.

Taegan's hand moved from my arm to my waist as I turned, and though I wasn't sure if he meant to, his fingers pressed into the curve of my side, making me step closer to him.

My heartbeat quickened.

"I'm glad I could do this one thing for you. To protect you

in this way, at least, after I failed you so many other times before."

My brows knit together, and I threw my arms around his neck, stretching my body over the length of his. I wasn't sure what to say, but I needed him to know I did not blame him, not really. Not so much anymore.

His arms wrapped around my back, pressing me to him. The moonlight moved from behind a cloud, casting silver light over us.

Taegan took a deep breath, holding me tightly. "Relina, I know this might come as a shock to you, but I think I'm in—"

Clapping reverberated through the garden as Logan appeared from the shadows.

"Now, now, Tae, don't rush things. Life can be long, and you really ought to choose carefully."

Taegan released me, moving me behind him as Logan approached. I wasn't in my suit, didn't have the dimming serum, and I was outside. I reached for my power, letting it warm in my chest for the first time in months. I had gotten so used to not having it that I hadn't even thought to use the gift right away.

"Two against one. Sorry, that's not fair." Logan shrugged, picking a pear off a nearby tree and taking a bite. "I'm afraid I don't have time to fight you both and still get the ritual completed. Tae, grab her and let's go."

Taegan turned to me, yanking my wrist painfully.

"What are you doing?!" I looked up at his labradorite-blue eyes and shivered to find two violet orbs instead. I loaded power into my arms, ready to use it on them both, when Logan laughed.

"I gave him a little taste of the serum we have been giving you." He tossed the half-eaten pear on the ground, using his free hand to tap the side of his head. "He's all in there, seeing, remembering, just as you did."

If my face could get any paler, it would have. How had Logan done it? When? Did Taegan know he had been given the serum? Had he been forced to take it this whole time? Was that how Logan controlled Taegan too?

I clenched my jaw. If I fought Taegan, he would know everything, see everything, trapped inside a shell he had no control over.

My hands began to shake.

"If you fight him, Princess, he will watch every single time he hurts you, makes you bleed, because you and I both know you are no match for him on a regular day, let alone with a Wraith inside him."

My breathing came fast and quick as I registered the truth in Logan's words. But the Taegan I knew, the Taegan I had come to care for, would want me to fight, would want me to escape, even if he had to hurt me in the process. He would want me to at least try.

With a scream, I lunged for Taegan. My charged punch landed against his shoulder; before he could respond, I landed another on his side. We were close enough to the dirt wall that I twisted out of his hold and flipped back, my bare feet connecting with the dirt.

I had little to no chance of winning—that I knew Logan had not been lying about—but I had my power, and though it was dark, it might just be possible to climb my way out of the garden. I didn't think, didn't look back. Like a beast loosed from its cage, I climbed with a single purpose in mind; freedom. Willing my power into my legs, I pushed off the wall. While in the air, I moved the vibrations through my body into my hands, so when my palms connected with the dirt a few feet higher, I scrambled vigorously for a hold. It wasn't easy; the earth was damp and slick, so I slammed my feet against the wall, adjusting my power into my legs to thrust out and up again. I had no time to look and see what Logan and Taegan were doing below, no time to second-guess this strategy. Up was the only way out, and I would have to use all my concentration, all my strength to make it up the vertical surface.

I didn't know how long I tried to climb the wall. The light of the moon was my guiding focus as I careened myself towards the opening.

"Tae, put her in the suit and let's go." The words sounded far away, but only moments after they were said did an explosion burst the wall of dirt next to me.

My concentration broken, I slipped, clamoring to find something to grab. I had no idea how high I had climbed, but I knew it had to be enough to break something if I fell to the ground below.

Another burst of dirt ruptured next to me. Little rocks pelted my sides, across my face. Another burst and another. Finally the vibrations the Wraith had been throwing at me hit true, slamming into my back. I screamed as the vibrations ripped through my muscles, bones, organs, till they all felt like they were splitting open inside me from the pressure.

I fell.

Familiar arms wrapped around me, cradling under my knees and back. I looked at the violet eyes staring down at me and coughed, blood tangy and foul filling my mouth. "I'm sorry," I wheezed as air tried to fill my lungs. Some of my ribs had to be broken.

Taegan carried me into the lab and placed me on his bed. I trembled, moving to sit up as the Wraith turned Taegan's body away. Logan was nowhere to be seen, and then his words from before registered. *Put her in the suit.*

I looked down at the white shirt, muddy and slightly ripped.

"Taegan, no."

The Wraith turned around, the suit I had been wearing for weeks in his arms.

Embarrassment and fear warred inside me.

"I'll do it, I'll change, you don't have to," I begged, knowing it was futile. The order was clear. The Wraith would put me in the suit, regardless of if I was willing to put it on myself.

Tears of frustration and anguish filled me. Taegan wouldn't ever do this to me, he wouldn't, but looking at his face, his hair, his hands, his body, it was suddenly very hard to separate the boy inside from the Wraith coming towards me with a blank expression.

CHAPTER 22

Exposed

Three weeks ago...

Taegan's hand reached out to me, grabbing the collar of the once white shirt and ripping it down to my hip. I couldn't help it—I screamed, stumbling off the bed and backing into the stone wall behind me. I curled in on myself, trying to cover my exposed skin.

"Please, please, stop," I cried, tears spilling over my cheeks.

The violet eyes stared down at me, void of any remorse, any emotion.

Taegan would never shame me like this. He would be hating himself for every tear, every moment of fear he gave me now.

So for him, for his sanity and for my own, I closed my eyes and stood up straighter, even as my body throbbed and ached with brokenness. My ribs rebelled, making me grit my teeth with pain. I stood anyway, eyes squeezed so tightly shut, they hurt.

This was punishment for what Taegan had done for me. It was obvious Logan was angry that he could not use me anymore, so he used the one tool he had left in his arsenal to make us both suffer.

Though I was embarrassed and afraid, I would not let Logan win, not this time.

I closed my eyes tightly for us both, knowing that Taegan was unable to shut his eyes inside, unable to look away from me, from the things the Wraith would make him do. I knew all too well there was no looking away, no hiding.

So I would not make it harder, would not add to the shame this memory would leave in both of our minds. I would not make it as if he forced himself on me.

Slowly I slid the tattered shirt from my skin, letting it fall to the floor. I flinched despite my effort to be composed, and shivered from the cold in the room, from the shock and nerves coursing through me.

When his hands touched my skin, they were neither rough nor gentle, but I winced nonetheless.

The top of the suit slid over my head, and I moved my arms around, finding the openings for them to slip through. Fingertips pulled at the hem, smoothing the fabric down over my waist. Every place his fingers touched trailed with sensations foreign to me.

I reached forward, needing something to lean on in order to lift my feet for the pants. My palms found familiar shoulders, and I gripped them, trembling as I lifted one foot, then the next. The knuckles of Taegan's fists skidded up along the outsides of my calves, thighs and finally my hips. I swallowed hard, eyes pinched so firmly I was afraid they would never open again. I had never been touched by a boy before, not like this. Fighting I understood; fighting didn't make my skin tingle and a nervous pit form in my stomach. And even though this moment was forced on both of us, I could not deny that being touched this way felt good; dizzying.

As soon as my vibration power muddled and faded, I knew it was over.

I was shaking from head to toe. No matter how much I wished I could make it stop, I could not help it. I was terrified. The tight fabric clung to me like a second skin, and though it left nothing to interpret, it was significantly less exposing than standing naked before Taegan. He had seen everything, every curve, bump, imperfection, scar and blemish. But the horrors of the night were only just beginning as I opened my eyes to see unfazed violet ones looking down at me.

———

The Wraith carried me through the lab and up through various tunnels, till finally we stopped in a room lit by candlelight. It was a grand room, like a ballroom or some kind of ornate theater, as a small stage was off to the right. Opposite the stage was a long banquet table covered with a white sheet, as if this room hadn't been used for a long, long time. The floor was patterned tiles inlaid with golden vines. A coffered ceiling with murals, like the ones in the library at the manor, spanned out over our heads at least eighteen feet high.

The Wraith put me down, but held my arm solidly so I would not move, would not run away.

Logan appeared then, holding the yellow journals and a long dagger. The hilt glimmered in the flickering candlelight.

"Will you behave now, Taegan?" he asked, examining the blade as if he was a little bit bored with the whole situation.

I looked at Taegan, his eyes fading from violet to blue. He shuddered next to me, releasing my arm and collapsing to the floor.

He was breathing heavily, shaking as vigorously as I had in the lab.

I dropped down next to him, brushing his hair out of his eyes, needing to see that they were blue, the blue I had come to admire, the blue I trusted.

He shrunk back, his trembling hands pulling mine away from his face. He stared at me with widened eyes filled with self-loathing.

"Relina, I'm sorry, I'm so so sorry." The broken boy I had seen that day in the garden was crumpled before me, the one who had watched too many horrors. Had suffered through too much alone.

I wasn't sure if he was apologizing for hurting me physically or for shaming me emotionally, or perhaps he finally understood what I felt each and every time I went out and watched the city burn at my hands, helpless to stop it. Most likely, it was all of the above.

I shook my head, even as anguish and humiliation roiled at my chest.

"Now, Tae, let's do this and fulfill all our promises and deals, okay?" Logan said, standing in front of us, the blade outstretched in his hand.

Taegan fisted his hands to stop them from shaking and stood, taking the blade. "Curse your plan," he spat, flipping the blade and cutting into Logan's arm, which had come up at blinding speed to prevent the blow from hitting his heart.

"Ahh!" Taegan yelled, stepping forward, his gift pumping through him, trying to force the blade into Logan's chest.

Logan slapped Taegan hard across the face, the sound reverberating in the mostly empty room. The force of the hit had my heart in my throat as Taegan was knocked across the dusty floors and into the burgundy papered walls.

Blood dripped from Logan's wound and Taegan's mouth as they stared each other down.

I hopped to my feet, reaching for the dagger that protruded from Logan's arm, but like a striking serpent, his uninjured hand grabbed my hair, yanking me back.

"I have Wraiths on standby to possess the children upstairs in case our little experiment disrupts their sleep. So in other words, *stop making a fuss*." Logan's voice slithered, his fist jerking, pulling at my roots. Tears brimmed from the corners of my eyes.

"You swore you would not harm him anymore," Taegan snarled, and I realized the children, or at least one of them, upstairs Logan had referred to was Rei. Were we inside the manor? For the last four months, had I been trapped, underground, beneath Rei's feet?

Logan discarded me, tossing me by the hair to the once glossy floor. "Then bleed her before I make the Wraith bleed her through you."

The ferocity in Taegan's eyes withered at the threat. He straightened to his feet, wiping the side of his mouth as he walked over to me. He took the blade from Logan's outstretched hand without meeting his eerie gaze.

Satisfied, Logan began speaking in a language I did not recognize, the words echoing in the ornate room.

Taegan lifted me from the floor, gently smoothing my

hair. "I'm so sorry. By the Strings, I never wanted this for you," Taegan whispered, his voice raw.

I lifted my hand to his pale cheek. "I'm okay, I'm okay. We can fight him together, I know it," I encouraged and shifted into a Krav stance, turning my back to Taegan.

Taking a deep breath, I prepared myself to attack. Prepared myself to stop Logan's plan once and for all but Taegan wrapped an arm around my waist, pulling me against his chest as he had done so many times before.

"What are you doing?" I hissed, then froze as the blade, cleaned of Logan's blood, lifted in his free hand. I wriggled and jerked against his hold, but he was using his gift to root me in place. Panic fluttered in my chest, quick and wild.

"If I do it, I can at least be sure it won't kill you. If the Wraith bleeds you, it will cut you in whatever way is most efficient." His breath was hot against my neck as he whispered. Understanding widened my eyes. The Wraith would slit my throat. The Wraith *would* kill me.

"After this we are both free?" I said, resigned, knowing that if there was a way out, Taegan would have thought of it, would have acted on it. His surrender gave way to my own.

"Logan!" Taegan shouted as he held me securely to him. "I have one more deal I want to make. Take the memories of the last four months from her," Tae begged.

I writhed against his hold. "NO! You said you wouldn't, you said you *wouldn't!*" I twisted in his arms, trying to see his face, to look at him.

"She won't remember you, that you love her. You will lose her either way." Logan tsked.

"Better to be a nobody to her than to be remembered for all the horrible things I made her do, had her be complicit to."

"By the Strings, Taegan, it is not for you to decide!" I screamed and tried to break his iron grip, but it was useless.

"Very well, but you know this indebts you to me again."

Taegan clenched his jaw but nodded. "Of course." Logan looked back down at the two journals in his hands. "May I have a few moments with her, please?"

Logan's eyes narrowed, a sneer on his lips as he warned, "Kiss and say goodbye, but that's all you get. My patience is wearing thin."

"Let me go!" I hissed, wild with anger and fear. I didn't want to forget, didn't want to lose Taegan.

He picked me up, taking me a few feet away from Logan. Turning, Taegan deposited me in front of the long banquet table, positioning us so neither of us could not see if Logan was watching.

His blue eyes bore down on me, stilling any words I might have wanted to say. He had dropped the blade a few paces back, freeing his hands to block me in against the table.

"Relina, if these are the last moments I have with you, I need you to know that every second, every minute I was with you was like fresh air filling my lungs. If these are the last moments I have with you, I need you to know everything I did was for Rei. To protect him." Heat radiated off him as he spoke in a low, urgent voice. As if he was afraid there was not enough time to say everything. "I am forever broken, forever tilted down a path that will only end in my destruction, and I was fine with it. Fine being the villain, being the one who destroyed and broke others." Candlelight licked warmth over his pale skin, casting shadows over his sharp features. "Then you came along. I didn't want to love you. Didn't want to save you, but more than anything I didn't want to break *you*. Your carefully crafted armor. Your passion and faith, your zeal to fight. You are fire, you are light, you are made to be so much more than you can see right now. I *can't*, no, I *won't* have the things that have happened to you these last months keep you shackled and broken. I *will not* be the one to break you. Not you." His eyes were fierce with a promise.

I shook my head, unsteady on my feet. My insides felt like they were snapping apart with pain not unlike the agony of the Wraith attack earlier. "T-Then why does it feel like I'm breaking right now?" I pleaded, my voice quavering.

He closed his eyes, looking like he was in so much anguish that my heart squeezed, nearly taking me to my knees. "Because you love me." He whispered like a caress, like a curse.

"No!" I said immediately. "No, I don't." *I don't. I don't.*

His eyes opened, and shards of labradorite cut through my disbelieving gaze as he lifted his arms from the table on either side of me, taking me instead into his arms. This embrace was different from the others we had shared. His palms were hot, pressing into my back, pulling us chest to chest. "By the Strings..." he breathed, his head tilting down to mine, breath brushing over my lips, "I wish that were true."

Then his lips were over mine. As if my body was possessed, knowing somehow what to do, my hands wrapped around his shoulders, crushing him into me. I had never been kissed, and yet it felt like the easiest thing to do with Taegan. Like, why had we not been doing this all along? His lips were full, firm as they moved against mine. I responded, breathing headily into the kiss.

I was floating and was only fleetingly aware that I was literally off the ground when my rear was placed onto the banquet table. My knees pressed into the sides of Tae's lean form, urging him closer. His tongue found mine and a fire ignited in my chest making me gasp. He was everywhere, hands against my skin, in my hair, behind my knees, pulling me closer. Closer to him. Closer but not close enough. I needed more. I was sinking in an ocean of sensations and would, no doubt, have drowned had he not pulled away.

"Relina, you are so beautiful," he panted, a huskiness to his voice that had me whimpering for him to draw near one more. Instead he pulled back further, his forehead against mine. "I have wanted to kiss you since the moment you yelled at me in the headmaster's office, it having only taken a few hours for you to piece together what was going on between my brother and I. So clever, so forthright." He smiled sadly. Slowly, his lips brushed against mine again, and the hunger to kiss him had me shuddering in his arms. "I don't deserve you. Not even a little bit. So please tell me to stop," he begged, the desire in his voice snapping me back to reality. To our situation. To Logan, to my memories, the ritual, all waiting.

I slowly, painfully leaned away from him. His blue eyes, dilated and wild, almost had me pressing my lips to his again in reckless abandon.

I didn't fully understand when my heart had begun to change, when I had stopped trying to find a way to escape the lab, to escape him. Perhaps it was the day in the garden, perhaps it was the day he brought me blankets, perhaps it was the moment he stepped out into the courtyard that very first time.

"Stop," I whispered, the word strangled.

With more strength than I had, he stepped away, the flexing of his hands the only indication that this was difficult for him too.

"Thank you," he breathed.

With those two words, my heart cracked, and I knew I

loved him. How and when it had begun wasn't clear, but I did love him and he loved me, but our situation was impossible. He would never sacrifice his brother for me, and I could never ask him to. "What do we do now?" I asked, wishing he had a plan, something that could free us all.

"I have to let you go." His eyes glittered in the dim light. "Go back to my brother."

The dagger he had dropped flew through the air. Taegan reached out to catch the hilt at the same moment he grabbed my arm, pulling me off the table and back to where Logan waited.

In the moments we had said goodbye, Logan had completed reading the ritual; a strange pulsation surrounded where he stood meditating. The language hung from his lips, a guttural, spectral sound that permeated the air.

Thick, stifling black smoke filled the room as we got closer to where Logan hummed.

We stopped a few feet away as a gust began to sweep through the room, wrapping around Logan. The room trembled and groaned as if the vibrations rolling off of Logan could not be contained by the wood, stone and brick.

"Logan! The deal!" Taegan yelled over the wind and groans. "Take her memories!"

I looked at Taegan sharply. He didn't mean for Logan to take my memories *now*, did he?

Logan's eyes opened, sickly pale green, sunken in and starved.

The moment they locked with mine, I felt it, like a thread being pulled and bunching up the other threads, over and over and over again. The sharp pull, the threads behind my eyes twisting and pulling and knitting up. It didn't hurt so much as it was anxiety-inducing. I blinked rapidly, my body shaking from a sudden chill.

I looked at blue labradorite eyes, a hand tight around my upper arm as cold metal sliced through my skin. Blood poured out, and I screamed, whether from the pain or confusion, I couldn't tell. The scream was deafening. Why was I screaming?

The room flashed and warmed as if the summer sun had just appeared in front of me.

A mass of inky purple formed from my blood on the ground. It moved towards Logan and seeped into his pale skin, his white blond hair turning to feathered scales, his hands darkening into black claws, and even in my bleeding state I could see clearly when his eyes turned from a man's to a beast's, the irises becoming narrow black slits.

Then the world plunged into darkness.

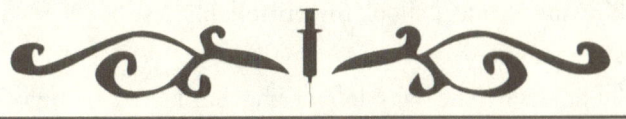

CHAPTER 23
Healing

Present day

"Rina?" Rei asked, his hand on my back, the other gripping my arm. "You look like death. What is it?"

"Was the kiss that bad?" Aaron snorted.

Tears filled my eyes.

Rei's eyes widened, and he quickly extricated himself from the intimate hold we were somehow sharing, shifting instead so he knelt in front of me, hands clasping mine, just as I had done with Taegan in the garden so long ago.

"Rina," he said, tone humorless, "whatever you remembered, you were possessed, okay? Just like when you attacked me, you are not to blame, you are not at fault," he said softly, but he didn't know. He didn't know anything.

I looked away from Rei and around the circular yellow-and-pink room. My eyes landed on Aaron, and I hiccuped through my tears as his blue eyes lost all humor.

"You remember it, then?" Aaron asked.

I nodded, grateful Aaron seemed to understand. He'd

had his heart broken too. On some level, he knew what was happening to mine.

Rei, not understanding, pulled me into his chest, his hand stroking my hair as I shook uncontrollably. "What is it? What did she remember?"

"The night she was left at the bunker. The night the dragon attacked," Aaron answered for me, leaving out the piece he and I knew was there, even if he did not understand who or how. One broken heart knew how to see another's.

———

I couldn't speak for a week. I just couldn't. The minute I opened my mouth, I began to sob, silently at first, then body-racking screams of anguish. Taegan had said he didn't want to be the one to break me. He had thought he had spared me this pain. He was wrong. He was completely wrong.

Aaron had explained to us that Sir Liam was returning with an army to take back the city. That that was the only reason he would have gone to the capital. So we waited, day after day, for news of the army's arrival.

The desire to disappear, to fade into nothingness was just like the crippling isolation I'd felt after losing my father, after murdering him, except Taegan wasn't there to bring me back from the edge, and that thought alone sent me careening over it.

Rei held me, read books from the library to me, asked me questions, only to get no answer. I barely noticed his presence most of the time.

One night, after an especially bad episode, I overheard Aaron and him talking about my condition.

"I thought Sir Liam was helping her, but clearly having

her memories is killing her. What can we do? There has to be a way to fix this. Make her forget again or something?"

"You felt how messed up her vibrations were; they are finally healing, coming back to a normal color, straightening out. You would subject her to live the rest of her life shrouded in darkness while wearing an ignorant smile?"

"No, I just mean, there has to be a way to help her."

"Time, Rei. Rina is strong; she has to find that strength again. We can't do it for her."

It was Aaron's belief that I could find my strength that helped me eventually to believe I could.

About two weeks after remembering what happened that night, I called Aaron to my room and told him everything. All of it, from the abuse, the serum, the possessions, the people I'd killed, the murder of my father, the attack on Rei, Logan, the ritual, the journals, and how I fell in love with Taegan. Everything but what happened the night my mother and Rei's mother died. I concluded that that memory was not something I had a right to share.

Aaron took it all in stride, listening intently as I sat curled up in the dark corner of the room Rei had given me to use. The irony of the corner was not lost on me. It reminded me of my cell, except this time instead of escaping, when I was in the worst pain, I would crawl out of the comfort of my bed and into the corner; into the cell.

Aaron watched me from the edge of my bed as I sat wrapped in a blanket, as I had been most of the last four months. When I finished, tears were in his blue eyes, a grim expression on his face.

"You have not remembered everything," he said softly.

I glared at him. I didn't want to remember any more; if there was more to know, I didn't want it.

"My uncle told me he would need to treat you one more time after he arrives, and that should be it; you should finally be free of the hold Logan cast over your soul."

"I don't want to remember anything else," I confided. I had thought I could handle it, knowing everything, and maybe Relina, the girl I had become over those four months, could have. But I hadn't been Relina for the last few weeks. I had gone back to being Rina the student, the girl with the dream of becoming a commander in the Shamar army. The girl who wanted to prove her worth. I didn't know how to reconcile these two people. I remembered nearly everything, so I could have easily stepped into the girl I had become, but she had been caged and forced to accept her fate. I had a choice, and choosing to be Relina again was something I wasn't sure I wanted. "I don't think I can handle it," I admitted.

Aaron's skin caught the firelight from the hearth, making his ebony tone glow with warmth as he said, "Most people do not know how strong they can be until they are faced with something that breaks them. That is when true strength is found. In that brokenness and your ability to overcome it."

I shivered from the floor even though the fire kept the room as warm as a summer's day. I nodded, acknowledging the truth in his words. For the many days after, I considered his words carefully.

———

A messenger arrived at the manor a few days later, telling us that Sir Liam and the army had arrived. Seojin, Rei, Aaron and I set out to the encampment only a few miles north of the border. As we crested the hill, breaking the tree line, we looked out at the thousands of Shamarian soldiers and tents below.

The messenger directed us to our tents to freshen up before meeting the commander.

I felt the eyes of nearly every soldier as I walked by. I paid them no mind; it was no doubt a strange sight for a Golan girl to be walking about a Shamarian military encampment. The side-eyes, the whispers and stares— nothing had changed in the way the people of Shamar treated me, but now it wasn't unwarranted; I deserved it all. I had taken these people's homes, families from them. I deserved far worse than their muttered words of confusion and distrust. I deserved their vengeance. I would not fault them for it either, if they took it.

I walked into my assigned tent. The space was cramped, pitched in the middle with a thick beam. A simple cot lay on the floor and a table off to one side with a small plate of food on it. The thing that caught my attention most was the uniform draped over the back of the chair. It was a slick black Krav uniform, the King's crest emblazoned across the chest, threads of gold were woven down the length of the sleeves in intricate twists. Out of every suit I had seen, it was the most beautiful. I traced the pattern, lifting it up to see; sitting in the seat of the chair were two black metal pauldrons, and arm braces.

I noticed the straps on the suit, made to snap the metal armor in place. Shaking my head, I put the suit back, certain I had walked into the wrong tent.

Behind me the tent flap opened, and I turned to see Sir Liam, his long dreads draped over one shoulder, his eyes, pale as the moon, watched me curiously.

"Sir," I breathed, glancing between the suit and the man

who had found me and set me on this course. "I'm sorry, I think they put me in the wrong tent."

He smiled a little, the scar that spanned from brow to lip crinkling. "They were not wrong."

"But this is a suit for a general, I can't wear this."

"If you don't wish to accept, you certainly do not have to," he advised simply.

My mouth opened and closed in astonishment. Why were they offering me this honor, to be a general? I hadn't even graduated; moreover, I was the one who'd destroyed the city. I hadn't done anything to earn this right.

"I can't. I can't dishonor Shamar by accepting this. It is a prestigious gift and I am of no consequence. Strings, I am responsible for the fallen city."

Sir Liam's eyes narrowed slightly, but not in anger. "Then take responsibility." He gestured to the suit again.

My heartbeat quickened. What did he mean? Becoming a general was not how I'd thought I would take responsibility for my actions. Imprisonment, trial were more the expectation I'd had.

"Make up for the lives lost by protecting the soldiers here with you, as their general. No one knows the strategy the enemy used to take the city better than you."

His words were true; even as he said them, the memories of the ways the Grieving and Wraiths took the city night after night raced through my mind. There had been a pattern, a method to their carnage.

My hand fisted around the suit and I nodded.

"Then dress—we are to meet the commander shortly to go over the plan, but first you and I have some unfinished business."

CHAPTER 24
A Strategic End

I dressed, and Sir Liam began the last session to restore my memories. It wasn't nearly as long of a process as it had been those first few weeks. Only a few hours had passed, the sun still high overhead when he finished. However, he looked as drained as he had been every other time. I didn't feel any different, hadn't recalled anything new while he had been working. A part of me was relieved—perhaps there really was nothing left to remember.

We walked through the camp and the stares I received felt very different as I passed tent after tent, soldier after soldier, the metal of the armor over my arms glinting in the sunlight.

I wasn't sure how to feel, but a sense of wonder filled me as I realized my dream was coming true. Rina's dream at that moment had become my reality, and it left me feeling a little sad and a whole lot proud.

The commander's tent was in the center of the camp, much bigger than the rest around it.

Though it was much the same as mine on the inside, the major difference was the size of the table, which took up most of the room. Maps and markers covered the long surface, and the chairs around it were all empty save one.

The man stood. He had Long golden hair, a sharp square jaw, ageless skin and gray eyes set in a gentle brow. He was unbelievably handsome in a golden-boy kind of way. He wore a suit similar to mine except he had more metal adornments covering his back, chest and legs.

"I'm Commander Callum McClain, and you must be the girl we have been waiting for."

———

Much as I had done with Aaron, I explained everything to Commander McClain and Sir Liam. I left out my falling in love with Taegan, my lineage and the blood trait, choosing instead to focus on Logan's strategy and the attacks on the city.

"Then Logan has the ability to turn into a dragon. By the Strings!" Commander McClain slammed his fists onto the table, breathing heavily.

"Callum," Sir Liam cautioned, "you can't go back there, your fight is here."

"I know that, old man, but I have to tell them." Commander McClain scribbled furiously on a parchment. He exited the tent with the letter and returned moments later, eyes on me.

"What about this Taegan character?"

"He is not the enemy."

Commander McClain's eyes narrowed slightly but

nodded. "Very well" He sighed, still a bit distracted and concerned.

I wasn't sure what the commotion had been about, but clearly it had unnerved the commander. "There is one other thing. The night in the hospital, the night I was taken, there was a boy named Theo, he did something to the Wraith that possessed Rei. He forced it out of him and I think he perhaps killed it somehow. I don't know how, or if what I recall is even really what happened. It all happened so quickly. If that boy is still alive he might be able to give us an upper hand against the Wraiths."

Sir Liam and the commander shared a look of weary knowing.

"Indeed, Theo was a wealth of knowledge now lost to us. He did not survive the attack that night."

My stomach churned. "Are you sure?"

"Positive." Commander McClain nodded grimly.

"But the ability you speak of," Sir Liam encouraged, "is not lost to us. Aaron knew Theo as well and Theo shared the ability with my nephew. I found out the night in low-town when the Wraiths came for us. Aaron protected us and shortly after the Wraiths vanished."

I bit my tongue from saying that Taegan was the reason the Wraiths left us alone that night and focused instead on Aaron having known how to stop possessions since the moment we met. Why had he not shared it sooner?

"Aaron as my nephew is part of the King's Court. He made a vow to tell no one about the power Theo possessed. His life was bound to that vow, it's hard to explain." He looked to the commander for help but the commander shook his head slightly. Whatever Sir Liam wished to tell me it was clear the commander did not give his approval. "As soon as Aaron was able to share the knowledge with me I hurried to send word to the capital, which is why I left with such haste. However, Callum and the court already knew about the power."

I turned to look at the commander. "Shamar knew all this time how to defeat the Wraiths but didn't use this strategy when the city was being overrun?" I accused.

The commander stood, hands splayed over the map of the city. "I'm not sure what you know of the state of affairs in the capital but we only just learned about the ability shortly before Sir Liam came to us and unfortunately word had not reached the capital of the Erasmus's need for aid until a few weeks ago, about the time when you woke up in the bunker."

His tone was final and showed his station, putting me quickly into my place. I was bestowed the honor of wearing the uniform of a general but that did not put me on the same level as the commander. Not even close.

Humbled, the topic shifted back to the strategy we would use to take back the city, and before we knew it, the day had given way to night.

"Well then, that's the plan," Commander McClain said, gesturing to the map we had used to chart the takeover. We had concluded the best plan of attack to be a four-way surround. We would enter the city from the four major routes at dawn.

Sir Liam patted my back as if to say good job, and I couldn't help feeling proud.

As I turned to say good night to the men, my hands began to tremble. My vibration built inside me like a wine bottle pressing against a cork, about to burst open. I gasped, falling on my knees, vision blurring. Neither man looked surprised as the last of my memories crashed through my mind. Not as painful as the many that had come before but just as jarring.

Taegan and I were in the lab. He was working on the serum to activate my trait when I snatched the vial he was working on from the desk. I smiled wickedly, looking at the vial.

"Relina," Taegan said like a chiding father, "come on, give it back. The vial of blood is critical to our getting out of this mess."

I gave an innocent look. I was so bored, and Taegan had been working all day. "I have more blood," I teased, clasping the vial behind my back. Taegan was always so serious—and rightfully so, our situation was life or death—but in that moment, all I wanted to do was make him smile.

Not leaving his stool, he reached for it a few times, not even really trying, and then the strangest thing occurred. He began to pout.

He sighed, exasperated, his blue eyes heavy from lack of sleep, his lower lips pushed out as he frowned.

"Are you... pouting right now?" I asked, incredulous, stepping around the table so it was between us.

He looked taken aback. "Of course not."

I scoffed, amazed at his lack of ingenuity. "You're how many times stronger than I am right now?" I rolled my eyes, gesturing to the suit I was wearing. "If you want it, come and get it," I emphasized, lifting the vial over my head, wiggling it just so.

"Don't shake it like that!" he warned, finally standing and coming towards me.

I shifted from side to side, my small frame making me quick even though he could easily catch me if he used his gift. But he didn't; instead he chased me around the lab, a smile spreading over his face as our game of keep-away grew playful.

I shifted and shimmied all round the lab till he finally used his gift to come right up behind me. His arm locked around my waist.

"Cheater!" I laughed, falling back into him. The force wasn't much, but we tumbled onto his bed, and he rolled us till he was on top of me.

He was warm all over, our breaths fast and quick from running around.

He reached for the vial in my hand, and in a last-ditch effort to keep playing, I stretched my arm high over my head.

My smile faltered as he leaned forward, his chest pressing into mine, hand moving up along my forearm.

Suddenly I couldn't breathe. My hand slackened overhead as his fingers laced through mine, the vial pressed between our palms.

He wasn't smiling anymore either, his blue-eyed gaze unwavering in its intensity, as if waiting for me to admit something. When I said nothing, did nothing, he rolled the vial from my hand into his and lifted off of me, disappearing out into the garden.

The next memory was fast, as we were in the garden under the fig tree, Taegan swinging and punching at me as I focused on dodging and blocking. When an opening came, I threw punches of my own. We sparred frequently. At first I relished the idea of hitting him, then over time as we trained together, I found I could learn a lot from his fighting style. The way he moved through Krav was sharp and cunning, different from the manner we were taught at school, slow and methodical.

I recognized the move I had used in low-town as one I

had learned from him in our training sessions. He swung his leg up at me during an especially vigorous session and as his heel came down over my head, I knew there was no way I would be able to block it, so I yelped, hoping he would stop before the hit landed.

Of course he did, his leg swinging just past my head at the last second.

"Ah, I haven't let loose like that in a while, I'm sor—"

I cut him off with a swing kick of my own, which naturally he caught, tossing me onto my back in the dirt, but not before I had grabbed the collar of his shirt, dragging him with me.

When we fought, he never used his gift, as I couldn't use mine.

But in the last moment, he used his gift to shift us so he slammed into the ground first, with me landing on top of him. Our sessions never ended with Taegan in the dirt—that was my role—but this time he had reversed our roles, and I couldn't help but laugh as I lifted myself off of him.

Another bunch of memories rolled through my mind. Moments of us cooking and baking Golan meals together as he taught me time and time again about the southern people.

"Could you teach me to make the spiral jam cakes?" I asked one day, recalling the sweet rolled jam cakes he had given me in the car after I visited Rei in the hospital.

"Let's make some right now." He said.

"Now?"

He pulled me over to the small kitchen and lifted a bag out of the cupboard. Inside were all the ingredients for the cakes. "Happy Birthday Relina."

I blinked. "My birthday isn't till—"

"It's today." I took in his words realizing then just how

long I had been missing for. How long it had been since the night in the hospital. "So," He hesitated as he watched me process, "shall we make the cakes to celebrate?" He smiled.

I smiled back nodding, and somehow, when we had finished, the jam filled desserts were more sweet the second time around.

The last memories trickled into my mind like a sink being turned off after having been at max pressure.

Taegan and I climbed the fig tree towering above the garden together, the smell of earth all around us. Crisp and fresh.

"I like it up here," I announced, lifting my arms wide even though there was no breeze.

"Careful, you might fall if you're not holding on to something," he said sardonically.

I raised a mischievous eyebrow, noting the lack of branches to hold on to. "What should I hold on to? You, perhaps?" I teased.

He chuckled, holding out his arm like a gentleman. "If you wish."

"What will you hold on to?" I asked innocently.

His blue eyes glittered in the sun as a warm smile spread over his face. "Why, you, of course," he answered cleverly.

My heart pumped wildly in my chest, as somehow I did not think we were talking about staying up right in the tree anymore.

Startled and unnerved, I shoved him unceremoniously from the limb he perched upon.

For a moment I was surprised by my own actions, before I laughed, seeing him fall unharmed to the ground below.

I climbed down quickly, meeting him at our bench.

"I could have broken something," he fussed impishly.

"Oh, that was payback from shoving me off the roof at the manor," I answered conspiratorially. "You will get over it."

"Falling from any height is a hard thing to get over," he responded, a weightiness to his words that gave me the feeling he was not talking about falling from the tree.

CHAPTER 25
A Need

"That's all of it, then," Sir Liam said, lifting me from the floor. The commander had left the tent at some point during the memories returning, leaving me in the care of Sir Liam.

I looked up at his clear eyes, nodding. My vibration warmed happily in my chest. I closed my eyes, feeling it move through me with ease and a levity I had almost forgotten.

It was like breathing at sea level after being in the mountains too long.

"Are you okay?" he asked, brushing the dirt from my knees the way a father would a small child. I laughed a little, amazed by the family I had found myself in. Sir Liam, Aaron, even Rei, people I hadn't known I needed. People who had picked me up and dusted me off, giving me a way to rectify my wrongs and heal the brokenness in me.

By the Strings, I was grateful for them, having lost so much and gained so much in such a short time. It was unthinkable, but here I was, standing at the end of those challenges feeling more prepared, more ready to take on the next, as long as they were beside me.

There was only one person missing from the equation, and if by chance I could, I would bring him into this family with open arms.

"I actually think I am," I breathed, not quite sure it was completely true but feeling like it could be, or rather it would be at some point.

Sir Liam smiled and patted my shoulder. "Hurry along now, sleep. We go to war tomorrow."

I agreed, wishing him good night, and left the tent.

I moved through the dark encampment, my eyes heavy from strategizing and remembering.

"Rina," Rei called while jogging up next to me. He was in combat gear specifically designed for the border's dusty warm climate and terrain. The fabric had various tones to help blend him into the dry scenery. Even in the dark, he stood out, though, his long hair tied at his nape, strands of black falling over his shoulders. "How did it go?"

"We leave at dawn," I answered. I was too tired to go into more detail.

He glanced at my clothes, seeing the metal, and the look of surprise and admiration that crossed his face was quite adorable. He gently took my hand, watching the soldiers that passed by us carefully.

"Can I talk to you privately?"

I nodded, unsure what he needed to talk about.

He pulled me into his tent. The space was exactly like my own, dimly lit by a lantern.

He turned around to face me, looking very nonplussed.

"What's wrong?" I asked. Was he hurt? Would he not be able to fight?

"Liam finished repairing your memories?" he asked, his two differently colored eyes searching mine.

"He did, but there are some things that still feel fuzzy, but I know it's all there," I answered, unsure why he looked so uncomfortable. I was the one who should feel uncomfortable; I was the one who'd attacked him and had kissed and fallen for his older brother.

"You were held captive by Tae because of me, because I asked you to spy on him," Rei said, looking down at the ground.

"No!" I said quickly, unable to bear him blaming himself for anything that had happened to me. Not when I knew so much more than him, not when I was the one keeping secrets. "No... they needed me for my blood, to destroy the city—it was not your fault. Tae had planned for me to go to T.R.E. from the beginning," I said honestly, using Tae instead of Taegan, knowing that would ease Rei's mind. He had to know that Taegan had planned everything long before Rei had shown an interest in me, or had asked me to spy for him.

Rei seemed to realize something, his eyes narrowing. "I played right into his hands." He turned, slamming his fist on the table. "Right into the game he was orchestrating," he growled, finally seeing how Taegan had planned for Rei and I to meet, planned for us to have an altercation. Because Taegan knew his brother well, well enough to know that if I went to the hospital, Rei would ask me to spy for him. "He knew I was watching him all that time on the roof. He knew all these years that I didn't trust him."

"Yes," I whispered, knowing now that it was all true. Taegan had moved us like chess pieces, into the roles we needed to play. All so he could protect his brother from the truth of that night years ago.

"From the moment we met, this was all a game to him? I was just a tool?" Rei concluded, sinking to the cot, his face twisted in pain. "Everything was to get to you, to your blood," he whispered.

I sat down next to him and sighed. "Tae was not all bad towards me. He helped me bury my father. He prevented Logan from doing worse things with me..." I trailed off, knowing Taegan had done more for me than he should have, and we were punished time and again for it.

"You give him credit where he deserves none. He held you captive." His fist clenched and he shook his head, disgusted by the thoughts in his mind that I could only imagine. "I didn't ask you to come here to talk about *him*." He spit the last word like it was a curse.

I put my hand on his shoulder, trying to comfort him. "Then what?" I smiled, trying to lighten the mood.

"I..." He lifted his head, his hand moving to rest on my knee. "I have not been shy about my feelings for you." His voice was melodious as his hands slid under my knees, lifting both up and over his lap.

I braced my hands back against the cot, taken completely by surprise. "R-Rei?" I asked, unsure what he was doing but leaning away from him all the same. He wouldn't try to kiss me again, not after everything that had happened with his brother, right? But he had no idea about any of that. No idea that my first kiss hadn't been with him but Taegan.

He leaned his head against mine, his arm wrapping around my back, holding me to his chest. "We are going to war tomorrow, and I don't want any questions between us. I want you to know how much I care for you." He pulled back, eyes searching mine for reciprocation.

I put my hand on his chest, making some space between

us. "Rei, we *are* about to go to war tomorrow, and I just got my memories back. I'm confused and dealing with everything that has happened. I need time," I answered with a cowardice I was ashamed of. I was being weak. I should tell him the truth. If I had never fallen for Taegan, this would have been so easy, because I did have feelings for Rei. Real, strong, magnetic feelings for him, but I didn't know how to reconcile that with the feelings I had for his brother.

The last time I saw Taegan in low-town, he saved us from the Wraiths and had such compassion in his eyes. He still cared for me, even though he had let me go, but I wasn't sure I was ready to let him go just yet.

Rei closed his eyes and nodded. "I understand, but for tonight can I have this?" he asked, a pleading in his voice I didn't know how to say no to. So I closed my eyes and let him lean in to kiss me. Soft and gentle quickly became urgent and desperate, as if on some level Rei knew—knew I had feelings for someone else and wanted to erase them from my mind.

His hand slid down my side, sending shivers through me. The fabric of my suit seemed to vibrate, the tension of our gifts mingling as he lifted me up, turning to lay me down on the cot, his body hovering over mine. I gasped as our lips parted, his hand under the small of my back, the other pressing into the pillow by my head.

The light of the lantern cast shadows over his face; his one blue eye glittered in the light, and a pain stabbed through my chest.

"Rina, you are so beautiful," he whispered, his head dropping to my neck, trailing kisses as he buried his face in my hair. Tears filled my eyes as Taegan's words filled my mind. "*Relina, you are so beautiful.*"

"Rei... please stop," I whispered, my heart breaking as I said the next words. "My heart isn't mine to give."

He pulled back immediately, sitting rigidly.

I moved my legs over the edge of the cot and stood up, creating distance between us. "What do you mean?" he asked.

"I-I need time, and this war needs both of our attention right now. *This* can't happen," I answered like an absolute coward. I had never thought I could be so cowardly but I guess backing down from a fight and this situation were two very different things.

I couldn't tell him about what had happened with Taegan. My mind was still trying to understand all of it, come to terms with it, even as my heart understood. This wasn't just about who I loved anymore, this was about the person I wanted to be. Was I Rina or was I Relina, or perhaps was there a way to be both?

"Rina, I'm sorry if that was too fast." His jaw clenched, and he looked so distraught. I knew he hadn't meant to push me.

"Time," I repeated. "Get some sleep, we go to war tomorrow," I answered with a small smile, hoping he understood that this meant I wasn't mad. I turned and left his tent, my body trembling. With a speed I had missed, my feet carried me as I ran straight out of the encampment and into the trees.

CHAPTER 26

Relina

I stopped in a clearing that looked out over the border. The blue volcano seemed to glow in the distance.

"You're here." A voice like a thousand needles stabbed into me. I whirled around to see Taegan, his short dark hair pushed back in that clean sort of way he'd had at T.R.E. His clothes, though not a pants suit, were still a suit. A Krav uniform. I blinked, surprised by the way the black material molded to his lean muscle. It had no embellishment and needed none, as he alone was opulent enough.

"Taegan," I breathed. The sound of his name on my lips was like water after a deep, dry thirst.

"You remember everything, then." He sighed, his labradorite-blue eyes sad even as a small hesitant smile lifted one corner of his lips.

"You were a fool to think I wouldn't," I replied with a smile of my own. Suddenly I wanted to tease him to make him blush.

He guffawed. "No, I knew you were too stubborn to

forget, but that is actually why I'm here." His face fell slightly as he walked towards me.

The old me would have stepped back in fear of him, but this time when I stepped back, my hands clasping behind my back, a wicked grin lifted my cheeks.

He paused, seeing my expression. "What are you doing?" he asked, taking a tentative step forward again.

Again I stepped back.

He tilted his head at my smile, then his eyes flashed a brilliant blue as he caught on to my teasing.

We danced in a swift flow of moves as he tried to catch me, just like we had played before in the lab, after I snatched the vial. Just like then, he was unsure at first, but quickly caught on to the levity. His laughter mixed into my own as he worked to reach the nothingness I had clasped behind my back.

This time though, we both used our gifts, flying and tumbling around the clearing. It was no real competition, though—he was much more skilled in his gift than I.

He easily caught me after a few moments, wrapping his arms around me, chest to chest, as he used his gift to unclasp my hands from behind my back. We twisted and fell onto the patchy clay ground.

His hands pinned mine as he straddled my hips. I panted and continued to chuckle even as Taegan stopped laughing, his eyes shifting from playful to pained.

"I felt it when you got your powers back; I could feel your gift every time that Wavemaster loosened a memory." He closed his eyes, and my heart fluttered at the knowledge that he had been keeping tabs on me.

"Taegan?" My laughter died down into a smile. Was that

why he was here? Because he'd felt me get my memories back and wanted to see me?

"Logan let me go. I am free of him, no deals, no more bargains." He opened his eyes, sliding his hands through mine. And the memory of him lacing his fingers into mine just like this had my heart hammering. "I had to see you." He pulled back onto his heels, lifting me by our entwined hands to sit in front of him. "Rei can never know. I needed to see you to be sure you would keep the secret of that night. To never tell Rei what happened."

I sobered, realizing that he wasn't here for me, but to make sure I would keep Rei's secret. My heart pulsed painfully in my chest as I looked at our interlaced fingers.

Taegan continued, "If he knew the truth, if he knew he was the one who killed his mother, he would not recover from it. He's not as strong as us. I have to stay his villain."

I thought of the hospital when Rei had been possessed, how when he saw the nurse I had watched him kill, he shattered, realizing what he had done. The lost look in his eyes, the way it would forever haunt him, and he didn't even know how he had killed her. This truth would destroy him and make him a shell. Taegan took that shame and guilt, bottling it up so it was a punishment only he could drink.

"You were wrong to take my memories, and I believe you were wrong to take his, but I will keep this secret," I answered.

His fingers pulled from mine as he stood up. "You remembering is a pain I never wanted either of us to have to live with, but... I am sorry for acting against your wishes," he said, bowing his head slightly as I looked up at him from the ground.

"You!" Rei's venomous voice bellowed into the clearing.

"Get away from her!" He moved at an enhanced speed, and though I knew Taegan could avoid his brother's punch, he didn't. I heard the sickening crunch as his fist connected to Taegan's face.

Taegan flew through the air, tumbling a few times before righting himself and skidding in the dense clay dirt, barely coming to a stop. Rei was on him again crouched over, fisting Taegan's collar.

Blood dripped from Taegan's mouth; scraps from the brush left little cuts along his pale skin.

"Brother..." Taegan whispered, a smile that looked pained curving his cheeks. "Glad to see you're still alive."

"You selfish bastard!" Rei yelled, lifting his fist to punch him again.

"Rei, stop!" I sprinted to them, grabbing his raised hand and using my vibration to prevent him from throwing the punch.

"Give me one good reason I shouldn't kill him after what he did to you."

"He's your brother!"

Rei turned to look at me, his eyes softening as he threw his brother down into the dirt, letting go of his collar. "He is no brother of mine," Rei said, standing, taking my hand in his.

I could feel him relax the moment he touched me.

I looked down at Taegan, but he wasn't looking at me. Instead, his eyes were on his brother, whose eyes were on me.

"Rei—" I began, but was cut off.

"Are you okay, did he hurt you?" I moved my gaze back to Rei, my chest squeezing so painfully it was hard to breathe. I shook my head, unable to use words. "We'll take him back to the encampment to stand trial for his crimes," Rei said coolly.

"Rei, if he stands trial, you know he will be executed."

"Perhaps, but he should pay for his transgressions in whatever way the court sees fit."

My brow furrowed, and I moved away from them both angrily. "Then shouldn't I? I shouldn't be wearing this armor with the King's crest." I lifted my arms, showing the honor they had given me in place of condemnation.

"You were possessed. You know crimes while possessed are not punishable," Rei answered icily, his hand lifting to my cheek to tuck my hair behind my ear.

I clenched my jaw, ready to fight for Taegan, but I knew it would be pointless and Taegan wouldn't want it, so I lowered my arms testily. "How will we take him back?"

Rei's expression turned vindictive. "You remember this trick, right Tae?" Rei turned, bending down to grab the pressure points on Taegan's neck.

Taegan looked past Rei at me before blacking out, a morose smile on his lips.

CHAPTER 27

A Choice

We carried Taegan to the cells at the edge of the encampment, built for runaways or captured Golan soldiers. Rei alerted Commander McClain to Tae's presence, and he met us at the cells with Sir Liam.

"After the battle tomorrow, we will send a small party to Romath with the prisoner," Commander McClain directed, handing a syringe to Rei. "He is your brother; though he seems to be cooperating right now, give this to him if he tries to use his gift."

"What is it?" Rei asked, holding the syringe.

But I knew all too well what it was. The serum that would keep me on the edge of consciousness and prevent me from accessing my gift. I had thought it was something Logan had conjured up, but it seemed even Shamarian military had such foul methods.

"It will keep him powerless," Commander McClain

explained to Rei, though his eyes flitted to me. Had he noticed the show of disgust on my face.

I glanced at Taegan, who had woken up once Rei dropped him in the cell. He had not looked up once, his eyes fixed to the ground the whole conversation.

"Come here," Rei said between the bars. Taegan took a long deep breath and lifted his chin to meet his brother's glare. His face was bruised, the blood on his mouth smeared and dry. Giving off the air of someone else, the person I knew Taegan pretended to be, he squared his shoulders and walked up to the bars.

Rei reached through the cell and yanked his brother's arm. "This is for Seojin," Rei threatened and jabbed the needle into Taegan's arm, "and Rina."

Taegan's stare was unblinking as he looked at Rei, but he flinched when the needle pierced his arm.

"Relina," Taegan sighed, correcting Rei, eyes closing as he slid down the bars to the floor.

I shuddered at hearing my name. My resolve crumbled, and I took a small step towards the cell. Aaron was there, placing a hand on my shoulder, squeezing softly. "Let's get some rest—the battle is tomorrow, remember?"

I glanced one last time at Taegan, barely conscious on the floor, before following Aaron out into the night.

We all went our separate ways, and I knew Rei wouldn't come to find me again tonight. I had asked him to give me some space as we carried Taegan back to the encampment. Because seeing Taegan again had given me exactly what I had hoped it would: assurance of who I was and where my heart truly lay.

I slept only a few hours, too restless to let sleep be a sweet refuge. Attaching the metal plates onto my suit, I made my way to the cells. The sun would rise soon, and the biggest fight of my life would begin, but before that I needed to help Taegan escape.

The tents were quiet with sleeping soldiers as I shifted with stealth through the encampment. The guard of the cells had dozed off, not realizing that the serum only had an effect for a few hours and would be wearing off soon. I peeked inside the tent first to make sure Rei or another soldier wasn't waiting inside.

It was clear, so I slipped through the opening.

Taegan lay against the bars, eyes closed, his breath steady and even. For just a moment the anger in me flared, and I felt somewhat vindicated seeing him behind bars, as this time *I* was on the outside. I quickly shook it off, because though it felt somewhat good to see our roles reversed, a larger part of me desperately wanted to set him free and ached at the sight of him caged once more.

He was finally free of Logan, only to be locked up again for a fate that might be deserved but was still not fair somehow.

I pressed the code for the lock and flinched as it clicked loudly in the quiet morning. The bars opened, and I stepped into the cell, my heart hammering with residual fear. I closed my eyes, taking a few deep breaths before kneeling down to wake him.

Taegan shifted, brow furrowing as his eyes opened.

He swallowed, his throat bobbing, the suit he wore ripped at the collar and along his front, showing the bumps and valleys of his toned chest and the faded scar Logan had given him.

The fabric must have ripped from the force of Rei's grip earlier that night.

My eyes lingered a little too long on his exposed chest.

"Relina..." he whispered, still sleepy and slightly drugged as he took in the open cell door, the cloak and satchel in my arms. He blinked rapidly, sitting up straighter.

"Drink this." I handed him a canteen, and he tipped it back, some of the water dripping down and loosening the blood on his chin, turning the water pink. I used the end of the cloak to wipe it away.

He froze, his rich blue eyes looking up at me, searching, questioning, and that something else that made me feel like a thousand bees were nesting in my stomach.

"Put this on," I diverted, unraveling the cloak and clipping it shut around his neck. "Can you walk?" I asked, lifting him from the floor.

He nodded, but his arm wrapped over my shoulder nonetheless.

"Let's go," I said, helping him as we shuffled out of the tent past the sleeping guard.

We were silent as we made it to the tree line, and once we were clear of the outpost's view, we ran.

Rather, I ran and Taegan clung to me.

I stopped in the same clearing as before. The sky blooming with morning light, filling the small space, stretching languidly across the dry ground.

"I'm okay now," Taegan said gently, stepping from my hold. I could see his eyes had cleared, the serum nearly out of his system. "Why did you come back?"

"I couldn't leave you there. Not to die," I explained. "Though I'm not sure if I can forgive you so easily for taking my memories when I told you that it wasn't what I wanted," I added honestly.

He nodded approvingly. "I would be disappointed if you

let me off the hook too readily. Still, I would have thought you would find more enjoyment at seeing me behind bars." He smirked. "If I recall correctly, you had promised to make sure I knew what it felt like."

I rolled my eyes and nudged his arm. "I did relish it a little bit," I confessed.

"I deserved to be there." He sobered looking up and out at the blue volcano far in the distance.

"We both have been caged too long," I reasoned. "I was not about to let your freedom from Logan be exchanged for a Shamar prison. Not if I could do something about it."

He closed his eyes and took in a deep breath, lifting his chin to the breeze, the smell of earth and birch on the wind. "Thank you for getting me out."

"Where will you go?" I asked.

His blue eyes flicked to me, uncertainty in them.

"I see, then, you don't intend to come with me?" He asked a coy tilt to his full lips that made my insides twist up with unfathomable joy. He was asking me to go with him? I wanted to yell, shout and dance to the mountains, to the moon, that I would follow him anywhere. That wherever he would go, I would go, and wherever he would stay, I would stay, but I knew, at least right now, those desires could not be.

"My place is here, fighting for Erasmus. I said I would face my mistakes." I turned to stand next to him, gazing out at the blue volcano. Our shoulders brushed and he sighed.

"Like I told you before, I'm going to try to deserve you." He reached over and took my hand in his. "I'm going into Golan to find out more about the yellow journals, perhaps there is one that can free Logan."

I stepped abruptly in front of him. "You are free of him,

why by the Strings would you help him?" I dropped his hand angrily.

Taegan only smiled, the hand I'd abandoned reaching up to cup my face. "Because I know what it's like to be held captive, caged by circumstance and forced to submit in order to protect the people I love. I won't leave him to that fate, not if I could do something about it." He answered, throwing my words back at me.

"Some people don't deserve help; some people are past saving," I said fiercely in his defense, knowing full well it was just my protectiveness of him talking.

His other hand threaded in my hair. "You don't believe that—if you did, you would not be standing here, right now, in front of me. You would not be staying to fight for Erasmus."

I melted at the truth of his words. "What can you possibly do?" I asked, angry tears filling my eyes. Even though he had been playing the monster for so long, his true heart was so pure and hopeful, he would set out on a quest to help the man who had controlled him with fear for seven years. Was that kindness or delusion?

His thumb brushed my lower lip. "I will go and find my mother's family. I will find your family's tribe in Golan and see what they know about the yellow journals. Perhaps it is in Golan that I can finally understand who I am and get a better understanding of who you are as a descendant of Gilead, as heir to the kingdom." His eyes turned sultry. "But most of all, I want to know who you are to me."

It was my turn to smirk. "As if you don't already know."

He moved his hand from my cheek down to my waist. "Besides the little Golan girl that I have come to love." His gaze dropped to my lips.

"I'm not so little." I protested weakly. My heart skittering at his confession.

His blue eyes flashed teasingly as he patted the top of my head accentuating our dramatic high difference. "I suppose you grew a fraction." He offered, lips lifting on one corner, drawing my attention to how full and smooth they were. He may have spent the night in a cell but it took nothing away from his opulence, even the slight bruising on his cheek only added to his mystique.

"I'm not so little." I insisted again, lifting to my toes to brush his lips with mine. His hand tightened on my side, our lips like the breeze on our faces a moment ago; soft and fleeting.

I pulled back to check his reaction but his mouth chased after mine and I blinked as his tongue dove between my lips making my head spin with his sudden passion. All the need and hunger from the night in the banquet hall rushed back as I closed my eyes clinging to him, kissing him with everything I had.

We were moving, shuffling clumsily till my back found support against a tree.

I arched into him, needing to be closer, desperate. A vibration shot through me, but it wasn't my gift, it was Taegan's. I gasped as I felt his gift all around, pressing, searching me, as if trying to seep into my bones.

"Relina." He rasped pulling away, severing the connection. "I want this, Strings knows I want all of this, but I'm on the edge of a knife here. My ability to hold back is paper thin," he warned, a fervor in his hold, in his tone, that demanded attention and caution. "You have chosen to stay and I have chosen to leave, but if you kiss me again I won't be able to let you go."

A thrill rushed through me at his words. I had power over him? Someone so many times stronger than me? The temptation to wield that power, test it, war within me. If I kissed him, he would have no hope of leaving me again.

His blue eyes dilated, waiting for my answer, begging me to end the misery of indecision between us.

I dropped to my heels. "I don't know what the future holds for us, but right now, our paths take us in different directions." I gazed at his knowing blue eyes.

His smile was somber. He had seen this coming.

His hand in my hair moved to the nape of my neck as he nodded. "You are not just Rina Rinehart. When you are ready to embrace all of who you are, you know where I'll be." Tenderly, he pulled me into an embrace. "I will have the answers that you seek."

"I know you will." I wrapped my arms around him, feeling for the first time in a long time I was headed in the direction I was always meant to, even if that direction took me away from the man I had come to love.

CHAPTER 28

An Open Wound

Perhaps if I hadn't been his captive, if I hadn't learned more about my people, about myself from him, then maybe Rei and I could have had a real chance at something great. But now, with my memories fully intact, all of that pain and hardship molded me. I knew who I was, and I knew who the man was that I had just let go free.

As I walked back to the encampment alone, I thought back to the moment I had fully fallen in love with Tae.

I lifted my face, the sun cresting over the hills, and let its rays warm my cheeks as I invited the memory to come like a long-lost friend.

"So you forgive him, then?" I asked, sitting on our bench under the fig tree.

"Yes."

I blanched and stood up, anger and judgment seeping into my bones. "Why?"

"Because I don't want to live with hate."

I glared at him, feeling like I needed to defend myself,

but feeling all the same how foolish it was to want to defend and get angry at him for his words.

"I have done terrible things too, and though I do not have to trust Logan once he is out of my life—I will be glad to have nothing to do with him—I know forgiveness is not the same as reconciliation. *He* is separate from the things he did to hurt me, and those I love. The real evil in all this is Skithian. We are merely his puppets, destroying at his whim. True freedom is recognizing the real enemy and not casting hate on those who are merely unwitting reflections of that adversary."

I softened despite myself. "Then what I've done, the horrible things... my father..." Tears threatened my eyes. "How can I ever forgive myself?"

He shifted on the bench, reaching out to me and pulling me down into his arms. I folded onto his lap. The pain and brokenness of my shame ripped into my chest like a beast with claws, desperate to have its pound of flesh.

"Relina..." Taegan whispered into my hair. "You can forget all of this. All this misery—you can be free just like Rei." The huskiness of his voice rumbled in my ear, which lay against his chest.

I pulled back to look at him. "Forget?" It was tempting. It was a freedom of its own that could give me peace, but did I really want to forget? "Do you know how?"

"I don't, but Logan can do it. I can ask him to release you from the last few months now that we have what we need, now that we can do the ritual."

"So another deal?"

"We can add it as a stipulation," he explained, taking my hand. "Then we can disappear..." His voice was small, hesitant, and I marveled at seeing his real age finally show through his bravado and self preservation—he was just a person looking for a home, just like me. Hungering for acceptance and a place to no longer strive to be seen as worthy of love.

I took his hand. "I don't want to forget. I will do the work to forgive myself, even if it takes my whole life. I will correct the wrongs I have committed."

He breathed out. "You are"—he came close, his eyes full of reverence as he leaned his forehead against mine— "everything a queen ought to be. I will endeavor to deserve you, should you grant me the right."

I sighed and lifted my chin, meeting his eyes with a deep sense of acceptance and agreement.

Taegan saw me, and for the first time I wanted to truly see all of him. I was Relina Gilead, descendant of the old king, of Skithian himself, of evil incarnate. But I was not the darkness in me, I was the light that rises out of the dark to overcome it.

I opened my eyes to the present moment as the horns of war sounded over the encampment.

Today I would fight, not for redemption, reconciliation or forgiveness, but because I did not want to live with hate.

Today I, Relina Rinehart Gilead, was a general in the Shamarian army and would save the city of Erasmus.

The city I had brought to its knees.

THE STORY WILL CONTINUE IN...
From Amalgamation

Taegan's POV
A Beast Is Born

The grand eighteen-foot ceilings of the ballroom trembled. The room shook and groaned against the force of Logan's ritual and subsequent transformation. The beast he'd become thrashed, black talons swinging wildly as smoke and flame burst from its snout. A broad swipe of its clawed hands crashed into us, throwing Relina from my arms.

The force knocked the wind out of me as I rolled across the patterned tiles inlaid with golden vines.

I had to get her to safety.

We'd done as Logan asked. Though, I did not believe this was what he had intended to happen. No, this was Skithian's plan all along. We were merely pawns, Logan worst of all, as now he was host to the evil that had plagued this land for thousands of years. Skithian's power was now inside Logan. Though Skithian was said to be gone from this plane of existence, his influence had remained, and now that his power had returned, soon the darkness himself would take form. How this could happen, how it was even possible for Logan to become this beast was beyond my understanding.

Relina, having been tossed from me, lay unconscious on the ground, next to the banquet table, blood pouring from the wound I had inflicted on her arm. I called out to her but she did not stir. With agonizing slowness I crawled to her.

The beast bellowed, shaking the whole manor. I looked up as Logan's eyes finally changed from the human pale green, to a putrid yellow marred by vertical black slits. It was this that told me Logan was no more, only the beast remained.

Rei, Emilia and Seojin were upstairs in the manor and would surely not be able to sleep through this. I had to get out of here before anyone came looking. If they were wise, they would not attempt to come here but instead run, as I was doing now.

Scooping Relina into my arms, I tore through the tunnels at an enhanced speed. Once back in my lab, I laid her on my bed and hastened to stitch her wound. I had thought I had been careful not to hit the ulnar artery. I thought I was better than the Wraith, but at the rate she was bleeding now told me I was just as loathsome as the Wraith would have been.

With shaking hands I thread the needle. My heart broke a little more as I pierced her skin again and again with the small instrument. It was not clean, not easy, not what we should have become, but what was inevitable, from the moment the Wraith delivered her up to Logan that night months ago.

Her gray agate skin was almost white. Under her closed eyes were dark bruises. If I was not quick, she would die from blood loss, and Golan blood was not kept in ready stock in Shamar.

"Relina," I whispered hoarsely, my bloodied hand cupping her cheek, feeling the clamminess of her skin under my palm. It would not be enough, she needed medical attention. More than what I could give her.

I could not lose her, not now, not after everything. She had a chance at a normal life. She had a chance at freedom from this nightmare. I'd meant what I'd said when I told her I would let her go back to my brother. If she chose him, I would not get in the way.

Shamar may not have Golan blood, but I did. In my own veins.

Quickly I gathered the supplies, much as I had done all that time ago, the last time she was bleeding out before me, on the roof of the school.

They had not kept any prisoners of war after the attack at the front line. I had persuaded the nurse to say that, rather than to say I had handed her many bags of my own blood. It had taken much longer than I would have liked to recover, but Relina had needed as much of my blood as I could spare then, just as she needed it now.

I made quick work of setting up the transfusion and gave her some directly from my veins before filling a few bags of blood to send with her. The medical center had been destroyed after the attack four months ago, as much of the city had been since. But there were still the safe zones, bunkers, outside the city, where most of the injured had fled to during Logan's—no, Skithian's—rampage against Erasmus.

Spent and a little dizzy, I finally stopped the transfusion. Taking a deep breath, I forced my power throughout my body, compensating for my weakened state. I leaned over her, her curls spilling over my pillow. My hand cupped her check again. She was still frightfully pale, but her skin was warmer.

"Let's get you some real help now, huh?" I whispered, gathering her and the supplies.

I carried her from the lab, through the tunnels, and back to the manor, where my father's other automobiles sat, unused for months. Placing her inside one, I drove to the nearest safe zone.

Pulling out onto the main road, I slammed on the brakes as vehicles piled up and crashed into one another. Behind us at the center of the city, the beast tore into what was left of Erasmus, and these people fleeing from their totaled automobiles were desperately escaping the destruction.

But it was night, and there was no place safe from the Wraiths, from the Grieving, and like a swarm they descended onto the highway. Possessing. Killing.

I reversed, bent on escaping the carnage. I knew a few old mining roads and took those through the leafless trees. When the road split, taking me away from the direction of the bunker, I swerved the vehicle onto the clay dirt, forging my own path.

Trees and endless night spun around us in a blur as I raced to the shelter.

Jerking the wheel, I stopped alongside the rusted door of the bunker. Car idling, I leapt out and hammered on the metal door. Turning, I scooped Relina and the supplies from the polished leather seat.

Carrying her to the flaking green-painted door, I laid the love of my life down in the dirt.

I gazed for a moment at her face, etching it into my memory. My thumb curved over her soft lips. "I love you, Relina," I whispered as her dried blood, crusted over my hands, mocked me. One did not put the person they loved through all that I had put her through. Still, I had lost two mothers in my life, was hated by my brother and shunned by my father, and yet this moment, this pain eclipsed them all. "I hope to never see you again." Tears pooled in my eyes as the last words shook loose from my lips. "Live and be free."

I kissed her once on the forehead, letting the pain of this moment nearly drown me, because even if I stayed with her now, she was no longer my Relina, I had already let her go, already lost her, the moment Logan took her memories.

I stood up, and on stiff legs climbed back into the vehicle. I peeled away in it, getting only far enough to watch the circular door open and a nurse call for help. I watched them carry Relina inside and into her new life.

One void of my presence, void of my darkness, or so I could only hope.

———

I hadn't lived in my father's house for years. I did not belong there after everything that had happened with Rei. Once I'd gotten the gift at fifteen, I moved out to a flat in the city.

It was better that way, for everyone.

I rolled once more in my bed, uncomfortable, heavy with sleep but unable to settle. I had many things to be unsettled about. Logan was gone. His plan ruined, even though he'd gotten what he wanted in the end. The journals, the ritual. Now he was a beast flying around the continent, doing the Strings knows what.

I was free, at least for now, to do as I wished, but her blood... her blood was still on my hands, though I had scrubbed them raw after leaving her that night in front of the bunker. After stitching up the gash I'd made along her forearm. After watching her forget me. All of it still haunted me.

The sun was beginning to set outside. Night would fall in Erasmus, and the Wraiths and Grieving would claw about like the vermin they are. Though, I had nothing to fear from them, they would never touch me, at least not unless they were told to. Because I belonged to Him. Still. Still I belonged to Skithian.

A flash of the last time I was possessed flickered in my mind. Her skin bare, trembling before me, before the Wraith inside me. My sweet desert rose, withered and afraid.

My stomach churned violently inside me at the memory. Disgusted, I rolled off my bed, taking the two quick strides across the room to the kitchen sink, and vomited the little food I had eaten into the basin.

Hands braced on either side, I forced my mind to clear. Forced the feel of her skin along my fingertips from my mind. By the Strings, she had been so soft. I retched again. Shame bored under my skin like a living creature I would only be free of if I took a blade and cut it out. The only solace I had was that she did not remember, would never remember the unspeakable things done in those four months. My punishment was that I would. But I could bear it, I could bear it because she was free. I could bear it because I had borne it for my brother as well. Glutton that I was, I could not seem to help but eat others' pain, others' sins, my own, all to keep those I love blissfully ignorant, blissfully safe.

By the Strings, I missed her, though. My little Golan girl, my desert rose, my heiress, my queen.

Wiping my mouth, I collapsed back into bed, desperate for sleep, bone weary, but unable to succumb to sweet rest.

As my treacherous mind thought of her again, of seeing

her, running my fingers back into those curls, a jolt of familiar power, familiar vibrations, hovered over my skin.

Relina. I sat up, looking around for her. It was not possible for her to be here. My eyes scanned the room, but she was not there, and yet I could feel her. Dread filled me, because even though her memories were gone, her soul still knew.

Her soul still sought mine over the many miles between my flat and the bunker. Her Nephesh sought me out just to tell me that she was finally awake. That she had survived and I could finally sleep.

———

It was a fitful rest, only made worse in the days that followed.

Relina's vibrations were slowing, clearing up, becoming whole. Piecing together what I had taken from her. It was the worst at night, as if somehow in her sleep she was breaking through the walls, the knots Logan had woven through her memories. How it was even possible, I had no idea. I had no idea how or why I was still feeling her vibration so strongly either, even over such a distance. Was it because we were both Golan? I had read about how the Golan people were more connected, more harmonious than those in Shamar. But I had never felt this with anyone else before, not even with Seojin, and she was Golan too. It just didn't make sense.

I sighed, running my hands over my face. I had been holed up in my flat since the night I left her at the safe zone, wallowing in self-pity and self-hate. First that she might be dead, now because she might end up remembering everything. Stubborn, clever girl. I should have anticipated she would find a way to keep her memories.

I sat up.

If she could remember, did that mean Rei could too?

I shook my head.

"No, no way." Not possible, Rei's memories had been altered, not taken. And it was only one night, not four months of memories. Perhaps it was harder to forget four months, whereas one night would be easier to forget—people forget many nights in their lifetime. Plus, it had been years ago. If Rei was going to remember it on his own, it would have happened by now.

I relaxed back down onto the bed and watched the sunlight dip in streaks of orange gold across the wall, climbing higher to the ceiling, signaling the end of another day.

Ugh! I grunted, mouth dropping open in pain, as a force like a powered kick to my ribs slammed into me.

Relina's vibrations flooded my senses. A memory, an important one, was loosening in her mind, though there was no way for me to know what that memory might be. I could sense her nearness, closer than any other time before. I shivered because she was somewhere in the city.

I stood, clutching my stomach, hunched over to look out the window at the ruined streets below. I leaned pathetically against the window frame, willing the needling sensation all over my skin to pass. I closed my eyes and reached into the pain, sent my vibration out to hers, searching. But I was not a bygone Wavemaster, and I could not find her if she was any real distance from me.

As the pain ebbed and I straightened, a thought hit me. Relina, without her memories, would be looking for the last person she had left in the world. Her father. A death and burial she would not recall. I felt sick all over again. If she went back to her townhome, she would not find him there.

Despite myself, despite my need to remain removed from her life, I found my hands grabbing a coat and my feet carrying me out of my flat to Lowtown. I skittered over the rooftops, keeping my senses on high alert, because not only was Relina in the city, but I highly doubted she would have come alone, and if she was with my brother...

My jaw clenched, because I had no right to feel the pang of jealousy swirling through my chest. I had let her go—no, more than that, I had erased myself from her life. Every moment we spent together the last four months, every look, touch, that single kiss. I pursed my lips, refusing to think about that kiss. That kiss that had undone me. That had rattled my brain of every intelligent thought.

I had never felt so overcome before, so out of my element. I'd wanted to take as much as she would give; I was a gluttonous villain, and in that kiss, if she had not asked me to stop, I would have taken her from that blasted ballroom and done all the things her whimpers and gasps seemed to be asking for.

I stopped running, frustrated at my inability to let it be. Let her be.

Then I saw him dashing across the streets below. I slunk into the shadows of the setting sun. It was Rei, but he was alone and running in the same direction as I, to the street Relina lived on.

He wasn't with her? Could she be in trouble?

My pulse quickened. The diminishing sunlight sent my mind into a frenzy. She would be okay, *she* couldn't get possessed, I had made sure of that with the serum that activated her blood trait... but... Rei could.

I followed after him, finding her moments after he had. She wasn't alone—two other men were with her. An older man with dreads who looked vaguely familiar, like I had seen him a long time ago at one of my family's parties, and a younger man with muscle on muscle. He had to be at least twice my size, and I was no peanut. The younger man wore a Krav suit with a unique crest across the back.

I swallowed thickly. I knew that crest. Not because I had actually seen it before but because Logan had told me about them. About the secret order of the late King Roark. Claw and Wing, the name fitting to the etched golden thread along his suit.

Why was Relina with someone from the order?

"Rei!" Relina cried out, drawing my attention. The look on her face as she gazed at Rei took me back to the day she once looked at me with such wide-open hope.

5 months ago...

I heard the girls calling for Shila to stop.

I had been preoccupied all day with thoughts of Rina after she had barged into my office, rightfully accusing me and telling me she was done with me.

I hadn't been sure she would still meet me after school, but I decided I would go wait for her in the courtyard nevertheless.

What I hoped for and what I found were so glaringly opposite I stumbled down the steps to the greenery, my pulse light and quick beneath my skin.

Rina was pinned against the large oak, face pressed into the trunk.

"Disgusting Golan trash, die die die already! I hate you, ahhhh!"

"Shila!" I hollered, as the girl, blinded by rage, slammed her enhanced fists into Rina's spinal cord. By the Strings, Rina could be paralyzed from that blow.

"Headmaster!" the girls around yelped, backing away as I ran past them.

With an enhanced kick, I whirled on Shila, slamming my foot into her side, sending her flying.

She smacked into the brick wall of the school, but I did not bother to see how badly she was injured because I was already turning, reaching for Rina, catching her crumpled form in my arms.

Pumping my vibrations into my legs, I carried her through the courtyard, up the stairs on the east side of the manor and across the entresol to the nursing lounge, for treatment. Since the school day was over, no one would be there, and I could treat Rina's wounds in private.

The space was not much: hardwood floors, yellow walls and antiquated equipment for testing the health of the students. I would need to allocate more budget to this facility. Especially since Rina was bound to be coming here a lot. I should stock up on Golan blood too.

I laid Rina down on the first of the two cots in the room.

It was then that I really looked at her. Her face was bruised, puckered with splinters, and her shirt was askew. Her ribs were definitely broken. I could only hope her spine was not badly damaged.

With a deep breath I moved to the intercom on the wall. They were not common in the main part of the school building, but we were in the section closest to the manor, and all throughout my father's house there were these channels to speak with someone in another room.

Seojin had her own private channel.

I pressed the worn golden button. "Seojin, you are required in the nurse's lounge immediately." I released the button, knowing it would take her about three minutes to get here from her room if she ran. Which, I knew, she would.

I raked my hands through my hair wildly assuring myself Rina would be fine.

Dawning a blue lab coat left hanging by the door, I set to work removing the spikes of wood from Rina's face. She seemed to stir once, eyes fluttering briefly before tilting her face away from my ministrations.

"Please don't move. I'm trying to get the splinters out," I advised, hoping she would not panic, but instead her eyes closed and her breathing stuttered. She was unconscious again. It was probably for the best, because just then the far wall clicked and slid open.

"Master." Seojin bowed.

The servants' corridors ran all throughout the estate; though not used by really anyone but myself and the girl before me, they proved very useful. Enough so that I'd prevented my father from permanently sealing them off after Rei's mother died. At first because they were a fun place to play, and then later, once I was older, because it was these hidden passages that led to my lab. My lab, a secret place deep within the tunnels, probably used for prisoners hundreds of years ago, as the space was not much more than cells till I'd spruced it up. Of course, the things I studied there were not always the most humanitarian. Seojin understood that well enough. She was absolutely terrified of me. At first, it hurt some, her being the only other Golan person I knew, the closest thing to my lineage, but her fear was necessary.

"Seojin. Heal this girl," I ordered, my voice stony.

"Right away," she squeaked, coming to Rina's side only after I moved away. Seojin's dark gray cloak swished along the floor, the heavy material a way to hide her skin from others and most likely herself. I had deduced over the years that she was more than a little ashamed of her skin.

Her dark eyes flicked to me and then to the girl lying on the cot.

"This is a new student," I offered, knowing full well she knew exactly who Rina was. I also knew there was no way she would not report this encounter to Rei. So I had to spin the story just right. "She is of great interest to me, being Golan and all. As you can see"—I gestured to the bruising along Rina's face, her broken ribs—"some of Golan descent have far greater endurance than others." My hand lifted to suggest I might be alluding to Seojin as being inferior to Rina.

Seojin's already dull face paled.

Cruel but necessary, I reminded myself.

"Of course, Master." She blinked quickly, reaching across Rina's ribs, and as if she were pulling a fine string across the gray blouse, the bones began to set in place.

Intent on understanding more about both women in front of me, I sat on a nearby stool and closed my eyes. Dipping into the vibration dimension, I waited, going deeper and deeper into the darkness. Then, like the world was being birthed before my eyes, strings of light blossomed and swirled before me.

Seojin's soul was not new to me—the green threads that made up her gift floated in a mass before me—but it was Rina's Nephesh that stole my attention. It glittered in front of me like golden hour light over a river. I watched in the vibration dimension as Seojin gathered more of the fine strings that made up Rina's golden essence and reordered them. Knitting her body back together before my eyes.

When she was finished, Seojin heaved a huge sigh. It was very taxing for her to heal someone so injured.

"Report?" I asked, wishing to know just how badly Rina had suffered, so I could be sure Shila's punishment was just as severe.

"Abrasions to the face, hands and arms. Two broken ribs, and..." She hesitated.

I opened my eyes then, the vibration dimension disappearing back into reality. "And?" I pressed.

Seojin flinched as if I had hit her. "The nerves in her lower spine were detached. Had I come any later, I would not have been able to help her. I have repaired the damage. A full recovery will not be an issue."

My stomach dropped. If I had been a moment sooner or a moment later, this conversation would have gone very differently.

"You are dismissed."

"Yes, Master." She bowed, looking between me and Rina. I knew what she wanted, but I would not give her the answer she sought; better for her to draw her own conclusions and report as she wished to Rei.

Rina stirred, making Seojin jump. Alarmed, she averted her eyes and exited the room through the hidden door.

I pulled the curtain around the cot partially closed and took the tray of splinters tipped in Rina's blood to the microscope. Nicking my own finger, I set to work making slides with her blood and my own. She would wake when she was ready, and in the meantime, I needed to verify that the paper on my desk earlier was correct. To be certain that Rina, child of Nivera, was truly a descendant of King Gilead, of Skithian, that she might carry within her blood the trait to end possession for all mankind.

I made quick work of developing the slides, relishing the satisfying click of the glass as I slid it in place under the scope. I took a steadying breath and leaned in toward the specimen.

By the Strings, there it was.

The very blood trait described in the yellow journal. The one only a descendant of Skithian would have.

My pulse quickened with the possibilities. So engrossed in the process and the discovery before my eyes, I completely missed that Rina had gotten out of bed.

I could feel her eyes scanning the room.

"Hello," I greeted, my back to her. Could she hear the joy and wonder in my voice?

Her power flooded the room, and I could not help but grin. She was magnificent. A marvel, a miracle. I relaxed my face, schooling my features to be as unassuming as possible.

"What did I tell you about fighting me? Oh, yes, you will lose. Now put the clipboard down, Rina." I sighed, turning to face her, her eyes wide, and her stance that of a fighter.

"You're the blue-coat mad scientist?" She guffawed, her scrunched nose surprisingly adorable.

"Have to keep the old folklore alive—keeps the students in line." I smirked. That wasn't true, in fact I cared very little for the rumors at T.R.E, but I was in a teasing mood. A playfulness I had not felt in ages crept over me. Could she see it? The way her mere existence sparked new life in me.

"How did you—" she wondered, distracted by her healed skin. She looked into the mirror on the wall beside her in awe.

"The pain will stay for a while," I cautioned, hoping she might take it easy from· now on. "My healer came and patched you up."

"Why?"

She gazed at me through the mirror, and when our eyes met, I knew I was in real trouble. I had the overwhelming urge to see her smile, a giddy kind of thrum in my chest making me want to be... coy. Me... Taegan Kang, coy? It was unthinkable, and yet... "I'm acting headmaster, as you know..." I alluded to the conversation she had overheard. By the Strings, if this girl ever began to trust me, I might fall apart entirely.

"Shila?" she squeaked. Was it nerves for her too? Did I affect her as well?

"Is suspended until an apology letter is written." I shrugged, ignoring my delusional thoughts and answering her question. I hadn't yet officially issued the statement but would before the school day began anew. Urgency filled me then—Shila was not the only threat to Rina. No, she was in more danger from me, from what I had discovered on that slide, because if Logan knew what her blood could do... Ugh, I didn't even want to think about it.

He already knew she was special, that she was Nivera's daughter. His curiosity was already piqued.

I lifted the beaker with my blood solution. I would need to hide the evidence of Rina's blood from Logan. Tapping a beaker, I dropped the pink liquid onto the slide with her blood, mixing ours to destroy the evidence. To be sure I had erased my findings, I placed the mixed blood back under the microscope.

"What is this place?"

"My lab," I lied, and leaned in to look through the scope.

Her trait was masked by my blood, but could still be discovered if one looked hard enough. I would have to burn it.

"What are you going to do to me?" she gasped, complete terror in her voice.

By the Strings. This girl. Here I was saving her, and she was terrified of me. No, that wasn't right, if I didn't want her to be terrified, then I wouldn't have said that this was my lab. Which it definitely was not, but lying was safer. For so many reasons. First, because I would never want her in my actual lab, partly because Logan always met me there and partly because it was very isolated, and having her so alone with me would not be good for my health. Because of this, and because I knew Rei wanted her to spy on my lab, I needed her to at least think she had been there once. She had no idea this was the nurse's lounge, and I would make sure to keep it that way. Perhaps I should just remodel the whole room?

I looked up, putting on my best annoyed face. "Gosh, Rina, how many times do I have to tell you to trus—"

"But I don't!" she screeched, making my blood freeze in my veins. Of course, of course she would never. Rei had already dug deep into her. They'd only had one day together, and she was already completely infatuated with him, believing everything he told her about me.

"I said we could help each other. You have a trait, special to only a specific line from Golan. It is critical to helping save Shamar." I pushed the microscope away and took a few steps towards her. "That is what you want, right? To help save the people of Shamar, to prove your worth?" I demanded, knowing better than anyone else those feelings, those desires.

"My blood?"

She did not move away from me as I advanced towards

her. Her caramel eyes were wide, drawing me in. "Naturally I should have asked, but I needed to be sure first that you were the right one. I tested the blood left on the splinters from your face. You do have the trait. There is no doubt about it now," I confessed, taking another step towards her.

"What will my blood do?"

I closed my eyes, deliberating. This was the moment to tell everything, but I doubted she would believe me about her mother. She did not trust me, just as she'd said, and Nivera was too important to us both. If I poured out the truth now and she rejected it, I would not be able to stand it. So I gave only what I believed she would accept coming from me. "Your blood," I began, halting my approach and looking her square in the eyes, "will stop Wraith possessions."

I waited as she processed. Then she advanced towards me, and I was not sure what she would do, but I braced for it nevertheless.

"I lost my mom too," she whispered. "She wasn't killed by a Wraith possession—at least, that's not what the report said. She died while working as a maid. Her heart just... gave out, they said." Her voice wavered, cheeks flushing as she fought the unshed tears pooling in her eyes.

I felt sick, like I could turn around and heave all over the floor. My father had covered up what had really happened that night to Nivera. Logan had killed her, and I could do nothing to stop it, as I was wounded, helpless, on the ground. I could tell her, I *could* tell her... but I wouldn't. Not yet. Instead I reached for her, hoping to offer whatever comfort I could.

She looked at my outstretched hand and smiled. Then she wrapped her thin elegant fingers around mine. "It hurts all the time. If what you say is true, about my blood, then take it. I can think of no better use than to save people." She shifted our hands till her wrist was upturned in my palm as if in surrender, in offering, in trust.

A swell of something powerful, incandescent, filled me as she looked up, her gaze full of hope. Hope to save mankind. Hope and faith in me to assist her. It was like nothing I'd felt before, absolute bliss and so alluringly attractive. In that one look I was seduced; if she asked me to string her up the moon, I would beg the Creator on my knees for the power to do so.

It was all this madness that led me to do what I did next.

Smiling, I bent down and kissed the smooth skin of her wrist.

Did I imagine the delightful jump in her pulse at the contact?

"What are you—" she balked.

"Not tonight, Rina," I breathed against her skin, a pit forming in my gut as I inferred another meaning my words could have. Because I was loving a little too much the feel of my lips caressing the pale curve of her skin. "You have school in the morning, and it's quite late," I amended, needing to put some distance between us. I walked to the door, my eyes catching on the eye mask Miss Reed, the resident nurse, used to take naps on her lunch break.

It was a simple strip of black fabric.

I lifted the cloth, and feeling very clever, turned to face Rina. She took in the blindfold I was holding, her cheeks warming to a delightful shade of pink.

"Take a breath, Rina. My lab is secret. I will walk you out, but you have to be blindfolded." I grinned, hoping it didn't look as wicked as it felt.

She nodded, standing in front of me. I actively hid my

surprise, as she was not even trying to question or fight me. So this was trust, then? How intoxicating, how empowering.

I tied the cover over her eyes, feeling the plushness of her curls.

When I finished, she lifted her hands and swallowed loudly.

"Lead the way?" she asked, a slight shake in her voice.

I looked at her open palm for a beat before squaring my shoulders and taking her hand in mine. By the Strings, the jolts passing through me were like a current pushing me to kiss her again.

I cleared my throat and squeezed her hand slightly, pulling her closer to my side. I walked us through the tunnels, knowing it would be faster than going around the outside to the courtyard.

"Have you learned how to meditate with your gift?" I wondered conversationally.

"Um, no, but I can sense someone's gift if I concentrate really hard," she offered.

"Hm. What about the vibration dimension? Can I assume you have never learned how to enter that?"

"That's kinda advanced."

"It is," I agreed.

"Do you know how?"

"Yes." I glanced down at her face, watching the curve of her lips as she asked the next question.

"What's it like?" Her voice lilted, telling of her excitement. I smiled, leading her through the archway and onto the path of the courtyard. We were outside. The dark night wrapped around us, whispering secrets, seducing in its own way. I shifted us around a bend and moved so I was behind her, guiding her forward with my free hand on her shoulder. I leaned into her.

"It's peaceful. Every living thing gives off a sound, like a song. A unique frequency that sings. In the dimension, you can hear it all, the cacophony of sounds, and yet it is soothing. Then there are the colors."

"Colors?"

"Every song has a color. Your vibration gift, mine, everyone's has a distinct color that swirls around in the darkness."

"I don't understand."

"What do you see right now?"

"You're joking, right?"

"No, tell me, what do you see?"

"Nothing, it's all dark, obviously." She was annoyed, and I couldn't help but smirk.

She was so fiery.

"That's what the vibration dimension is like. Dark, black, nothingness... and then colorful shapes begin to grow out of the nothingness." I stopped walking us forward, as we had made it to the courtyard. Holding her still, I closed my eyes, falling into that darkness, into that nothingness, looking for her there. "The sounds mix together, the colors stretch and move about like streams of liquid light." Painfully slow, her vibration strings blossomed before me. The gentle hum of her soul was a soft lilt, the strings twisting in the dark; caressing. Though I could not see my own—no one can see their own soul—I could feel how mine searched for hers, reaching out; needing her. The strings of our souls bending and weaving around one another in a desperate dance. My hand slid from her shoulder along her collarbone, till she was wrapped against my chest, pinned to me by the palm I splayed just under the hollow of her throat. "The strings of one's soul glowing, growing and expanding like a deep inhale." I relished the rises of her breath against me, breathing in with her till we were synced. "Falling and sinking like an exhale." I felt the thrum of her pulse beneath my palm—full and quick, in rhythm with my own.

"Are you there now?"

"Yes," I answered, my voice as breathy as hers.

"What does my soul look like?"

I opened my mouth to answer.

"Never mind," she huffed, pulling away. The golden strings of her soul recoiled from mine, her withdrawal a much needed slap to my senses.

I had taken things too far. If she had any idea of what I was doing, by the Strings, she would never forgive me. The strong pull to her was reprehensible. Bonding our souls was the last thing I should be doing. I hadn't even realized I had been. What was wrong with me? Disgusted with myself, I hastily turned her around and removed the blindfold.

She looked up at me, dazed, the same hopeful look in her eyes. A look I did not deserve.

With a quick pat on her shoulder I departed, needing a very cold shower.

Water sprayed down from a busted water pipe over my head, bringing me back to the ruined streets of Erasmus. Below my rooftop perch I watched Rei hold his own against a horde of Grieving. Scanning the darkened street, I looked for Relina. The two men she had been with were skilled fighters, taking down one monster after another. Then I spotted her, framed by a shattered storefront window.

It had been weeks since I had last seen her, and though

she looked the same, I knew the girl before me wasn't my Relina.

Then, as if to prove that thought wrong, she rose up and twisted into a move I knew well. A move I had painstakingly taught her. The crown kick, aptly named because it resulted in one's heel connecting with the opponent's head. I watched as she flawlessly whipped through the air, her foot connecting with the Grieving's skull with deadly precision.

She was as beautiful as ever, a warrior princess.

"Sir Liam!" she yelled to the older man in the street, but her warning was too late.

The Wraiths had arrived.

Panic painted her features as she disappeared into the store. My brow furrowed, and on instinct alone, to make sure she was alright, I made my way down to where she had slipped into the darkness. Finding a hole in the roof, I dropped into the empty store.

Glass and debris littered the ground. The smell of rot and death mixed in my nose. I covered my face with the collar of my coat.

Where had she gone?

I closed my eyes, seeking her out in the vibration dimension. Slowly the light of her soul met me in the dark, but it was not what it once had been. A thick mass like thousands of tiny clawed hands clutched her strings, knotting and clumping them together in unnatural ways. This was what Logan had done. Then I saw a few that waved and hummed free of the tangled mass.

This was what I had felt? This was her soul freeing itself from Logan?

Shame, hope and fear pulsed through me at what I had

done to her, but more than anything, I feared what might happen to her once she remembered.

Could she possibly remember everything?

The hair on the back of my neck rose, and I shivered from the chill filling the air.

I reminded myself she was safe. She could not be possessed.

I opened my eyes, sensing the Wraiths in the store. A soft whimper made me flinch. I drew closer to Relina's hiding spot, noticing how similar it was to the cell she had been in. Even down to the way she sat curled up in the dark hole.

She did not know she was safe, and her fear was like a shot of adrenaline to my heart.

I moved to her. "We had a deal... Not them," I ordered the Wraiths harshly. They would not listen to me, but Relina did not need to know that.

"T-Tae."

She knew my voice, then? So much for keeping my distance, then again, what had I really thought would happen after following her into the store?

"You should have never come back," I whispered, offering my hand to take hers once more. The feel of it was like coming home. Soft and welcoming. I lifted her to her feet and out of the hole she had curled into.

Though I knew I should have schooled my face into the calculated features of Tae, the person she expected, I just couldn't. Instead I drank her in, gazing at her with all the adoration and longing I had wrestled against the last few days.

In my observation of her, I noted the cuts along her arm. Wanting to get a better look at her wound, I peeled back the fabric of the new Krav suit she wore, revealing the stitches I had etched through her skin along her forearm.

A wave of nausea hit me.

"What—" She glared, readying to pull away from my touch.

With deft ease, I moved my hand to her neck, chopping sharply into the pressure point there.

She fell limply into my arms, unconscious.

I cradled her to my chest for a long time, till the shuffle of footsteps met my ears. If they got any closer, they would be able to sense my vibration.

"Aaron, look for Rina over there," an older voice, Sir Liam's, ordered.

"Rina?" Aaron called. "Rina, it's okay, but we have to hurry and get back to the manor." The steps drew closer. "Rina?"

"Did you find her?" Rei's voice joined in.

How had they escaped being possessed?

I looked down at the girl in my arms. I didn't have time to question how they'd done it, as long as she was safe. Letting her go once more, I laid her down, and I disappeared back into shadow, but not before hearing Aaron whisper.

"Thank you for protecting her."

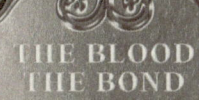

CASSANDRA CIELO

FROM
AMALGAMATION

THE BLOOD
THE BOND

FROM
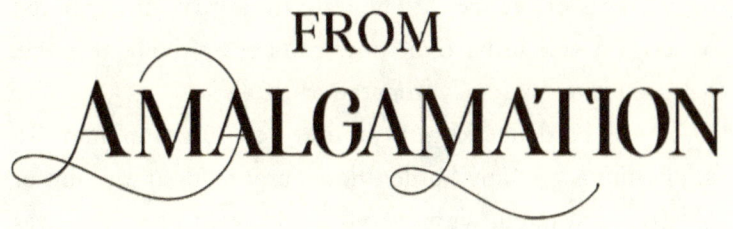
AMALGAMATION

SNEAK PEEK

Chapter 1 : Secrets We Keep

The rising sun warmed my face; the horns of battle rang out, waking the earth and the sleeping soldiers of the encampment.

The metal arm plates of my uniform clinked together, instilling in me a sense of duty, responsibility, and pride. The horns sounded again, and inside my heart swelled, my vibration power rising and heating in my chest, eager to be used after being weighed down and crushed by dampening Krav suits and serum for months.

I was finally free.

I was finally ready to fight back.

A battle awaited before me. A battle I must fight and win to redeem myself, to prove to myself I really was more than I appeared. More than my Golan skin or the destruction I had caused while possessed by Wraiths. To earn the metal adornments strapped to my arms. To show a certain blue-eyed man I was able to overcome my darkness.

The blue-eyed man I had just said goodbye to lingered on the outskirts of my mind. The only thing that—if I dwelled too long on—might have the power to defuse the fight in me, to cause me to turn away from the battle ahead.

It was hard not to turn around and run after him. To follow him across any border, down any road, to my ruin or salvation. I wanted, with everything in me, to go, but I was determined to not let everything in me be stronger than my sense of duty and responsibility. I was a warrior through and through, and I would not abandon the city I'd had a hand in destroying.

My place was here, on the cusp of battle.

My body tensed, mood shifting the minute I entered the camp. Rei was yelling at the guard who was supposed to be watching the cells, the ones I had helped Taegan escape from. It was clear from the anger on Rei's face that he was well aware his brother was gone.

To avoid the drama I skirted a few tents, when the side of my face slapped into a smooth black Krav uniform. I looked up at the man I had crashed into, coming face to face with Aaron. His bright blue eyes and knowing pearly smile warned that he had been expecting me to bump into him.

"Now I wonder where you went off to this morning?"

"Aaron, I can explain," I said, confident there was no lie I could think of that he would possibly believe.

He gave an exaggerated yawn. "As much as I would love to hear what deceit you have concocted, I'm afraid my curiosity will have to wait till after we have won back the city." He tossed his arm around my neck, hiding me with his massive muscles, and helping me sneak past Rei and the guard who appeared to be desperately trying to assuage Rei's fury.

I sighed, relieved to be avoiding Rei's wrath for now. Though I would have to face him sometime. It was inevitable.

"Thanks."

Aaron leaned down and whispered for my ears only. "He better be worth it."

My face flushed.

I didn't know how to answer that. The truth of the matter was Taegan was long gone, across the border by now, so it didn't matter anyway. Was it worth it to betray Rei? Was it worth it to let Taegan go without me? Only time would tell, and until I was sure it was worth it, I wasn't ready to disclose anything. "I don't know what you're talking about."

Aaron scoffed and slapped me hard between the shoulder blades.

"Of course you don't."

—————

One Month Later

"Drop your shoulder," Aaron ordered.

I dropped forward into a lunge, my shoulder dipping as commanded. A quick succession of *thunk thunk thunk* had me grinning as I chucked three short daggers from between my fingers into the bark of a tree across the training ground. Aaron circled around behind me with a low whistle.

"That's it. Now again but from a spin kick."

After twisting on my heel and lifting my leg to chamber, I kicked with added force from my gift. With a swiftness I was getting more precise at controlling, I plucked another knife from my hip and, midswipe, flicked it under my leg into the tree beside my previous targets. The satisfying crack of wood splitting affirmed what I was already suspecting. My gift, my skill might finally be at a level where I could take on Logan and possibly win. Even despite his dragon ability.

Panting, I landed in a low crouch as the sun cut across the grounds, illuminating the city of Erasmus and our military encampment, now located in the city center.

The plan to win back the city had been relatively simple. Blockade the four major entrances, ensuring we could wipe out the Grieving first. And when night fell we'd had a small force gather in the city square. The group was composed of those who had been possessed before because only those possessed could see the Wraiths. I had told Callum about the yellow journal about Logan becoming the dragon, but I'd left out some key information, not ready to reveal all my secrets. No one but Aaron knew about my lineage, or about the blood trait Taegan had activated in me. So when asked if I would be in that small group of people who would face down the Wraiths, I'd gladly volunteered knowing full well I would be immune to their possession.

Our orders were to destroy as many Wraiths as possible. Aaron had shared how to force a Wraith out and turn it to dust. The skill was particular, but the assembled team was well versed in how to use their gift, and we'd each picked it up quickly before night swept over the city that first day. Our small team would not take them all out in one night, so it was a long game strategy, with the weeks following the initial attack consisting of nightly raids that drew out the Wraiths for their destruction. Those not on the small team stayed at the major points of the city, preventing any reinforcements from Golan. Once we'd been able to hold the city for seven days without new hordes of Grieving entering, we'd begun the rebuilding process. Romath had craftsman crews on standby, and when the all clear was given, they'd gotten to work.

Callum said it would take months to get the city habitable again, for families to come back, but so much had already changed in the last month since the battle began. Some parts of the city were just barely habitable, and families of soldiers were welcomed in as official residents of New Erasmus.

"Rina, that was excellent. You're looking more and more like a general everyday." Aaron chuckled, but I didn't. In fact I wasn't even wearing the armor that signified my rank; too many eyes ended up on me when the shiny metal glinted on my arms, so I had taken to only wearing it when absolutely necessary. Training with Aaron was not one of those times.

Since we had won back the city, Aaron and I had made a habit of training together every morning. It was comfortable at first. He was a wealth of skill and knowledge, but mostly his company was relaxing, a safe place I could be my whole self with. And for every skill I gained I got to ask a question about Claw and Wing, or anything else I wanted.

"So you were talking about the yellow journals, how they were written by King Roark..." I panted, moving into another Krav stance and starting again with throwing my knives.

"Yes, the originals we know of are in Castle Judahall, but the less sensitive information was duplicated and can be found in libraries around the kingdom," he explained, pacing the length of the training grounds. He wore his standard Krav gear, but since we arrived at the encampment he also wore a cloak that covered the Claw and Wing emblem on the back of his uniform. "The journals are mostly a personal account of King Roark's time as king. After he passed, the steward thought the people should have access to some of the king's writings."

"Then the king wrote about how to become a dragon using Gilead blood?" I accused while straightening out of the Krav flow I had been shifting through.

Aaron shook his head. "No, based on our knowledge passed down, King Roark and King Gilead both wrote in the yellow journals; in fact the language used in certain tomes is wildly different from the others. The journals found in the strange language were few, but after some study it was concluded they were written in Old Golan. King Roark would have known the language, but from what we could translate, the writings in those journals did not have his voice."

"So then the yellow journal, the one Rei had all those years, was actually written by King Gilead?"

"That is what we believe."

I considered this. Though I hadn't gotten to look at the yellow journal Logan had used for the ritual, I did recall the sloping scrawl found in the corners and margins of my grandparents' journals. Could that writing have been Old Golan?

"Each king pursued a different path with their gifts from the Creator. From what we can tell it seems they followed mirrored trajectories."

"How so?" I asked, shaking off the memories of my grandparents' writing.

"The Wraiths and Grieving were Gilead's distortion of the vibration power, while the Wavemasters and Orators were Roark's creation. Roark, however, was guided by the Creator, and so people are born with the gift, as opposed to the Grieving, which is something you become."

"Then did Gilead have a king's court too?"

"It is possible, but my uncle would know the details. I am not privy to *all* the kingdom's secrets."

"He will be returning soon?"

"Today, actually. I think he has something he wants to talk to you about, so be prepared to have him sneak up on you."

"Right, and you're sure he would be okay with me using these?" I plucked the throwing knives from the tree and holstered them on my suit.

"Of course." He waved me off. "We have plenty of unique weapons, and since you will be officially joining you get to enjoy the benefits of our stash."

I had been training with the knives for the last few weeks after I agreed to join Claw and Wing in the hopes they could help me get more answers about my lineage. When I had asked Aaron about the use of weapons he explained using weapons gets you up close and personal with your enemies. He said to be a part of Claw and Wing one has to approach battle with the intent to overcome fear. That it is critical to survival. The way one overcomes fear is by truly facing your enemy, literally, up close.

So along with utilizing Krav and my vibration gift, I now throw knives like I'm juggling cotton balls.

"Still, I'm not officially a member yet," I hedged.

He walked over to me and flicked my shoulder where the pauldrons should be. "The moment you accepted responsibility you became a candidate—that's good enough for me and my uncle."

I rubbed my shoulder with a half smile, remembering how Sir Liam had encouraged me to take on the role of general. It had been a hard decision, made easier when I considered how much good I could do as a general instead of a lone soldier who'd never even made it to graduation.

I had come to learn over the last weeks that though I was a general I had very little power in the encampment. The pauldrons put me above the soldiers, but I was still the lowest ranked general in the whole camp. I was more of a decoration at the general meetings than a real player. Still the title gave me access to information I would have never been able to get. It was an honor but a humbling one all the same.

I sighed, holding one of the six lightweight knives. "When are you going to show me how you made a weapon out of your suit in low-town?"

Aaron rolled his shoulders and backed up before vaulting onto the small platform used for meditation. "When you can tap into the vibration dimension." He pat the seat next to him, and we began the next round of our training. Aaron had told me there was a way to tap into the vibrations around us. In the vibration dimension most were only able to see and hear the powers around them, like Taegan had explained to me all that time ago. But some were actually able to draw in the vibrations from others, from nature itself, and harness it.

"It takes time to see and hear the vibrations, but once you master that you can take it further, you can reach out and wield the power beyond yourself," Aaron had explained. "Most don't know it's possible, or even where to begin, but with me as your teacher you will be wielding in no time."

He had been right about that—in only a few short weeks I had been able to draw in the slightest bit. Nothing substantial I could do anything with, but it was something.

"There is only one rule," Aaron had warned me. "Never reach for another person's vibration."

"Why?" I had asked.

"Unless you want to be bonded to them for the rest of your life, just don't do it."

The way he'd said it had me so unnerved I hadn't wanted to ask anything more at the time, but now it was bothering me.

www.ingramcontent.com/pod-product-compliance
Lightning Source LLC
Chambersburg PA
CBHW062010190726
48283CB00002BA/640

* 9 7 8 1 7 3 5 2 5 0 9 7 7 *